Given

Given

SUSAN MUSGRAVE

thistledown press

Thistledown Press Ltd.
118 — 20th Street West
Saskatoon, Saskatchewan, S7M 0W6
www.thistledownpress.com

Library and Archives Canada Cataloguing in Publication

Musgrave, Susan, 1951-
Given / Susan Musgrave.

Issued also in an electronic format.
ISBN 978-1-927068-02-1

I. Title.

PS8576.U7G58 2012   C813'.54   C2012-904714-7

Cover illustration by Judit Farkus
Cover and book design by Jackie Forrie
Printed and bound in Canada

 Canada Council for the Arts   Conseil des Arts du Canada   SASKATCHEWAN ARTS BOARD   Canadian Heritage   Patrimoine canadien

Thistledown Press gratefully acknowledges the financial assistance of the Canada Council for the Arts, the Saskatchewan Arts Board, and the Government of Canada through the Canada Book Fund for its publishing program.

Given

For Given

We lose our children not once, but over and over again.
— Neil Gordon, *The Company We Keep*

People sleep, and when they die, they awake.
— Mohammed

PART ONE

Of all escape mechanisms, death is the most efficient.
— Henry Ward Beecher

SHOELACES ARE THE MOST POPULAR WEAPON IN prison. With no elasticity and a high breakage point they can be used to hang yourself or strangle other people.

My shoelaces had been taken away from me when I was moved to the Condemned Row — the State didn't want me turning myself into a wind chime before the governor had signed the warrant. I had grown accustomed to walking around with my shoes loose, flopping open, but now, standing beside the prison transfer van, I felt, in a strange way, naked.

"What's the first thing you plan on doing, you get yourself freed?" Earl, my driver asked, as he unlocked my waist chains and manacles and helped me into the back. There were, I saw, no door handles, which was why he'd felt secure enough to remove my shackles.

I told Earl I'd always figured the first thing I'd do if I were ever released would be to return to South America to find my son. "Right after I get finished buying shoelaces."

Earl, a big man with grey hair mussed up as if he'd been tossed out of bed, and everything he felt hidden behind chrome mirrors, hefted my prison-issue duffel bag marked "Property of Heaven Valley Correctional Facility" onto the seat beside me. "That's a long way to go to look for somebody," he said, giving me an opening, but I wasn't about to tell him I'd had to look in a lot more farther away places since I'd left my son's body behind on Tranquilandia; I'd had to begin the search in the shrunken rooms of my heart, to find myself first, the hard way.

"As long as you keep moving you can get anywhere you want," Earl said, looking up at the sky. His view was that most people went from being alive one minute to being dead the next, without knowing the difference. "Half the people walking around, they don't even know they're already dead. The rest of them die before they ever learn to live."

He turned on the radio, volunteering, over the static, that he had some knowledge of my case. In his opinion "women of the female gender" didn't belong behind bars; being locked up didn't make them any easier to get along with. He said he believed prisoners of all genders should be set free and given jobs, so they could make themselves useful. In his country, for instance, during the ethnic cleansing, they had enlisted men serving life sentences for rape and murder, because they made the best soldiers. "There are men who like to see blood. Lots of it."

Officer Jodie Lootine, the guard everyone called the Latrine because of her potty-mouth, slid in next to Earl; it was her job to make sure I reached my destination without making a jackrabbit parole, the reason my destination remained a secret, surrounded by a bodyguard of lies. All I'd been told was that I was being transferred to a remand centre where I would be held pending a new trial.

Years before, when I was first admitted to the Facility, I had been given a pamphlet called the *Inmate Information Handbook*. One of the first rules, right after "If you are a new inmate only recently sentenced by the courts, this will probably be an entirely new experience for you," was "Don't ask where you are going, or why, they will only lie to you anyway." We had *our* rules, too, the rules of engagement with prison guards, wardens, classification officers, or even the all-denominations chaplain who came to wish you *sayonara* in the Health Alteration Unit, a.k.a. the death chamber. *Don't ask questions. It spares you the grief.*

Something else I'd learned from the *Inmate Information Handbook.* "You will feel completely alone, because you are."

I checked my Snoopy wristwatch — bequeathed to me by Rainy the night before she took her trip to the stars: it was still ticking. "Within a week you will forget you ever had friends." Months had gone by since I'd lost Rainy and Frenchy, *the two best friends I could never hope to find*; (a Rainyism) but though they'd been executed they had never stopped being with me, carrying on the same way they did when they were alive. Sometimes it seemed they hadn't really died so much as I myself had become a ghost.

I know this much is true — Rainy and Frenchy never stopped suffering for their crimes. Rainy, who looked so frail it was hard to imagine her giving birth to anything heavier than tears, had borne conjoined twins who'd needed a medical intervention, one she couldn't afford. When they were six-weeks-old she left them in a Glad bag on the railway tracks where, she hoped, they wouldn't know what hit them. When a reporter asked Rainy to compare being given the death sentence to being run over by a train, she said "the train was quicker, the train was softer." Rainy believed she'd one day be reunited with her joined-together twins. She was saving all her hope, she said, for the afterlife.

Right until the very end Frenchy insisted *she* deserved to die for killing her son. They'd been robbing a bank, which they probably shouldn't have been doing since they were both high on pharmaceuticals and also on probation at the time.

The gun went off by mistake, Frenchy said. If her son had lived she would have made it up to him, though she didn't know how you could say you were sorry enough times to make up for shooting a family member in the head.

The newly dead use up a lot of our skull space. They were the ones we talked about when we got together, once a week, for mandatory group therapy. Rainy thought group therapy on Death Row was a joke; an even sicker joke was their insistence upon cleaning your arm with an alcohol swab before giving you a lethal injection. "It don't look good, you die first from some bad-ass infection," Frenchy tried to explain.

"Can I ask you a question?" our care and treatment counsellor always asked, instead of going ahead and asking the question itself. "If you love something, aren't you supposed to let it go free?" She talked like a fortune cookie and was something of a know-it-all. Rainy used to say she was so full of herself she didn't have room to eat.

We can be free of life, but can we ever be free of death? Rainy, who'd expected nothing from life ("one door closes, another bangs shut," she was forever saying) and hadn't been disappointed, didn't think death would be all that different, just more of the same walls painted avocado green, televisions tuned permanently to the God channel, and guards who tortured you with jokes you had to laugh at if you didn't want them horking in your soup. In prison we learned to laugh about everything that had happened to us in the past, because not laughing hurt too much inside. You had to let it out, the rage that was ready to split you apart, like a wishbone, one way or another.

Without acknowledging me the Latrine took a pair of aviator shades, Oakley's Eternal, with opaque pink frames, out of her handbag and put them on. Earl, who kept stealing glances at my escort's breasts, started the van and we pulled out of the Admissions and Discharges lot. It was bad luck, I knew, to look back, at least until the prison was out of sight. I didn't intend to look back. Not now, not ever. Visitors to Heaven Valley say it's the most beautiful prison in the world, but those of us who've done time inside that place know — the only beautiful prison is the one you are leaving behind.

As we headed into the early morning smog that hovered over the City of Angels, Earl offered the Latrine a bottle of mineral water. She shook her head, dismissively. "Bottle of water costs more than a gallon of gas," Earl said, as if he didn't appreciate the rebuff. He rambled on about the hard time he took from the War Department — his pet name for the wife — how having that cancer hadn't improved her disposition. She still tried to shove breakfast down his throat every morning when he'd sooner watch the TV. He said he had to drink bottled water to wash away the taste of the sausages and beans he choked down before leaving home, because eating was easier than arguing. "Some women think the way to a man's stomach is through his mouth," he said.

He paused and took another swig, as if to prove his point, his eyes straying back to my escort's breasts, groping at their yeasty rise and fall, and resting there.

"I go along with it. I mean, if she wants to force breakfast into me so I'll live longer, I'll eat. It's easier than paying for a divorce." He made a face, as if the water had an unexpected bitter taste, too. "You married? Kids?"

My escort stared straight ahead out the window. "Was. Once. Dickwad had kids but not me, personally. Fuck, no."

The traffic had slowed and Earl switched to a more philosophical mode. We hadn't really made much progress out here in the modern world — a commuter on this six-lane freeway

GIVEN

moved more slowly than an old-time horse and buggy, he said. When we rounded a bend in the road I saw the cause of the congestion: two women trying to hitch a ride beside the broken-down body of their van. One of them held a crying baby; Earl said "sorry ladies." What with all the "criminal element and their ilk at large all over the place," he said, you'd have to be crazy to pick up hitchhikers these days, even the fairer sex, because it could be a trap. "You pull over and the next thing you know you're driving them down the road where they have a murdering party to go to. No sir. I've got enough problems in my life without stopping for more."

The Latrine turned her face, trying, I imagined, to block out our driver's monologue, and lowered her window all the way. I took a big breath of the dust-and-eucalyptus-smelling late summer air as we entered a tunnel where the words NO MORE ACCIDENTS had been sprayed in day-glo red. "No such thing as an accident," Earl said. He accelerated until we were back out in the hazy sunlight.

"One daughter, she's a hairdresser in Stockton," he continued, in answer to a question I hadn't heard asked. He switched lanes. "The son's predeceased. Suicided himself." He switched back again. "From the day he was born I never understood him."

I stared through the bars at the planes coming in for a landing, and saw the sign saying, "Airport Exit Ahead". Earl lit a cigarette, then stubbed it out. "I'm supposed to stay quit," he said.

He didn't continue right away but studied the road in front of him. "The boy, he was a peaceifistic kind of kid, hated guns, any kind of violence. He wanted to play the piano. You know what they say about kids. They don't come with instructions."

Earl said a day didn't go by when he didn't wish he'd been more of a father. He wished he could have accepted his son the way he'd been. If he could turn back the clocks again he'd even pay for piano lessons.

I could see planes circling overhead. Earl increased his speed, seeming not to notice the roadworks up ahead. The Latrine grew more agitated as the freeway merged into one lane. I wondered if she was worrying about the same thing I was thinking: what would happen if we met another vehicle coming the opposite way?

Earl narrowed his eyes, as if the white lines were leading him somewhere he had never intended to go. I followed his gaze, saw the world floating towards us on waves of breath, and when I glanced at him again his eyes had become hopelessly fixed on the Latrine's breasts.

"Holy fuck," she cried; Earl had misjudged the distance between her side of the van and a tree covered with brilliant red blossoms. As he tried to get control, he missed the Exit to Departures and pulled a sudden, rash, U-turn on Airport Boulevard. I saw the giant billboard with its bigger question looming up in front of us:

ETERNITY
WHERE DO YOU THINK YOU'RE GOING?

Earl, as if entranced, gunned the van towards it.

After the crash I saw, in the shattered mirrors of his sunglasses, three red blossoms reflected, as if each one had been placed there in memory of our lives. I'd spent my life feeling that I was hanging on to the side of the planet with suction cups, and now all of a sudden I had been hurled into the luminous hereafter and my singing heart was full.

Then came the usual crowd of the morbidly curious, like worms after rain, straining to get a closer look, a vicarious taste of mortality. A putrid, steaky smell filled the air. The volume on the van's radio seemed to be getting louder with each breath I took. I looked at my watch, but the face had been smashed off.

I lay for the longest time where I had been thrown clear of the wreckage, intoxicated by the pure feel of blood coursing through my veins. I tasted my own flesh, and heard sirens winding down. After a while my thoughts became the colour of water; I got to my feet, brushed myself off, and looked at the scene from my new perspective.

Fate always gives you two choices: the one you *should* take, and the one you do. Earl had made the wrong choice, and now he lay face down in the stubble-grass next to my lifeless escort, his body so black it stood out like a hole in the day. How long, I wondered, before the police notified the War Department, who would forever wish she hadn't forced breakfast down her husband's throat before he'd left the house that morning, and would always feel guilty for not having kissed him goodbye?

Fatty be fucked like a bologna pop tart, Frenchy whispered in my ear.

Then my thoughts of Earl vanished, merging with the traffic that was, once again, beginning to flow. I picked up my escort's purse and her aviator shades that lay on the grass a few feet away from me. I put the aviators over my eyes — I remember thinking then that nothing, not even your life, looks as beautiful as when you are leaving it behind — and turned to face the terminal building.

§ § §

Given time we begin to lose all interest in our past, but I still remember those first hours after the accident with a kind of detached curiosity. I expected I might feel everything more intensely than I had when I was a prisoner, but instead the world right away assumed an ordinariness that filled me with a mixture of homesickness and dread. For most of my life only the fear of death had prevented me from dying all the way. I felt afraid, now, of what I was about to become. Our care and treatment counsellor had reminded me every chance she got, "To free yourself is nothing, the real problem is knowing what to do with your freedom." By escaping, I knew, I had exiled myself to the lonely recklessness of the fugitive. Suddenly I felt as if I had been cast adrift in a leaky boat without oars, no charts, no stars to go by, only an endless emptiness, and the final consolation: sorrow and its truth.

The airport was under construction and I had to enter at the Arrivals level. Everything I looked at seemed to shine with its own light — the plummy grains of wood in the panelling on the wall, the red blouse of a woman walking towards me, the eyeless GI in the wheelchair, the chunky brown dog hunched beside him, the poster advertising HEAD, a kind of footwear, the sign advising against making jokes, particularly about bombs or hijacking. They had a similar rule at the Facility: when you wrote a letter you weren't allowed to joke — about anything: sex, politics, religion, or any aspect of institutional life.

Two of my faithful correspondents had stopped writing to me when they died: my father in my sixth year on the Row, of heart failure, and my mother, six years to the very day later, following a freak gardening accident. After twelve years — thirteen if you count the year I was a hostage on Tranquilandia — I had lost touch with most of my friends;

being on Death Row could be said to have tested the bound-
aries of what is meaningful between people and the way we
are tied to each other without ever understanding why. There
had been too much explaining to do, and in the end I had
realized I really didn't know anybody very well, not even
my estranged husband. These days when I closed my eyes I
couldn't remember what Vernal looked like, or the taste of his
skin, or the way he'd kept his eyes open when he kissed me, as
if he'd been afraid I might disappear if he so much as blinked.

The morning light struck the terminal windows like a
backhand to the mouth. I had become so used to being led
everywhere, having to ask permission or send in a written
request before I made a move in any direction, that now,
having abandoned myself to fate, I had become lost.

I let my shadow lead me, trying to see whether I could
catch the reflection of my face in other people's dark glasses, to
verify I was real. My shadow rounded a corner and I followed
it into a public washroom where I removed the Eternals and
hesitated for a moment, looking at myself in the wall of mirrors
over the sinks, my eyes the ice blue of power-line insulators,
my mouth turned down from the way things had gone. I put
on the aviators again (*What you do now? Win an Oscar?* Rainy
breathed in my ear) wanting to stay hidden.

I turned from the mirror, and locked myself in a stall where
I could go through the Latrine's purse in privacy. Along with
forty-five dollars in small bills and some change, my escort's
purse contained a collection of photo booth snapshots — her
ex and his two boys making faces for the camera — and her
Department of Corrections ID card.

I took my few possessions, including a toothbrush, a
change of clothes, prison issue pyjamas, a photograph of my
son, and a clean sweatshirt out of the duffel bag, then turned

the sweatshirt inside out so that the Heaven Valley logo didn't raise any red flags at the check-in counter. I put the ID and the change in the pocket of my jeans, and slipped the rest of the money in my sock, then stuffed the Latrine's wallet in the sanitary napkin disposer. I wasn't proud of myself for doing that, but at least this way someone might find it and turn it in to the Lost and Found. I repacked my duffel bag, and left the washroom without glancing again in the mirror. Then I found a pay phone and called Vernal at his office in Vancouver, collect.

I tried to tell him I'd been in a wreck but a gurgling, rattling sound came out of my throat, as if my breath were slogging through a slough of mucous. "My God, you sound terrible," Vernal said. "You should see . . . don't they have doctors down there . . . wherever you are? I'll try getting someone on my cell . . . just hold on . . . is there someplace you can . . . you still with me?"

I nodded into the receiver, furrowed my brow, wanting Vernal to stay calm, to know I was giving this question proper consideration, when really I knew he couldn't see me and I felt lonely as the furthest stars. Bullying muzak blared from a speaker somewhere near my spinning head. Vernal kept asking if I was still there, had I had anything to drink? At first I thought he was asking if I was drunk, then realized he meant water, that I needed to drink water so I wouldn't dehydrate. I promised him I would buy a bottle as soon as the world stopped turning so fast, and gave him the details, my new alias — he said he would book me a ticket home online. I waited until the dizziness passed and I could walk without drawing attention to myself, then rode an elevator up one floor to Departures.

All around me people shouted the intimate details of their travel worries into the palms of their hands. I felt conspicuous, even though I blended with the crowed that was dressed, for the most part, casually, in jeans and sweatshirts like the one I wore. The only noticeable difference was my shoes.

And my face, the face that had recently appeared on the cover of *Newsmakers,* a special issue profiling women waiting to die on Death Row. I'd signed the release forms though I hadn't seen a copy of the magazine to date. I was death's latest poster girl and my mug shot had been on TV, too, on more than one occasion — most recently on *Executions Live!* the night Rainy died.

Nearly everyone I saw carried a bottle of water — hard to believe the planet would have had so many pure mountain springs (as Vernal would have said, "Evian is naïve spelled backwards.") When I first met Rainy she used to wash her important parts with the bottled water we were issued, the tap water having been declared unpotable at the time: she claimed they made the taps in our cell sinks especially hard to turn on and off so that girls would break their fingernails trying to wash, and the institution would save money by not having to provide us with nail clippers. Frenchy said her logic didn't make sense, that bottled water cost way more than nail files.

Your point? said Rainy.

You stupid? Frenchy shot back.

I stopped at the first newsstand I came to, to buy my own bottle of water, and a copy of *Newsmakers,* then stood waiting to pay while the salesclerk, applying a layer of blue nail polish, talked on her phone. "When Carley broke up with him he wanted to kill himself so he ate a pencil." She looked up at me, spreading her fingers to let the polish dry. "He wanted to give himself lead poisoning."

My eyes shifted to a nearby table, piled high with books that had been marked down — how to die with dignity, how to cheat death, how to write a foolproof will, an etiquette book including helpful hints on everything from planning an after-funeral soiree to the right coloured flowers to send the deceased's family and *Why We Live After Death* — not the kind of escapist literature I could imagine anyone enjoying on their flight. The salesclerk must have read my thoughts because she removed her cell phone from her ear and volunteered that death wasn't real popular in airports, the main reason why her manager had decided to clear their stock. "When people are travelling, they don't want to think about, you know, not getting there type of deal?" I could tell she wanted to get rid of me so she could get back to her phone call, so I paid with cash and thanked her for her help.

I found the American Airlines check-in counter and joined the long line snaking its way towards the only available ticket agent. The man in front of me was watching a rerun of *Executions Live!* on his laptop and I found myself sneaking glances over his shoulder. Since I'd been convicted and sent to prison, executions had become a spectator sport; on the night Rainy was dispatched to meet her maker, a contingency of pro-death advocates revved their motor homes and honked their horns and set off fireworks outside the prison gates. We didn't know it at the time but Rainy, who had injected drugs for so long she didn't have an uncollapsed vein left in her body, was undergoing a "cut-down". Shortly before midnight as the pro-deathers fired up their barbecues and began grilling greasy slabs of bacon, corrections officers, who had no experience as surgeons, were in the process of slitting Rainy's arm open, searching, desperately, for a usable blood vessel into which they could syphon their lethal cocktail.

I'd been wrong when I'd assumed that in a culture as show business oriented as ours, televised executions would soon lose their appeal and be cancelled for poor ratings. More people watched Rainy die from a lethal injection than tuned in to the Super Bowl the next day.

A second ticket agent arrived to open another check-in desk, and the line moved slowly forward.

"Over here. Can I help the next person in line?" I saw she meant me, and toted my duffel bag up to the counter and placed it on the scales.

The agent asked to see some ID, and I gave her the Department of Corrections card. She glanced at it, and then began tapping on her keyboard, her smile retreating behind her teeth.

I took a deep breath, and removed the aviators so I could look her in the eye. She looked back at me, briefly, screwing up her face. She tapped on her keyboard again as if it refused to cooperate, then, without taking her eyes off the screen, asked me how many pieces of luggage I'd like to check.

"Just this one." I pointed at the scales, wishing I could fold myself like an old sweater and climb inside my duffel bag, worried that it was suspiciously light. The agent tagged my bag to Vancouver and apologized for the time it had taken to get me checked in; the system was making her life hell today, which accounted, I assumed, for her terse manner. She printed my ticket: Vernal had warned me that tickets were issued electronically now and not to act as if this came as a surprise to me.

"Any carry-on baggage?"

I shook my head. The agent gave me back my Corrections ID, and handed me my boarding pass. "Enjoy your flight to Vancouver, Ms Lootine," she said, pronouncing "Lootine" to rhyme with "shootin". When I stood there, staring at my e-ticket, unsure of what to do next, she lowered her voice and, as if sensing my hesitation, said, "You can go. You're all free to go. Enjoy the rest of your day."

I walked towards Security, knowing I should feel grateful for something, if for nothing more than for the miracle of having made it this far; I thought of the wholeness the word *free* implied. A lot of people seem to believe that in prison you're not allowed to have a life of your own. They are mistaken. In prison I had nothing *but* a life of my own. (Rainy argued that freedom was the only thing you didn't get on the Row, but even there you were given the freedom to make a limited number of choices — for instance, which form of capital punishment was best suited to your personality — lethal injection, gas chamber, electric chair, hanging, or the firing squad. When you couldn't make up your own mind, they chose for you. "Dead if you do, dead if you don't," Rainy put it.)

After clearing Security where once again I escaped being recognized, I headed for the departure lounge. I passed booth after booth, marvelling at how much was for sale — everything from sequin-covered running shoes to barbed-wire encased cigarette lighters. There was even a stand devoted to shoelaces — the kind you "never have to tie again" — and would have cost more than a month's wages in prison. When I stopped to buy a coffee at Hooked, I saw the posters. "Missing. Have You Seen This Child?" The photographs showed a smiling, inquisitive face, beloved of someone, last seen going out a door, waiting at a bus stop, peddling towards a corner store.

"Will that be a Blast or a Belt," said the boy waiting to take my money, after I'd decided on a macchiato, then changed my mind because I didn't know what a macchiato was, and asked for a cappuccino instead. I could hear the hint of impatience in his voice. "Blast or Belt?" he repeated, looking at me as if to say where had I been all my life.

"Small?" I said.

"The smallest you can order is a Buzz," he explained, the way one might speak to a recalcitrant child. "Small is really a Short. We call it a Buzz. Tall's what you get if you ask for, like, a small, but it's not really, it's like, that's why we call it a Blast. Large is a Belt, and Super Large is, like, a Bloat?"

"Okay, then. Tall."

"Excellent. You want a Skinny or a 2%? Sprinkles on top, extra foam, mini-marshmallows, cinnamon, nutmeg or chocolate crunch?"

"Surprise me," I said.

The boy rolled his eyes, exasperated with me, it was clear. I took off my shoe and reached into my sock for the money to pay for my coffee but when I looked up again I saw him staring at me, and my first thought was that now, knowing where I kept my stash, he would hunt me down later and rob me, but I had to remind myself: I wasn't at the Facility anymore. And people, citizens in the free world, didn't keep their money in socks, especially not in socks inside shoes that had no laces.

The boy wiped an already clean counter and rearranged a display of juice bottles — "Freedom of Choice — Big Gulp Brand." I cancelled the coffee and asked for a bottle of the turquoise-coloured juice instead. The colour made me think of the sky, the day I'd left Angel behind on Tranquilandia.

I'd spent my years on the Row not allowing myself to think of my son as being dead. What had helped me to live, at first, was to believe my son's life was going on somewhere without me, just as putting my own life in danger, living from moment to moment on Death Row, helped me forget what I had lost.

But now everything that reminded me of Angel went through me like a spear. I held him in my thoughts as I held on to life, clumsily, but with a big, "Open 24 hours" heart. In every child I caught sight of I saw what my boy might have become. I saw him as the baby in the arms of the woman in white shorts and a pink cardigan; I saw him in the frown of the two-year-old refusing to let go of a piece of chewing gum he had picked out of an ashtray; I saw him in the six-year-old missing his two front teeth.

Missing. One word but it summed up a lifetime. Missing my son was *how* I lived, and now I imagined him running on ahead of me and disappearing into the play area for children, hiding behind a purple cartoon plane cut out of plywood, with plucked birds poking their heads from the windows. The pilot looked like a demented child.

I saw all this but in my heart I knew: the dead don't age. They don't grow up, they stay stuck. Angel, his perfect earlobes, his fists, his soft baby-head, would never grow older. The curtain sighing in the slight breeze along the wall would always be enough to make him stop nursing, and turn his head from my breast, as if he were listening to something I'd never be able to hear. *Nació de pie*, he was born on his feet, born all-knowing and streetwise, and he would stay that way, for eternity, stretching his tiny limbs into each new morning, beating up the very air we breathed with his fists. Missing my boy was the black and endless night I had tumbled into. It was where I lived.

I didn't have long to wait before they called my flight. Two youths, who looked as if they'd been on Spring Break since February, slumped into the seats across the aisle. "What does a person have to do to get a drink around here?" the one with a watch tattooed to his wrist (perpetually 4:20) said, letting everyone around him know that it was his constitutional right not to fasten his seat belt, either.

"Dude," his companion replied. "This ain't no fuckin' disco, dude. We like left that, like I don't know when, you know, whenever?"

I sat back, thinking it would be a long flight to Vancouver, and heard the whumping of baggage being loaded into the belly of the plane as a man of generous proportions took the aisle seat next to me, looking anxious the way people do when trying to settle into the small allocation of uncomfortable personal space that will be home to them for their flight. I lowered the armrest thinking, unkindly, that a person of his size should have paid for two seats.

"I shouldn't have pigged out on that second helping last night," he said, as if he had, in his sleep, gained the weight. "My mother's always telling me, 'son, push away from the gravy'." His efforts at unnecessary conversation were answered by a measured sigh on my part, but not even that silenced him.

In the bowels of the plane a dog began to bark. "I hope he don't know something we don't know," my seatmate said. "Dogs have an inner instinct. They can sniff out things like epileptics and cancer." He was sweating profusely and kept mopping his brow with the paper towels he produced from his jacket pocket.

I nodded, once, hoping he'd get the hint, and reached for the safety instructions in the seat-back pocket in front of me and concentrated on the drawings of passengers calmly leaning forward, hands covering heads, to brace themselves for an imminent collision with Mt. Fujiyama. The cabin lights flickered, an alarm bell sounded, and the skyway was withdrawn.

Once we were in the air another attendant came through the cabin distributing pillows and headsets, and small hot towels. The captain piped up to say passengers on the right side of the plane would soon be treated to a spectacular view of the San Andreas Fault, as if the earth had heaved and shifted thousands of years ago solely for their benefit. This seemed of little interest to the two across the aisle who had stripped down to their wife-beaters and were refreshing their armpits with the hot towels the flight attendant had given us. I stared at the empty air on the left hand side of the aircraft, wishing I could escape my circumstances, then remembered I had the magazine.

"You on vacation?" my seatmate asked.

I shook my head.

"Business trip?"

I shook my head again.

"You look familiar," he persisted. "We meet someplace before? Dallas? Fort Lauderdale, maybe?" He volunteered that he spent a good deal of his time in the air because of the exciting and interesting nature of *his* job. *What he be, some kind of flu germ?* I heard Rainy sniff.

His company, he informed me, made plastic eyes for stuffed animals; he had a contract with Corrections because convict-made teddy bears had become hot commodities ever since executions started going live. "Eye-Yie-Eyes? You heard of us?" He seemed disappointed when I looked at him, blankly, and gave me his card. "Deacon Maplethorpe, Northwest Regional Rep."

Our fellow travellers across the aisle had passed out and were snoring. "Faggot dope dealers," Maplethorpe said, in a voice so full of disgust that I wondered, for a moment, what he was hiding.

GIVEN

Hope rhyme wid dope, I heard Frenchy snicker. *You got any?* Twelve years had gone by since the time I'd given up my life to the White Lady, but even now, at the thought it, my palms began to sweat and my mouth filled with saliva, remembering what I knew. I loved the ritual, getting high, being alone, way out there. But you never stop to think about what comes after.

Maplethorpe took two packets of pretzels from the flight attendant's tray and gave me one of them. "They don't even allow guns into Canada," he continued. "You can imagine how they feel about dope dealers." He had a high-pitched voice, hard to listen to, like a series of musical notes that kept getting higher, and slightly more off-key.

"Some of my ladies are featured in this," Maplethorpe said, pointing at my face on the cover of the magazine that lay, still unopened, on my lap. My cheeks reddened — I feared he might recognize me, even though the photograph had been taken over a decade ago, the day after my arrest. My hair had been described as "torrential" on the front page of every newspaper in the country (it had rained, and a muttersome wind had followed me from the detention centre to the court-house), my skirt "slit up the side" (it had torn getting into the police van) and my face "expressionless". Looking closely at my grainy image now, I thought: it was just that there had been no other way left to look.

I flipped to the magazine's centrefold that featured "Noosemakers: Seven Condemned Mothers Who Kill." In each photograph I could see the dark stain at the core of the woman's being, and the beauty fanning out from that centre. This beauty, the way the photographer had captured it, had a way of making pain seem almost desirable. The stain, and the same dope-sick look in their eyes, described the history of their hearts.

People don't hold grudges against drug-dealers or bank robbers given a decent lapse of history, but there's no such thing as "used to be" when it comes to murder.

"This girl — Charlene — I knew her back in Texas, she's just had surgery on her hands," Maplethorpe said. "Claims she can't even open her painkillers now.

"That's Deshawn. Met her once, too. She's *not* a cokehead, she'd be the first to let you know. She's only addicted to the *smell* of cocaine."

I turned the page and found more pictures of sick, beautiful women. "I seen a lot of ladies smile like this," Maplethorpe said, pointing to a woman covered in tattoos. "That type of smile, it don't live long enough to call itself a normal life span."

"That used to be Halo," he said, as I lingered on the page with her photograph. "A real angel before she became a drug addict of blood." Halo stood over a man passed out on a mattress in an alleyway. She wore his tie around her neck, and an evening dress. She appeared to be singing.

"She don't sing no more. She got cancer of the voice." I turned the page, wondering how much more I could take. "Bernadette." He inhaled, as if even his own fat body had no more space in it for memories as doleful as this, and tore open his bag of pretzels with his teeth.

"She always said she'd never stick a needle in her arm, or let any man make a bitch out of her. The gentleman she shacked up with made her clean the commode with her . . . " He paused, popped a pretzel in his mouth, licked his lips, "You want my opinion, guy like that don't deserve a good-looking lady."

Every photograph had a story, each one more desperate than the last. "This one, they mopped the floor with her hair before nailing her to a tree. She went back a week later and shot all three of them in cold blood. That one, she escaped a month before her date with Old Sparky. She was last seen getting into a car."

I turned another page, and saw my face again — wearing a tired and slightly embarrassed smile for the flashbulb, as if I were a celebrity arriving in Paris after a trans-Atlantic flight. I don't remember smiling, ever, on the Condemned Row, but here it was, proof. I had pretended to smile and by accident it had come out looking real.

Maplethorpe wouldn't quit. "If you ask me, which you didn't, she don't look to me like the kind of mother who could . . . " He stopped mid-sentence, as if incapable of sullying his mouth with words like *kill her child.*

What does she look like, the kind of mother who kills her child? I sped-read the article — not difficult since it was less than a paragraph long — and I knew everything it contained. New DNA evidence, unavailable at the time of my arrest, my lawyer said (the same lawyer, Pile Jr., who had promised he would get me out of prison if it took him the rest of his life) would prove, beyond the shadow of a reasonable doubt, my innocence.

I closed the magazine as the flight attendant came through the cabin with our Customs Declaration forms. I filled mine in, ticking NO to everything on the list — NO alcohol or cigarettes, NO dairy products, NO gifts, NO contraband, then put the form and my unopened pretzels in the Latrine's handbag, lowered my seat back as far as it would go, and closed my eyes. Maplethorpe didn't get the hint and kept talking. He told me he had a limo and a driver waiting for him at the airport. It would be his very great pleasure, he said, to take me where I wanted to go.

≤ ≤ ≤

I was not among the passengers who applauded because the captain did his job and put the plane down on the runway, not on the slopes of Grouse Mountain or at the bottom of Lost Lagoon. I was ready to vacate my seat the minute the engines went into reverse, but had to wait for Deacon Maplethorpe to solve the puzzle of how to unbuckle his seat belt first.

He told me to "go ahead," not out of courtesy, I think, but because he was not what you would call a natural leader; I led the way up the aisle with Maplethorpe close behind.

When I entered the skyway leading to the arrivals area I felt, for the first time since leaving the State Facility earlier that day I could look at the world around me and feel only a small ache. Perhaps this was freedom: to ache, but not to be incapacitated by pain, the way it is when you are locked up for days, months — whole seasons gone. Feigning normality, acting as if it were everyday, I walked through an airport not knowing what I was headed for, pretending to be in control: this was my single, certain task.

I followed the signs to Immigration with Maplethorpe still on my heels. A flight from Bangkok had come in ahead of us and I joined the line behind two young women smelling of unwashed hair. "Eau de travel," Maplethorpe said, sniffing. The one wearing the most beads had lost a sandal and kept bending to examine the heel of her bare foot as if she might have stepped in something.

The Immigration Officer barely glanced at my ID as she asked how long I'd be visiting Canada. I said a couple of weeks. Purpose of visit? Pleasure. Was I bringing any gifts, alcohol or tobacco? I said I had nothing. The immigration officer scribbled a code, in green, on my declaration and waved me through.

My duffel bag was the first piece of luggage onto the carousel. Maplethorpe insisted on carrying it for me since he had no luggage of his own. I gave up trying to convince him I could handle it myself, remembering what Vernal had said, how when you are kind by nature you end up attracting a lot of people you don't like. Together we joined the long line headed for the Customs hall.

I watched as passengers ahead of me handed their forms to a Customs officer and were directed one of two ways — to the left, to an area marked with a red "Stop" sign, or to the right where a green sign said, "Exit: Nothing to Declare". The young women off the flight from Bangkok had veered to the left as if they had been through this procedure many times before, spreading their souvenirs and the contents of their travel-worn backpacks on the counter, the way street vendors might display their wares.

I thought of the women I'd met in Tranquilandia, "cover girls" hired to pose as grieving mothers, rewarded with free trips to Disney World for carrying the gutted bodies of dead babies stuffed with cocaine, on planes to Los Angeles or Miami. Poor, broke, just wanting to offload their cargo and go home, they were paid a pittance in Tranquilandian pesos to walk with their *contrabando* through Customs.

Maplethorpe stood beside me, fidgeting with the straps on my duffel bag. He began, in his irritating high-pitched voice, making small talk about airport security, how he hated to see our human rights being eroded, how everywhere you looked you had a camera watching you these days. His voice grew more frantic the more he talked, the musical note now as constant and insistent as a canary's on its way down a mine shaft. It was then that I spotted the blue wall of police officers, some of them holding dogs straining at their leashes — lined up by the exit in the Customs area.

I felt my heart trying to slide out between the gap in my front teeth. I had come so far, allowed myself to hope. What had I been thinking? Just because I had risen from the walking dead, had I truly believed I could walk away from my past, also? *Evian is* naive *spelled backwards.*

Maplethorpe thrust the duffel bag into my arms as if he knew what was about to come down. I handed my card to the Customs officer who pointed me — no suspicious look, not even a question — to the right, and I turned to face what now seemed to me the logical conclusion of the course of action I'd taken.

I froze as the wall came rushing towards us, full, suddenly, of a new kind of fear, that from now on my life would be a series of small subtractions from what had been — for the last few hours at least — a taste of freedom. I felt myself being jostled and heard the sound of their keys, the sound that lets you remember, when you would most like to forget, that you don't exist, you are in exile.

I waited for what would come next as time stopped for me, the way it does when you have a near death experience or a spectacular night of lovemaking. From a distance I watched myself collapse onto the floor, and then a man wearing a turban — not a cop, not Deacon Maplethorpe — bent over me, saying, "You okay, Missus?"

He helped me to my feet, led me to a bench and told me to sit until I got my breath, he would call Security or was there perhaps a family member who might be meeting me? I shook my head, thanked him, said I'd be fine, and as soon as he left I got up and began walking. I kept walking towards the doors that opened automatically into a world where I could lose myself again, but I kept hearing Maplethorpe's pleading voice over the barking, and when I looked back I saw him being handcuffed by a police officer while another held the dog who had plunked himself in front of my seatmate's briefcase.

Maplethorpe looked terrified and I felt ashamed of myself for abandoning him. The dog handler spoke into a cordless phone, and then a dozen other men in black nylon jackets with DAS in white letters across their backs, had my travelling companion pinned to the ground.

I bolted from the Customs hall into the arrivals area where greeters with signs in many languages awaited passengers from all over the world; I looked around, desperately, for Vernal, who'd promised to meet my plane. I don't know why I expected him to be on time — he used to joke that he'd be late for his own funeral — but I had hoped he might have made an exception, just this once.

The airport didn't feel safe to me, and I headed outside. A black limousine pulled up to the curb and the two men who'd sat across from us on the plane jumped in. The pieces started falling into place: Maplethorpe had been a mule and this had been his trial run. I knew from my own experience — it had happened to me the same way — how *contrabandistos* worked. They have their lieutenants follow the drug runner through Customs — anything goes wrong they disappear. You get popped. It's you and the lions.

There was no smog, like there'd been in L.A. and a clean, quick wind blew off the distant, snow-capped mountains. I crossed the road to a miniature park, where a sign said, "Rest Area No Loitering". Two benches faced each other in a patch of grass bordered by flower beds full of petunias with sunburn. I sat down on the bench partially shaded by an ornamental maple, opened my duffel bag and took out the one photograph of my son I had ever possessed. You couldn't even see his face, only a blur of white, as if his soul had streaked away. There used to be more — one arm, his little hand knotted into a fist, poking out of his sleeve — but even that had been worn away from so much touching.

Now, as a breeze rose from the grass, I imagined taking my son's hand and leading him up onto one of those mountain slopes then stopping to look down on what we'd left behind. I caught a breath of him; he smelled the way a bird's wings smell of the wind long after the wind has died.

I heard a familiar voice, looked up across the parking lot, and saw Vernal sprinting towards me, calling my name. He wore a plain white T-shirt, freshly ironed jeans and hiking boots. From a distance, nothing about him appeared to have changed from the day I'd met him in a New York nightclub — the luckiest accident of his life, he used to claim. His face was still unlined, boyish almost.

Vernal, who kept himself in what is commonly called 'condition', had always maintained that if you look good and dress well you don't need a purpose in life. Today as he got closer though, I saw he carried in his body a kind of gentle weariness, a faint slump to his shoulders as if he were weighted down by doubts of some kind. I saw, too, that he was experimenting with a beard and a moustache, in keeping, I realized later, with his new, more leisurely, island lifestyle. (Vernal had been spending much less time in town since he'd acquired an old homestead on a small island "practically off the grid" where he went every weekend and most of the summer. "I can't wait until you see the place," he'd written me in his last letter. "You'll think you've died and gone to heaven.") When I got to my feet he hugged me, as if we were lovers who had been parted from one another for a long time, but not for the first time; lovers whose lives had become a familiar ritual of disruption and reconciliation.

I had tried to imagine, since I'd been gone, living with Vernal again. He had, after all, visited me and written to me, faithfully, since I'd been sentenced and begun my countdown on the Row. I went to hug him back, but gestures of affection had become foreign to me. In prison we avoided physical contact because when you felt good, if only for a moment, it would hurt even more afterwards.

Vernal picked up my bag and nodded towards the multi-levelled car park. "Let's get out of here, then. They take you to the cleaners in airport parking lots." Vernal had always had a parsimonious streak. I once heard him on the telephone trying to negotiate a better price for his own funeral, the one he'd already predicted he'd be late for.

I put the photograph of Angel, and the Latrine's ID, in my jacket pocket. I didn't know where Vernal was taking me, though I was sure it wouldn't be to our old house in the suburb of Astoria, twenty minutes from downtown Vancouver. When we bought the place I'd nicknamed it the Walled Off Astoria because of the security that included a gatehouse manned twenty-four hours by guards. Vernal had moved my mother into the house after my father died — "she's not going to be around forever, either," he'd written me. He had acquired a house sitter, a client whom he was helping "get back on his feet," and had put the house on the market the day he found my mother in her rose garden, impaled on a pair of secateurs on top of her turtle-shaped stepping-stones.

Vernal had been articling when I met him, but some part of me had always suspected his heart hadn't been in the practice of law. I think he would have settled for a black and white world, but the law confronted him, daily, with uncomfortable shades of guilt. "Nobody is innocent," he was wont to say, "but some are more guilty than others." Drug traffickers were his specialty. He charged exorbitant sums to make sure their guilt couldn't be proven beyond a reasonable doubt.

He had said the same thing to me when I was arrested; over and over again, in each letter he wrote: "you are only guilty if they can prove it." For me, once I'd lost Angel, guilt or innocence no longer mattered. I used to think there was nothing more that could happen to me. Until Frenchy said, "You think their dyin' be the worst thing that happen. Then they stay dead."

Some nights I dreamed Angel lay buried in the black earth under the guaiac tree where he'd once dozed, peacefully, the coppery blossoms settling on his sleeping eyes like coins. But then I would have to remind myself that even if my son had lived, he would no longer be a child; by now he would have grown into a young man with his father's black hair tied back in a ponytail, a hollow place in the centre of his chest that I would fill, if I ever found him again, with tears.

Vernal strode ahead, taking the steps two at a time, enquiring, over his shoulder, about the heat wave down south, what inedible meal had been served on the plane — the sorts of questions people always ask when they meet you at the airport and run out of things to say. I told him about Maplethorpe and the two lieutenants, and what had taken place in the Customs hall as he scanned the parking lot's third floor for his ride. "You're still the same old trouble-magnet" he said.

It was hard to miss, the Cadillac, black with stiffly folded drapery to match, and Ceese Fun (a ghostlike "erals" after the "fun" part) painted on the side. Vernal opened the rear doors to show me the cavernous interior, the rollers, embedded in a fake walnut floor, laid out in two straight lines. "To help ease the passengers out," he said, as if he had read my mind, then adding, hastily, when he saw my look, "You're not *that* kind of passenger yet. Go ahead. Jump in front. You're riding shotgun."

Vernal took an "On Appointment" sign from the glove compartment and put it on the dashboard where it could easily be seen. He said he'd got a deal on the hearse when Ceese, Sr., the funeral director on Kliminawhit, passed away. "His son sold off the old man's whole rolling stock and I took it instead of a retainer for some work I'd done." When we left the parking lot, the attendant doffed his cap after taking Vernal's money.

I noticed how people glanced at us then looked quickly away. Vernal said after a while you got used to it. Driving the hearse had given him a whole new kind of freedom — there was no chance of getting stopped at a roadblock or ticketed for speeding through a school zone, for example. I wondered why anyone would need to speed in a hearse?

"Nuns," he said, swerving to avoid sending two jaywalking sisters into their afterlives. "Sheep. One black one. Flock of starlings. Nuisances." Vernal still had a habit of pointing out things to me, without giving me a chance to see whatever he'd seen, for myself, first. "Cyclists. Over there. Repair job. Without a manual."

The outside air looked good enough to breathe. Vernal wanted to hear all about my great escapade (as he called it) and I told him it hadn't exactly been masterminded, there'd been an opportunity and I had simply walked away.

Half an hour later we headed onto a causeway that led to the ferry terminal. "Accident," said Vernal, pointing to the twisted wreck of a car with NO DRY GRAD 2000 spray-painted on its caved-in roof. "I see that," I said, a little tersely, thinking of my dead escort and driver, Earl. *No such thing as an accident.*

I hadn't thought about my own car accident since I'd landed in Vancouver but now I wondered if the Latrine's Dickwad would tie a ribbon to the maimed blossom-tree, if the kids would leave their favourite teddy bears on the spot where their stepmother had exited this life. Would Earl's bossy wife place a bottle of Evian water on the spot where her husband collided with ETERNITY? I saw myself, too, broken on the ground, trying to get up, the words WHERE DO YOU THINK YOU ARE GOING staring me in the face.

The trees all around us were beginning to be absorbed by the darkness. A great blue heron rose, like the ghost of a pterodactyl, and flapped off into the last remnants of an eggplant sunset, as Vernal paid for our tickets and pulled into the ferry line-up. We had an hour to kill before the ferry departed. I told Vernal I needed to stretch my legs and when I got out a fine mist of rain licked at my face, but I didn't mind; it felt like stars coming out all over my skin. The seagulls wheeled above me, around the flag that had snapped alive in the rising wind, and made me think of the congregations of dishevelled pelicans who kept dropping out of the sky like wind-blown umbrellas on the Tranquilandian coast, hundreds of them gliding south, that the locals told me meant rain. It rained the day I arrived in the City of Orchids and it rained the day I left. When all our other options had been exhausted, I'd taken Angel to a *curandero*, a faith healer, in that desperate place, an endless perfume factory of trees shedding their bright flowers on narrow roads where women fried fish on hot plates made from the ends of forty-four gallon drums, placed over dangerous-looking fires. I remembered rows of blackened huts, the passages between them stagnant chasms of sludge, silt and litter where small black pigs rooted for anything they could eat. And birds, wheeling above me that now brought back memories of my son.

Sometimes *any* memory of another can be godlike. I walked to the end of the wharf where I could hear the sound of each raindrop hitting the sea — each drip making a ripple that spread out from the centre — the lapping of waves. Looking down into the water I saw a white plastic bag billowing beneath the surface, caught in the current like a drowned swan.

A hard rain began to pelt the dock, the wind got up in gusts, and was soon whipping the flag so hard the *thwacking* sounds echoed out from the pole it was attached to. An announcement came for all passengers bound for Kliminawhit to return to their vehicles for loading. I wasn't dressed for weather like this, anyway, and sprinted back to the hearse, noting how much space the car behind us had left between his vehicle and ours. Not only do people dislike seeing a hearse, they especially don't like waiting in line behind one.

The lane next to us had filled up with a posse of RV's, with names like Rustler and Nomad and Wilderness Trails, implying their drivers spent a lot of time avoiding main roads, when the opposite was true. Parked beside us was a truck with MOTHER CLUCKERS painted on the side. The noises coming from the truck's cargo, packed together in crates the size of egg cartons, reminded me of the sounds some women on the Condemned Row made in their sleep.

I climbed in beside Vernal as the cars ahead of us began to move.

Rainwater beaded down the window as we drove onto the ferry like any ordinary couple riding towards their future in a hearse.

ॐ ॐ ॐ

Vernal found something to keep me dry — a grey waterproof cape he kept in his Emergency Preparedness Kit behind the driver's seat. It fit over my head and shoulders, and was several sizes too big. "It'll keep the rain from getting in, that's what matters," Vernal said.

We climbed the stairs to the main passenger deck. Vernal stopped at the purser's desk to pick up the key to our cabin and to book a table for dinner in the Fine Dining Lounge where he said he'd meet me in fifteen minutes. I stepped through two heavy doors onto the outside deck and smelled salt on the wind. A series of steel benches had been bolted to the deck and manacled to thick black posts at either end, as if someone were afraid the benches would be stolen. Piles of chain dotted the deck, coiled like great black helpings of spaghetti.

I heard the throb of the engine change pitch, and felt the ferry lurch beneath me. I leaned into the wind, pressing myself against the railing. As we slipped out of the dock and entered open water I reached into my pocket for the Latrine's ID, and dropped it over the ship's side, watching it stutter on the breeze until it landed on the foam and was swallowed in the ship's wake. *Ocean look way-blue, way it do on TV,* I heard Rainy whisper. *Any ocean blue, not just on TV,"* Frenchy shot back and then their otherworldly voices were drowned out by a recorded announcement welcoming us aboard.

I went back inside and followed the signs to the dining lounge where I leaned against the door, feeling self-conscious in my ill-fitting rain cape. I waited until I got tired of waiting, then fell in behind a party of revellers who stumbled into one another as they tried to negotiate their way through the Driftwood Bar door. I had never felt at home in a bar — Vernal's home away from home. I looked around for him, the way women for hundreds of years have done, standing lost in the doorway of a pub or lounge, wondering who they are married to and why it has come to this.

I spotted him at once. Vernal nearly always chose a corner table, farthest from the drink, as if trying to keep as far away from temptation as possible. Before I'd left him and moved into my own apartment, he'd always kept his commodity in the liquor cabinet in the living room and made the trip back and forth — from his office or outside by the pool or to wherever he did his drinking. He didn't like to have the bottle within arm's reach, believing this was the first sign of addiction, and that getting up and going to another room and then pouring a drink meant you had were not powerless over alcoholism.

On Vernal's right sat the most unattractive man I had ever seen, and I'd seen a lot of human ugliness, both inside and out. His skin, the colour of canned tuna, bore deep circular pockmarks.

A pregnant woman dressed in a short, sleeveless, loose-fitting tunic made of deer hide, combed the man's knotted waist-length mullet with the fingers of her right hand. She had eyes the same colour as the middle of a Mars Bar, so big they seemed to swallow the rest of her face, and cheekbones you could cut yourself on just from looking, and she cradled a little bundle in the crook of her other arm. She looked too young to be a mother, and to be expecting again so soon. Her own hair fell from her shoulders, a tantrum of red, which, if you weren't beautiful and fearless, you might consider an affliction. She was tall, almost too thin — *she be dying or else she be rich*, Rainy whispered. She'd slipped off her sandals, and kicked them under Vernal's chair.

As I stood watching, the woman leaned down and kissed the man I could barely stand to look at, the way new lovers do.

Maybe he hadn't always been so ugly, I thought. Maybe he'd been handsome once and then, after the acid had disfigured him, she'd stayed with him out of the goodness of her heart: when you were beautiful you could squander goodness. Perhaps, being so beautiful, she didn't know how to be unkind.

I considered sneaking out, going to wait for Vernal in our cabin, but then remembered — Vernal had the key. Besides, it was too late — he had seen me, and was signalling me over.

I slid in next to him, and he introduced me — as "a ghost from the past" — to Grace Moon and her friend, Al. Grace, who had a soft, feline quality, wore three carved gold bracelets on one arm, a giant key and a medicine pouch around her neck. I saw her scarred throat, the stitches stretching from one side of her neck to the other.

When she reached across the table to shake my hand, I saw more scars up her arms — slash-marks that followed her veins all the way from her wrists to her elbows — not just your run-of-the-mill cry for help. Rainy used to say Frenchy was lucky to have scars you could see, what was the use of having scars on the inside where you couldn't show them off to anyone? Where another girl might have had a broken heart tattooed on her breast, or a handcuff with a broken link on her wrist, Frenchy spent a lifetime tattooing her rage on her skin, bringing blood to the surface where everyone could see her pain.

I pulled my hand back, startled, as the bundle in Grace's lap let out an inhuman wail. Grace lifted him into the air and began rocking him with such fervour I worried she was going to shake to death the source of the terrible sound.

"I'd kill for a fix right now," Al muttered into his beer. His ugliness had not improved with proximity.

Grace's tawny eyes looked frozen gold, and her smile clicked off. "That's just Al," she said, looking at me apologetically, as if being "just Al" were an excuse for any kind of bad behaviour. She rocked the inconsolable creature in her arms; Al — not, I hoped, the baby's father — reached up and pushed his snagged locks out of his eyes, which was when I noticed his forearm covered in sores, the kind Rainy used to get from the repeated use of dirty needles. I *wanted* to feel sorry for Al, but I didn't have enough sorry in me for anyone that unpleasant.

"He can't help it — he's programed that way," Grace said, looking down at the bundle in her arms, and then back at Al. I didn't know whether she meant the baby, or "just Al".

Vernal rubbed the stubble on his chin with the heel of his hand. I could tell, by the fewness of his words, he was uncomfortable being around Al. Al wanted us to know this was their anniversary, the reason they were celebrating; he'd met Grace exactly one week ago when he was fresh out of rehab and looking for a buzz. Grace said she had stayed off drugs ever since her visit to the hospital to have photographs taken of the baby inside her — but she'd let him buy her one for the road. Grace drank her beer straight from the bottle, draining it, then, when the bottle was empty, picking at a corner of the label and peeling it off in little strips.

"She's drinking for two," Al said.

Grace lowered her eyes — now she was the one looking embarrassed. She said she believed her baby was going to be born with special powers — she had heard him drumming and singing from the inside of her. She reached into the pouch around her neck and took out a grainy ultrasound photo of her unborn child, stroking his tiny body, lightly, up and down, with her index finger, the way I had stroked my baby's eyelids when he was fitful or too tired to fall asleep.

The child in Grace's arms let out another *screak*, as if he sensed a threat. "Last night we couldn't get him to wake up for at least six hours," Grace said, wiping the baby's mouth, then tucking the photograph back into the pouch.

"She tried to blame me for looking at him," Al said, making his idea of an ugly face that seemed like an improvement over his real one.

Grace gave him a brief, tight smile. "We went to bed when it was getting light out, and Baby started to cry. I was glad. I thought we'd lost him for good."

I reached for the glass of water Vernal had ordered but hadn't touched, thinking of the babies on the planes from Tranquilandia again, and their mothers — mothers like me — praying that other passengers wouldn't come down the aisle and say things like, "Isn't she precious?" "Is he yours?" "Can I hold her?" or that a flight attendant might become suspicious, especially if the plane was delayed and the baby didn't fuss. I longed to reach across the table, lay my hands on Grace's full belly and feel the fists and the heartbeat of her child, his earnest limbs jerking in unison as if he were practising running away. I wished babies were contagious.

Vernal took my hand saying he hoped Grace and Al would excuse us but we had a table reserved for dinner. Al said go ahead, they were sticking to their liquid diet these days, and ordered two more beers.

Gracie's baby wasn't exactly her own, Vernal hastened to explain in the dining lounge where we were shown to a table by the window. It was a life-size model of a baby that cried at random intervals, came with all the accessories, and was inescapable. Gracie had volunteered to participate in the Baby-Think-It-Over Program, designed by Social Services to teach young, drug-using mothers the realities of parenthood.

As a trial parent she had to wear a "care-key" around her neck, and if she neglected her baby it would register in a computer chip inside the baby's head. A red light behind his eyes meant she was handling him too roughly, a yellow light that he had been left to cry longer than a minute, and a green light that he needed to be fed.

"If the lights go out, it means . . . what?" I said.

"Sounds like they had a close call last night, doesn't it?"

Our server set a pitcher of ice water in the centre of the table between us. I picked at the oysters Vernal had ordered for me — local oysters served on a bed of white rocks. I had no energy, or the desire, to eat the *steak au jus* that came next, especially after our server brought complimentary motion sickness bags.

Grace Moon's story got worse: her particular doll was underweight having been modelled on a crack baby, born addicted to the drug his mother smoked all during her pregnancy. The cries we'd heard were the tape-recorded cries of a real drug-affected baby, which explained why they sounded familiar. But not even Angel, as he lay sickening at the Clínica Desaguadero in the jungle, had screamed as desperately when I tried to quiet him in my arms after the faith healer swept his body with flowers and sweet basil, and suspended *amuletos* over his head to prevent the onset of *mal de ojo*, the evil eye.

"The program's supposed to change your mind about getting pregnant in the first place," Vernal said, "but if it happens . . . in certain cases . . . Social Services wants you to think pretty seriously about giving the baby up for adoption."

Vernal said Grace's social worker wanted Grace to sign her baby over before he was even born. Grace said no way, she didn't want anyone else raising her kid. "As you can imagine,"

Vernal continued, "that Al's not stoked about being a step-parent, either."

I asked what, if anything, Vernal knew about Al — if he had any idea why a woman like Grace would be attracted to such a man.

"Not much," Vernal said, in response to the first part of my question.

"He can dress himself, at least," I said. "He's got *that* going for him."

Vernal scoffed at my remark. "As far as I can see his best quality is his bank account. His father owns, I don't know, all the hotels in Mexico. Al can stay high off his interest, if he's motivated enough."

I laughed at this. Vernal came from old money himself, the kind so fusty with age and respectability no one remembers it was ever clean and new. Or how it was made, and who dirtied their hands in the process. We had argued from the day we met about the unfair division of wealth in the world. The Christmas we'd been burglarized the thieves took the telescope Vernal had given me so I could look out over the city to see how poor people lived.

"I say something to make you laugh?" Vernal asked. "I haven't heard you laugh like that since . . . I don't know when. Before we were married, come to think of it." I didn't comment, and then Vernal added that he thought Gracie was wasting her life when she could be making her own millions modelling for Victoria's Secret. I said I didn't imagine Victoria's Secret used pregnant, intravenous drug users to model their lingerie.

"Trust me on this one, Grace is flying straight these days," Vernal said, as he filled my water glass.

I watched as he took a drink from his own, then slipped an ice cube onto his tongue, and crunched it between his teeth. I hadn't seen ice since I'd left Tranquilandia. There it was generally believed that iced water must by definition be pure, regardless of its origins. At the Clínica Desaguadero it was offered to guests as a medicinal tonic, so clear and cold and western, so incompatible with the sticky cloying island heat. Buried in the ice cube, though, could be a germ that led to delirium and death. I learned quickly, because I had to: it's the thing you trust that does you in.

Vernal set his glass down, then reached for my hand. I could smell Grace's scent, like baby powder, on his skin.

The first time I'd slept with Vernal I swear I had to beg him to let me take his clothes off. He'd said he'd wanted time to think about it, to be quite sure, because he knew it would be more than just a casual undertaking. He actually used the word *undertaking* — as if I were a study in the dismal trade. And then when we finally did end up naked he told me to calm down.

In all things related to love and sex, Vernal exercised caution. A cautious lover was not what I had been looking for. I wanted the dumb thrust of life, not a man who apologizes for making you come so hard it hurts.

How could I have thought that marriage might be a solution? I was the one who proposed, though whenever Vernal told the story, he gave a different version. "I told her, this is for life. I want you to be my widow."

Vernal, I soon discovered, lacked a number of social graces. I blamed the private school he'd gone to, one where the future leaders of our country are sent to learn how to behave like gentlemen. Sex education, otherwise known as the facts of life, was reduced to a single scrap of advice: when you get to the trough, don't act like pigs.

Sex education in prison hadn't been much more enlightened. Our care and treatment counsellor used a strip of masking tape stuck to her arm to describe the effects of multiple sex partners. The first time she used the tape it came away from her arm with bits of skin and hair attached. When she put the tape on someone else's arm it didn't stick as well and came away with their skin and hair, also. "Stick the tape to yet another person's arm and you've got biological matter from three people and a tape that doesn't bond very well." People, she said, were like masking tape, too.

Our cabin had two bunks — an upper and a lower. Vernal sat on the bottom one, and pulled off his hiking boots. He wanted my opinion: did I think Grace capable of being a good mother?

"In what way?" I asked.

"I find other people interesting, that's all. I didn't mean to suggest anything *duplicitous*," he said, defensively.

I squeezed into the bathroom and sat on the toilet to let Vernal finish undressing in privacy, wondering what point he was trying to make. He said that if he was looking for a wife again he would expect her to make sacrifices and that he would have to be faithful, too.

I remembered from living with Vernal that the more intense his feelings, the more likely he was to say the opposite of what he meant. He wanted, always, to maintain a high level of tension by keeping the dialogue evasive, filled with suppressed information and unstated emotions. Conversations with Vernal were like icebergs: most of their weight, their substance, was under the surface, where they could do their best harm.

"Are you trying to tell me something," I said, pushing the door open with my foot. "Because if you are, get it over with."

Vernal froze, one left leg halfway into a pair of sweat pants. "You haven't changed, have you," he said. It wasn't a question.

The truth is, prison life detracts from a person's *savoir faire*. When you do years behind walls your idea of proper decorum becomes severely distorted. "Life on Death Row isn't all that conducive to personal growth," I said.

"You take everything I say so . . . personally."

"I'm a person," I said. "How am I *supposed* to take it?"

Vernal gave me an exasperated look. "Can't we just have a conversation? It's like you have to have an argument, or you don't see the point in talking."

I knew now for certain something was wrong. Ever since I'd got into the hearse he'd been looking at my face with a mixture of curiosity and pity, the way an undertaker would look at a face he was about to restore for viewing.

"You *are* trying to tell me something," I said. Suddenly I felt like a stranger in my own life.

Now he looked defeated, as if he were fed up with the whole world, tired, especially, of trying to get love right. "It's hard, when I'm still married to you, and people see us together, we get along so well. Dead lovers make tough rivals, you know what people say. It's hard on other women, you're hard for anyone to live up to."

It hurt that Vernal thought of me as dead, but I wouldn't let it show. "When in the last twelve years has anyone seen us together?" I said.

"They don't have to physically *see* us together to know I'm still *with* you." This was an old record: Vernal had always blamed me for the fact that none of his relationships outside our marriage had endured. I remembered, at Mountjoy

Penitentiary, in the chapel where my baby had been conceived, a sign above the altar that said, "Marriage is the voluntary union of one man and one woman to the exclusion of all others".

I had been married to Vernal, and yet — *I* had been unfaithful to him. It hadn't taken much. Just a man who looked at me, and smiled a particular way, as if there were no wound on earth love couldn't heal. Making love, that one time, with the man who was about to become the father of my child, was the beginning of my being something that no one else had ever been, or lived through.

I partially closed the bathroom door again so Vernal could finish getting into his sweats. "I'm not planning on remarrying . . . trust me . . . it's just that someday . . . in the future I might . . . want the option . . . again."

Vernal was always saying, "Trust me". But the fly side of trust is betrayal: how difficult to overlook indiscretions in one we had trusted ourselves to love. Then again there were women I knew, too, who believed that love, even love from the cruellest of men, was kind.

I told him I had to step more carefully around the trust part. Since I'd lost Angel I'd learned to set my foot down with distrust on the crust of this earth: it was thin.

"I didn't want to say anything when you were still . . . when you were . . . you know . . . where you were," he continued. "I thought I might have been useful to you . . . otherwise I would have suggested we do this ages ago." He paused as if hoping I would help him out, but I let him suffer. I could have dug my own grave and suffocated myself in dirt in the time it often took Vernal to finish a sentence. "It's a . . . just a . . . it would be a favour," he added.

We had been together a total of four hours, we hadn't even tried to kill each other yet, and Vernal wanted a divorce. Deep down this didn't surprise me: Vernal and I had been destined for divorce since day one of our starter marriage. I came out of the bathroom, shutting the door behind me and locking it so it didn't keep us awake all night banging open and shut during our tempestuous crossing, but I couldn't think of anything to say, except that the moustache he was experimenting with looked like a caterpillar paralyzed by stage fright halfway across a melon, and he should consider shaving.

"I'm trying to be a man about this," Vernal said.

At the moment I saw Vernal, not as a man, but as the abandoned boy who had fallen so far into himself that no one would ever reach him. I picked up my duffel bag and climbed the ladder to the top bunk. I slipped under the covers, still in my clothes. Everything — the sound of the ship's engine, the smell of toothpaste and work socks, even my grief — seemed alien to me.

A poet, blind and deaf from birth, wrote that in the odour of men there is something elemental, as of fire, storm, and salt sea. He was a romantic, who had probably never spent the night in an airless cabin crossing a treacherous stretch of water with a man to whom he had once been unhappily married. And I thought *this is how it is: we fall in love, lighter than air, marry in mid-air, divorce when we hit the pavement.*

I remembered a dream I'd had, not long after I got the news I was soon to be executed. I was on a tropical island with Vernal, and I'd been lured from my bed in the middle of the night by air pregnant with the scent of vanilla. I found giant cauldron-like orchids opening in the moonlight and thousands of tiny sphinx moths fluttering from one pod to another. In the morning, when I brought Vernal to look at them, the scent had disappeared, the orchids had closed themselves tight, concealing their mysteries. Vernal had tried to pry open the petals to get a glimpse inside.

In his own way I knew he still loved me and probably always would. I think he loved me in defiance, as if he believed reason had the power to banish everything that had gone passionately wrong between us.

PART TWO

Loneliness is a terrorist, except it has no righteous cause, no moral foundation, no God. There is no reasoning with it, none.

— Asha Bandele, *The Prisoner's Wife*

THE CHICKEN TRUCK WITH ITS FORLORN CARGO pulled off the ferry ahead of us into the wetting rain. As the truck gathered speed, the air filled with hundreds of small white feathers that stuck to the hearse as we drove. "What's easier to load, a truck load of fuckin' chicken feathers or a fuckload of dead babies?" The Latrine had been pretty pleased with herself for coming up with that one: dead baby jokes were the order of the day on the Row since most of the women were there because they'd killed one or more of their kids. (Her answer, when she'd finished slashing my pillow in search of contraband: "The babies. You can use a fuckin' pitchfork.")

I rolled down my window and took a gulp of cool, saturated air. Aside from a lone ferry worker in a yellow rain slicker directing traffic the only way it could go, and a small crowd of bedraggled protesters bearing placards that read "Right to Silencers" and "Say No to Noise," the place was still asleep. The silencers wanted to purge the island of anything that disturbed the peace, from wild geese to weed eaters, Vernal said. "There's a new cause around here every week. We had one group protesting for a protest-free zone!"

The road followed the coastline and I wanted to take it all in — the rain falling solidly, like cold, wet lead, the purple bloom of the common teasel, the proliferation of foxgloves in the ditches. I asked Vernal to slow down, so the world didn't go by in a blur — something else we'd always argued about, his zeal for speed. Vernal put the rattling hearse in cruise control as two ravens flew up from the ditch where they feasted on the night's casualties. "Look!" he said, pointing to a pair of eagles side by side on a branch at the top of a dead cedar. "I see the same two sitting there every time I drive past. A mated pair like that stays together for life."

I watched the eagles, thinking back on our conversation of the night before. What Vernal had been trying to say to me was that our marriage had become a life sentence without parole. My execution would have solved our biggest problem from his point-of-view — the need to retain a costly divorce lawyer.

Vernal didn't slow until we approached a sign, one I could barely make out through the rain: "Port of Mystic" and, below that, "Progress Welcome". Someone had inserted the word NOT.

At first glance it looked like any other sleepy Gulf Island town: on the south side of the main street a post office and a liquor store (both closed), a credit union "Open Thursdays to the Weekend", and Chubb's Used Body and Parts. "Everyone in this town knows everything about everybody else," Vernal warned me. "The liquor store employees can tell you what anybody here drinks, as well as how much." Islanders were a breed apart with a strong impulse to protect the outlaw — whom they perceived as the underdog — and a deep-seated hatred of mainland jurisdiction. He paused. "We don't even have a police force on the island — yet."

Ceese & Son Funerals, "Closed Until Further Notice", stood on the north side of the street, along with a walk-in medical clinic, a general store called Natural Lee's, the King Koin Laundromat, and a coffee shop, the Snipe. It was meant to have been the Sandpiper, Vernal said, as he pulled in next to a red pickup parked outside. Marg, the owner, had come up with the Snipe in an effort to economize.

A dog locked inside the truck barked at us, his breath steaming the windows. I slipped the rain cape back over my head when Vernal said we should grab a cup of tea — none of the shops opened until after nine. "I'll make us breakfast when we get home," he said. "You probably won't be surprised to hear it, but I'm still not much of a chef."

Home. When we get home. When I'd tried, over the years, to imagine reconciling with Vernal, I'd fantasized about going home to live with him, the way we used to be. I'd make Chicken Quito Ecuador — my old standby — and he'd polish off a bottle of Scotch. I'd have the run of the kitchen, it went without saying. Vernal's idea of a meal had always been a kind of comforting punishment, something you could look forward to for its entertainment value, and enjoy missing at the same time.

He got out and, I noticed, left the keys in the ignition. "Who in their right mind's going to steal a hearse?" Vernal said, when he saw me reach for my duffel bag; prison teaches you not to let anything out of your sight if you want to see it again.

The door to the Snipe was wide open and the rain came at us horizontally, following us inside.

"Leave it open, I'm letting the flies out." A woman who knew how to make stretch pants work for a living came out from behind the counter, a cigarette in one hand, a bottle of vodka in the other, and lowered herself into a chair. She looked first at Vernal then squinted at me, as if trying to decide whether or not she approved of serving a person she'd never seen before. Vernal said we'd like tea, and Marg looked at him as if life was hard enough. "There is no tea. Every morning's a Smirnoff morning around here."

Vernal laughed and said coffee would do, and Marg said he'd have to get it himself, she didn't move once she was down. "Tell you the truth, I'm celebrating. I had this cousin, eh? Up the road? She croaked." Marg was still scrutinizing me. "Couple nights ago. She et something that disagreed with her. I should have tried it years ago. Disagreeing with her, that is."

The coffee Vernal brought me tasted like tea, almost as bad as what you'd get served at the Facility. Marg complained about Ceese Jr. closing the funeral home right in the middle of what was supposed to be their tourist season. She thought it would discourage tourism.

"No one dies much this time of year, anyway," said Vernal.

"Not if they do it around here, they don't," Marg said. She'd had to pay for her cousin's body to be shipped to the mainland, which had cost her an arm and a leg. "You know what they say. Some things are just the way they are, and nobody knows what for."

Vernal and I were the only patrons, aside from a man who sat in the corner farthest from Marg, next to an artificial Christmas tree, one that appeared to be a permanent fixture. He brought his cup to his lips, blew on it, and then looked over the rim at me. I pretended to be reading the menu on the wall behind him, and wondered if the chickens in the truck that had covered us with feathers were destined to become Today's Special: Chicken Cordon Blues.

My attention shifted back to the man in the corner again as he stood up, pushed his chair in, and reached into his pocket to pay for his coffee. He wore a yellow toothbrush on a chain

SUSAN MUSGRAVE

around his neck, had long blue-black hair falling straight from a headband of red cedar bark, and eyes blacker than the inside of a raven. But it was his scent that attracted me most: even from across the room I could taste him — like the air before a storm, long before there is any visible sign of it.

He had on jeans, a denim jacket, and a pair of boots made out of cobra skin. Another snake had died so he could have a belt to match the boots. At a quick glance I figured the wardrobe was meant to draw your attention away from the fact that he was missing his right hand. He had a hook instead that stuck out below the sleeve of his jacket.

"We weren't close," Marg continued. I watched the man — who swayed as he walked, as if he'd just got off a boat — push open the door and disappear into the rain. "She always had to be first at everything — getting born, getting married, getting knocked up, having kids. Trust her to kick the bucket first." Marg said she was looking forward to death. She could use the rest.

Vernal paid for our coffees and told Marg to keep the change. "I can keep anything long's you don't ask me to keep a secret," Marg said. I heard, and saw, Rainy again in my mind's eye — Rainy in her baby dolls made of a padded quilted material not unlike packing blankets. "A secret ain't a secret unless keeping it hurts."

We went back out into the weather. Vernal nodded to the man with the hook who sat inside the red pickup with the window rolled down, watching us, smiling. Lips you wanted to lick under a moustache — a big moustache, one I associated with fierceness and a high disregard for the law, unlike the one Vernal was experimenting with — that kept you from ever getting quite close enough. Then the smile faded out and he looked at me with an expression of such stony sadness I half

~ 60~

expected a solid tear to drop from his eye and bounce across the hood of the hearse like a marble dancing on a drum.

"Who was that?" I asked, as Vernal grabbed my arm and pulled me to him, so I wouldn't be swallowed by a pothole.

"Hooker Moon," said Vernal, "Gracie's brother. He's the one they wrote that song about. 'Bad Moon Rising'?"

There was no doubt more to the story, but he didn't elaborate. We danced our way around the puddles, down the still-deserted street; I could feel the rain trying to take shelter on the inside of my cape. Sandwiched between Ceese Funerals and the medical clinic was a building I hadn't noticed until now, an unlikely, gaudy little shop painted purple with yellow trim, called Down to Earth. There may have been a downturn in death on Kliminawhit, but from the numbers of SOLD tags dangling from the caskets there was still a healthy coffin industry.

"There's a customer born every minute," read an ad in the window, next to a slightly bigger sign saying, "Open for Pre-Arrangements". Vernal pointed to an environmentally friendly unit called "The Chrysalis," woven out of willow twigs that could be "used as extra storage space until needed."

I keep meaning to take a couple of those home," Vernal said. "They hadn't invented the idea of cupboards when our place was built, way back when."

Home. Our place. We walked arm in arm against the rain as far as Natural Lee's, which had just opened. Vernal emptied his wallet and told me to pick up cereal, a ten pound bag of sugar, some fresh vegetables "to keep the doctor away," a piece of fish and anything I needed, while he went to pick up his newspapers. I needed deodorant and dental floss, two luxuries they didn't allow on the Row; I suppose you could hang yourself on a few lengths of floss strung together, but I never figured out what they had against deodorant. If you wanted underarm protection (as the guards called it) you had to stand by the door of your cell, naked from the waist up, arms raised above your head, at five to eight every morning. At 8 AM a nurse walked down the range with a can of Right Guard and sprayed your pits. I entered the store where a woman with thinning blonde hair and small crushed lines around her mouth glanced up at me, then at the clock, as if she hadn't expected anyone so soon. She told me if I was after anything fresh I would have to come back later — the produce that had arrived on the ferry hadn't made it onto the shelves yet because she was on her own here and she only had two hands.

The "natural" in Lee's appeared to be something of a misnomer. In the Foreign Foods section that shared a shelf with Personal Hygiene Products, I found soya sauce, ketchup, and two tins of China Lily Bean Sprouts. I also found a roll-on Ban whose expiry date had come and gone, and dental floss, and then took a detour through the Back to School supplies area where see-through backpacks were on sale, now regulation in the country I'd come from. Teachers maintained it was one way, at a glance, to see if their students were packing guns or other prohibited weapons. I picked up sugar, and a box of Fruit Loops for Vernal — his idea of having fruit for breakfast. At the fish counter a sign said, "Our fish is fresher than it is in the sea", but the display case was empty. I unloaded my shopping basket at the checkout counter and then remembered something else I needed. I asked the sales clerk if they sold shoelaces; she nodded her head as she removed a box labelled Canadian Mosquito Terminators — a fly swatter with a dart attached — from a shelf beside the till, and marked them down in price. "All out of them right now," she said, glancing up at the clock again with a bleak lack of hope. "People keep buying them."

GIVEN

❧ ❧ ❧

Vernal sat on a bench outside the post office, a selection of newspapers in his lap. "You get killed in a car crash, you become a saint overnight," he said, without looking up at me. For a minute I thought he was talking about Earl, or my potty-mouthed escort.

"'Teen Angel Dead: Driver Charged,'" Vernal read. "'She always had a smile for everyone.'" Why is it that kids who die are never the unsmiling miserable depressed ones who smoke crack and swear at their parents who nag them to take out the garbage?"

"You die, things get forgiven."

"You have to wonder."

A journalist I'd heard interviewed described how war had changed her life, because going to Bosnia, albeit to write about the war, changed the way others saw *her*. They took her seriously now, she said, as if she'd proven herself to be a person of substance.

Prison had been a test for me: there could be no doubt about that. And doubtless, too, it would change the way the rest of the world would regard me from now on. Had I died in the crash in LA, would I have gone from Killer Mom to sainthood overnight in the press? Highly unlikely, given my particular circumstances.

I felt like I'd been given a reprieve. We returned to the Snipe — the red pickup had gone. When we got back in the hearse Vernal set his newspapers on the seat between us and I remembered how different it had been when we were first together, how he would pull me close to him and drive, one arm over my shoulder, his hand inching down for a feel of my breast.

I thought, too, about a road trip to the interior one fall when the trees were turning, and we had only been married a few months. I'd fallen asleep and Vernal had shaken me awake to write down the lyrics to a song he'd started composing as we'd passed Hell's Gate. I scribbled his words with a purple crayon on our tattered road map. It had felt so romantic, as if love couldn't get any better than that.

We had our first fight hours later, at the only motel in Hope that had a vacancy, the Paradise Motel. My purple scrawl had been illegible, the words to Vernal's first and last love song, lost.

§ § §

We took the coast road north out of Mystic, with Vernal pointing out the sights — the blackened shell of the fire hall he said had burned down on Halloween, with the fire truck parked inside; the road to the municipal airport. The cemetery on the outskirts of town was growing even more quickly than the town itself, Vernal said. He saw an excellent investment opportunity in cemetery futures.

Next to the graveyard was a square grey building with barred windows overlooking a gravel parking lot.

"Church of the Holy Brew," Vernal said. The only way Father Tunney had been able to get a following had been to convert the Catholic church to a bar and off-license — there was no pub on the island and a lot of people liked to socialize when they drank — and it had become the place you could go and share a beer and a plate of traditional bar food during Holy Hour and gossip with your neighbours. The church still presided over weddings and funerals, Vernal said. Some things never changed.

Vernal chose this moment to confess he had made changes in his own life since he'd started spending more time on the island. He had stopped using drugs, and — "just for today" — stopped drinking. Vernal, who'd always said a room without a TV was like a room without a view, was learning to live simply, without a television. He hadn't weaned himself off the telephone yet. Since there was no cell phone service to the island he had had a landline installed so his clients could reach him if they had to.

He wasn't taking on many new clients these days, he had enough repeat offenders. As for money, he needed much less of it than he had done when we'd met, "in the beginning". He said *in the beginning* as if we had been Adam and Eve, oblivious in our walled Eden.

He had also started going to church. "It's not what you're thinking. I've joined . . . a support group. There's a meeting every night — in the church basement. Noon hour meetings, too. Over the lunch hour. Obviously."

In the past, whenever I'd suggested Vernal consider attending AA, he had resisted. If I tried having a conversation with him about how I was afraid he was drinking himself to death, he would say the graveyard is full of sober men. He'd once described an unusually sober judge as embodying all those characteristics that men found distasteful in other men, meaning he didn't drink. I had decided, long ago, that Vernal had chosen alcoholism over our future.

My window had fogged making me feel that no other world existed, for the moment, outside the car. We drove, each of us wrapped in our own silence — Vernal wiping his side of the window with a rag he kept on the dashboard just for that purpose — along the Bend, the winding, cratered road, named after a pioneer, Orbit Bend, that led from the Port of

Mystic all the way to the Yaka Wind First Nations village of Old Mystic on the northern tip of the island. Islanders' favourite pastime was enquiring of tourists, "What you doing today, going round the Bend?"

Grace Moon lived in Old Mystic, Vernal said. He wondered if her baby was going to be a boy or a girl. When I said I wouldn't hazard a guess, he went on to say he regretted not having had at least one child of our own; he wished he had had his vasectomy undone. When I'd married him he hadn't told me we would never be able to have kids, he saved that surprise until after we said our "I do's". He'd told me he hadn't had the courage to say anything *before* we got married because, back then, he had been too afraid of losing me.

Our marriage hadn't been altogether childless. There'd been Brutus, with Canine Attention Deficit Disorder, dog acne, a pacemaker, and low self-esteem. It probably hadn't helped that Vernal had named her Brutus. After she drowned in our swimming pool, Vernal had vowed that he'd never again fall in love with anything or anyone capable of loving him back.

The sky, as we drove north, became more foreboding. The paved road ended and I saw a sign in the middle of a field where a small herd of horses, with ribs like radiators, stared at the dead grass: "Christian Vegetables Ahead". As we hit the gravel Vernal swerved, but too late, and I felt the hearse juddering beneath me. "Potholes," he muttered, then swerved back into the right lane to avoid another one, turning right off the main road at the honour stand where a plywood square nailed to a stake bore the hand-scrawled message, "Count on the Lord," next to another, a list of commandments: "No Loitering. No Trespassing. No Soliciting. No Dogs." Vernal said I could count on one thing and that was getting a new self-serving platitude there every week. A man wearing a green beret and army fatigues stood guarding a bin of zucchinis the size of incendiary rockets. Yet another sign — this one not homemade — had been bolted to the bin and warned, "Video Surveillance".

"So much for honour," Vernal said. "I make it a point never to buy any of his wretched Christian vegetables."

He slowed over the washboard surface of the unpaved dusty road and then turned left at

PARADISE FARM B&B
Stay Here for the Rest of Your Life.

I recalled that after our aborted trip to the interior, Vernal had said "remind me to avoid any place that uses 'paradise' as an enticement."

"The previous owner's sign, not mine," Vernal said, as if he knew what I was thinking. "I keep meaning to take it down, but . . . well, it's on my list of things to do around here. I still get people driving in, wanting a room for the weekend, asking if we take kids or pets. I even tried locking the gates but that didn't stop them."

The long driveway, overhung with dark evergreens, ended in front of a barn. A marmalade cat sat washing himself, and didn't move until we were almost on top of him.

"Aged Orange. The only cat I know who plays chicken with a hearse," Vernal said, as he eased the Cadillac, with wet, white feathers still sticking to it, into the barn, as if bringing it home to roost.

The barn had been constructed of bottles, what looked to be 26er's. I assumed Vernal had found a creative use for his empties — before he found AA — one that didn't require him lugging a Blue Box as far as the end of the driveway every recycling day — but he hastened to explain how each bottle had been filled with nothing more potent than embalming fluid, once. The barn, he said, was another of his predecessor's many creative endeavours. Slab Ceese believed that a true artist — one at the height of his powers — ought to be good enough to bring death back to life. "He needed bodies to prove it — ergo the B&B. Problem was his guest book didn't balance. He had more clients checking in than checking out. "They checked out all right, but not in the usual sense of the term.

"No one ever found any bodies," he continued, "to back up the Crown's claim — it's all hearsay as far as I'm concerned. You know how irrational people can get about anyone who dares to be different. And at the end of the day, though, the judge didn't buy my artistic license defence either."

I wanted to say most people would consider killing your guests more than a little different, but who was I to judge? Vernal said Slab's wife had filed for divorce shortly after she had retained Vernal to act for her husband on the criminal matters. Vernal said he'd been warned by the real estate agent that he would be moving into a distressed house.

The air was filled with sweet-smelling hay, the scent of late summer rain on dry cedar, warm moss, and the punky forest floor. I could hear rushing water. A creek ran through the property on the other side of the house — I'd have a good view of it, Vernal said, from my bedroom window.

From somewhere beyond the creek, deep in the woods, I heard a deep-throated songbird singing his dark-hearted song as Vernal picked up my duffel bag and led me towards my new home. Silvered by time and exposure to the wind and rain it rose, mind over matter, from the earth. Even if Vernal hadn't told me about the artist who had found a way of bringing the dead back to life, it was, I could see, a house ripe for haunting.

Vernal's laptop lay face down in the driveway. "It crashed," he said, miming its descent from an upstairs window.

I stepped around the computer and an enormous hunk of cement at the foot of the front steps, a mounting block that Orbit Bend, who'd built the original farmhouse, had laid.

"Orbit thought motorcars were a fad. He went everywhere on horseback right up until the day he got thrown off his horse and ended up in a wheelchair," Vernal said, as we climbed the steps to the long shady porch my mother would have called a verandah.

He shouldered open the heavy wooden door and motioned me inside. I bent to take my shoes off just as Aged Orange darted between my legs, almost knocking me down.

"He's not used to anyone else being in the house," Vernal laughed. "It's been just the two of us rattling around together."

One glance inside told me there was not much space in which to rattle around in. Even the mudroom was piled high with boxes — Vernal said he had been emptying our house in Astoria bit by bit, but hadn't had time to properly unpack. He hurried me into the living room, apologizing for the chaos. He had tried to be ruthless, he said, but it was always hard to know what to keep, and what to give away.

He excused himself to go upstairs to make sure my room was "in order"; I plunked myself down on our old forest-green leather couch that faced a bare wall where, judging from the ganglion of wires issuing from a hole in the woodwork, the previous owner's entertainment centre had been. The liquor cabinet stood empty, too: in our old house it would have been crammed full, at all times, with every type of alcoholic drink we didn't need. Vernal's explanation for the wide variety was you got an hour's free parking downtown if you bought a bottle of booze.

After Brutus died Vernal took to leaving our bed in the middle of the night to quench his grief with a bottle. I'd find him downstairs in the early hours of the morning, his arms wrapped around his commodity, plead with him to come back to bed with me, where I could lie listening to him breathe, so exquisitely aware of his suffering that every detail on which my eye fell — the crease of the sheet, the fissure in a tile, the slight discolouration on the wall around the doorknob — commanded attention and became significant, as if my perceptions were trying to divert me out of self-preservation, in the way one might offer candy to an incorrigible child. Now I remembered an argument we'd had in a Vancouver café where I'd noticed, for the first time, the word "zen" in "Frozen". It became something for me to hang on to, as he harangued me about the fact that he didn't want to have kids. He'd seen enough unwanted mothers in this world.

Vernal came back downstairs and sat next to me, put his hand on my knee and said how happy he was I was home. I got flustered, said I'd like to settle in, take a nap. "I'm sorry. Yesterday must have been a long day for you and I don't know about you but I didn't get much sleep last night," Vernal said.

"I don't need an apology," I said.

"I know you don't, but it doesn't mean I'm not sorry."

Ever since I'd first known Vernal, his mantra had been "I'm sorry". Once I'd accused him of saying, "I'm sorry" instead of "Good morning" when he got out of bed. He actually said, "I'm sorry I'm sorry." The worst part was he meant it.

Vernal said he would sleep on the couch as he led me upstairs, my duffel bag over his shoulder, to the biggest room in the house, the only one with its own bathroom. I had a brief moment of panic when he stooped to kiss me, gently, on both cheeks. "I hope you'll be . . . as comfortable as you can . . . for now . . . if you plan on . . . we'll see what we can do . . . "

Once I would have completed the sentence for him, out loud, but now I did it, quietly, to myself: *If you plan on staying here any length of time.* I was only looking at staying here, I told him, for the rest of my life.

I watched Vernal retreat down the hall, wanting to call after him to stay with me, but doing my best to hide my disarray. Like anyone who has ever loved, I knew that the more I needed the less I would be likely to receive. When he had gone downstairs I reached to open my door, thinking how many years it had been since I'd been able to touch something as ordinary as a doorknob, amazed at how smooth and cold it felt, wondering how long it would be before I started taking it for granted. It turned in my hand; I edged open the door, then stood savouring the moment before feeling for the light switch. I had been deprived of so many other ordinary things, too.

The curtains were closed, though that didn't keep daylight from peeking in. I switched on the overhead light, and the room — with walls the colour of old teeth, stained, perhaps by smoke from the fireplace that had long ago been boarded up — shivered to life. Vernal had furnished the room with objects that made me feel at home. A clock ticked on the mantelpiece above the fireplace — the same clock that had been in our bedroom at the Walled Off. Night after night I had lain awake listening to its heartbeat sound, so constant that after a while it became part of the silence. Above the clock hung a photograph that Vernal had taken of me on our honeymoon. My hair was longer then and my eyes half open.

I wore a burgundy sundress and a smile on my face because Vernal refused to take the picture until I at least pretended to be enjoying myself. Vernal, like most people, wanted to deny any negative feelings, and always did his best to keep them out of the picture.

I flicked another switch and a fan on the ceiling began to *whirr*, making the staccato beat of a helicopter overhead, a throaty *thwap thwap thwapping* like the gunship that had landed in the big yard at Mountjoy Penitentiary the day I was taken hostage. On the night table beside my bed, between a stack of books and a radio-cassette player, I found my bracelet, a thick silver band with a frog design Vernal had acquired in lieu of a retainer from a client, and given to me for an anniversary gift. I slipped it on. It was the first thing I'd worn on my wrist in twelve years, other than handcuffs.

On the dressing table Vernal had left me a new toothbrush, a water jug and bowl, a hairbrush, and a black handgun-shaped hair dryer. I went to check out my bathroom that was twice the size of the cell I'd occupied for the last twelve years, the same length of time since I'd had a toilet that wasn't inches away from where I laid my head at night — a steel toilet that flushed automatically. I had a deep, clawfoot tub — I hadn't taken a proper bath since I'd left Tranquilandia, only inade-quate showers — and my own sink, above which hung another mirror.

In prison we were allowed a "personal mirror" but the rules were it had to be kept in an "appropriate place" where you wouldn't be distracted by looking at it. Rainy said mirrors were mostly for thin, rich people who felt good about themselves. If you went into a house like the White House, she used as an example, even though she'd only ever seen it on TV, there would be mirrors on every wall from the ceiling to the floor.

I stared at my face, hard and long. My lips were sealed so tight they looked as if they had been sewn together, like the lips of the shrunken head that had hung in the cockpit of the small plane that had flown me to Tranquilandia. My eyes, once cold blue, had become the colour of ash, edged with shadows, bruised by all they had seen. One thing I didn't have to worry about: no one who might see my WANTED poster on a Post Office wall would recognize the person looking back at me from the mirror now.

I opened the cabinet doors so I would no longer have to face myself, and set my deodorant and dental floss, side by side, on the one empty shelf. Vernal had stocked the cabinet with everything he thought I'd need — toothpaste, sunscreen, mouthwash, wax earplugs, tampons, laxatives, insect repellant, cough syrup, and a bottle of Extra-Strength Tylenol labelled "These have been on the floor," in my mother's failing handwriting.

I unscrewed the lid, poured them onto my palm and ate a handful — just because I could. It had been twelve years since I had been allowed to administer my own drugs. At the Facility they were stingy, to say the least, when it came to issuing any kind of medication for pain. A woman with lung cancer would be lucky if she received a baby aspirin to help her through the night.

I started a bath, then went back into the bedroom, turned the radio on, and heard a caller say it was time women every-where appealed to Jesus to ask his help in reducing. I fiddled with the radio dial, marvelling at my own freedom to make choices. In prison your corrections team carefully selected what you watched or listened to. It was either *Executions Live!*

or the God channel which, in my mind, amounted to the same thing.

Only four stations broadcast to Kliminawhit: *Weather or Not,* a community service that gave weather reports and ferry schedules; *Radio Peace and Love* that covered war and world hatred; *Radio Orca* transmitting the underwater squeaks and cries of migrating whales; and *God Listens*, with Christian oriented programming.

I settled on *Radio Orca*, where a human voice that also sounded as if it were coming from the depths of the sea, interrupted the whales. "Each pod has a distinct dialect," the voice intoned. "Scientists have lowered microphones in various locations off the coast to monitor the whales conversations." In the free world even whales were under surveillance.

I unpacked my belongings and set the photograph — the blur that was Angel — on my dressing table, propped up against the water jug. I had to struggle with the drawers that were swollen shut in the antique dresser, then laid out my pyjamas and the one change of clothing I'd been allowed to take with me when I left the Row.

When you first arrive on the Row, you are requisitioned three orange jumpsuits, one pair of orange sweat pants, five pairs of socks, useful for padding your three brassieres (white) that look like the mailbags they were always busy making and then unmaking (an exercise in futility that the guards called "making yourself useful") back in the general population. It was the most degrading thing of all for most women — to be issued brassieres that were several cup sizes too big for them, and Rainy decided to make the best of a humiliating situation. After she had finished cleaning the chow hall she would empty the sugar containers down the front of her shirt, hoarding it in her 42-D cup bra for when she woke up in the middle of the night craving a sugar fix.

You are also issued five orange T-shirts, one pair of shoes (no laces) and seven pairs of coloured underpants, a different colour for every day of the week. If a guard caught you wearing yellow instead of red on a Monday or red instead of blue on a Thursday, it was considered an infraction of prison rules and you were subject to disciplinary action, which meant spending time in a punishment cell. I got an extra three days when my red underpants fell into some bleach by accident and turned orange (Rainy was sterilizing her needle) because I said aren't *all* cells punishment cells?

Some of the girls sewed their own clothes and the ones who got really good at it, like Frenchy, were hired to help make the guards' uniforms. Frenchy used to cut the khaki-coloured material on the bias, on purpose; we got no end of satisfaction watching a guard stop and try to straighten her twisted pant legs when she thought no one was looking.

I undressed and got in the bath and lay for the longest time luxuriating in the hot water, looking down at the length of my body, running my hands over my belly, thinking about what the *curandero* had told me — that the uterus is the last internal organ to decompose. I closed my eyes, let every part of me but my head slip below the surface; even after my bath the clean surface of my body felt like a thin shell around everything I couldn't wash away. I got out, towelled myself off, then went back to my bedroom. The bed looked inviting — not like the kind I had become used to with the lumpy mattress that lay there rubbing it in — *you're sleeping Single-O tonight* — or a bunk like I'd had on the ferry, but a big-ass bed, as Frenchy would have put it. I rubbed my fingers on the chenille bedspread, a nubble like Braille under my hands, and then climbed under the covers.

The sheets were soft, creamy flannelette. My head fell in love with my pillow the moment we met, and I lay there, staring at the ceiling, the molding a pattern of vulvic tulips, thinking this could be the first pillow I'd slept on in twelve years that hadn't been stained with tears. I always imagined I could feel those tears and the marks they'd left, as if they'd never quite dried, but stayed wet in memory of the last woman who had cried herself to sleep. I'm making it sound like a pretty sad place, the Condemned Row.

I lay awake listening to a newborn killer whale on the radio crying for his stranded mother, thinking of my son. When I had turned the doorknob and opened the door to my new room it was if I had opened up the old place inside me where I'd locked my grief. I'd thought there was nothing you could have told me about grief I didn't already know. Until I lost Angel.

I thought of the ways he had reached for me, as if to say *stay here, with me, for the rest of your life.* There were places where the heart could not rest, where the best you could do was be at home with the rootless.

§ § §

When I woke the next morning, to a bird screaming in the trees beyond the house, Aged Orange lay curled at the foot of my bed. I'd spent most of the night in the fetal position to avoid kicking him. I stretched my legs out under him, but he didn't budge.

The whole room smelled sweet, a familiar unsettling kind of sweet, and when I looked around I saw that Vernal had filled a Wedgwood vase with Stargazer lilies he'd picked in the garden.

Their fragrance reminded me of my last days on Tranquilandia. Angel and I had spent the first night together at the only hotel in town, the Hotel Desaguadero (which translated as the Hotel Drain) at the end of La Camino de Penitencia, or the Road of Penance. The owner looked astonished to have guests and asked my driver how we had chanced upon the place, as if it were impossible that anyone might come to his establishment by choice. In the evening he served chicken necks, rice with gravel, and Coca-Cola on a patio under a crackling bug zapper; the scorched remains of flying insects fluttered down onto my plate. Our room, when we returned to it, was filled with orchids, orchids with bruised lips, slashed throats and bloodshot eyes. *Flores para los muertos.*

The day I left Angel behind on that island I'd boarded a plane filled with the same intoxicating and seductive odour of sex and death. The coffin holding the baby whose body had been emptied out and filled with cocaine had lain on a bed of crushed Medusa's Head orchids, each one wet, as if it had been picked weeping.

I pulled the curtains and opened a window, hoping the smell of Vernal's flower arrangement would fade. "Meow," I whispered, and the cat's ears twitched. The breeze ruffled his fur.

On the Camino de Penitencia I'd found a dog lying at the side of the road, tail twitching, oblivious to all forms of life going on around it — a Zen dog, slumbering in the sun, seemingly at peace. He was the first dog I'd encountered in that forsaken place who hadn't either attacked me or slunk away, tail between its legs, when I'd extended a friendly hand, but, when I went to pet him, I realized he was dead. The breeze that stirred his tail came from the traffic rushing by.

Two flies buzzed against the glass and another lay dazed on the sill, intoxicated, perhaps, by the Stargazer's lurid odour. I reached to stroke Aged Orange, and his tail began wagging the way it does when a cat's trying to decide whether to rip your face off or just scratch out your eyes. At the same time I heard the mournful bird crying again, followed by a scream that sounded like *"helllllllllp helllllllllp,"* then a more plaintive dove-like call, *"ohhhhhhhh ohhhhhhhhh."* I could hear other noises — the sound of life going on — below me in the kitchen.

I propped myself up and picked through the stack of books Vernal had left beside my bed, including *Beloved,* one novel I hadn't had the opportunity to finish on the Row because the copy I'd borrowed from the prison library had been missing its final chapter. Frenchy confessed: she had mutilated hundreds of books this way. If her life was to be cut short, she reasoned, she wanted others to know what it felt like. Rainy, who had never learned to read or write, who thought a sentence was something you had to serve, didn't think anyone was going to miss the last chapter of a book. "You don't know what a book be about before it get to the end, you ain't never gon' know," she said.

I read for a while, then turned on my side, and went back into a half-sleep, coming fully awake again when Vernal knocked at the door, sometime later, with a bowl of Fruit Loops and a pot of tea. Aged Orange scooted across my head, and then burrowed down beside me, between the bedspread and my sheets. Vernal said if he got too hyperactive to turn on *Radio Orca* — the whale songs had a calming effect. He asked if I needed anything else and I said no thank you there's nothing I need.

I stayed in bed, petting Aged Orange, who seemed anything but hyper, listening to the world going on without me as it had done during my absence. I wanted darkness to fall again, to silence the bird at the periphery of my hearing, hurting me with his cries. Later, when the cat wrestled himself from my grip, I recognized panic, like a rat the trap has snapped on, who hobbles to his hole with his freight of pain, dragging the source of it after him. Vernal had asked me once in a letter if I'd ever thought of "taking the easy way out." I said there never was, there never would be, an easy way.

When Vernal came to check on me, early in the evening, he found me with my eyes staring wide, full of a sadness I couldn't explain, except to say I missed something, the way you feel when you're a child and someone you love goes away, you watch them leaving in the rain. Vernal said I shouldn't expect to feel anything *but* sad. He touched my cheek with the back of his hand. In rare moments like this, Vernal took hold of my affections in a profound way.

When I woke again it was dark and he was lying beside me, turning his flashlight on and off, making little animals of light that prowled our walls. I rolled away from him. Vernal could be kind. Had I become a woman who believed that love, even from the kindest of men, could only be cruel?

I lived to kill time in those endless first weeks of my new life on Kliminawhit. Vernal brought me three meals a day and after the first week it seemed we had never lived any other way. I wondered if there would come a time when I no longer defined myself by where I'd been, but by where I intended to go. And if I would ever feel whole again, capable of walking down a flight of stairs without fear of falling into an imagined abyss, or opening a door that led to the outside world, or any door other than the one that opens inward?

When I slept I dreamed about Angel. In one dream I opened a can of sardines and found him curled up inside. I ate him — like eating an eyebrow — and woke up thinking *why would I eat my child*? So he would be safe, so I'd know where he was, inside me.

I'd wake from my dreams and lie still, until I was sure the waking up part was not the dream; it was often hard to tell, in those first moments. After I was convinced I was in bed, in the ripe-for-haunting house, I'd turn my head to look at that photograph, as if needing further proof I was where I had determined myself to be.

I slept, and when all the sleep had been wrung out of me, my mind would fill with thoughts. *Thoughts* is the wrong word: the lawless beauty of the imagination allowed me to lie in my bed full of drowsy pleasure, dwelling in the past; the future was something I could put off until tomorrow, like a chore I would get round to, eventually. But the future kept arriving; it arrived day after day, moment by moment, an assembly line of itself that kept me revolving with it.

Some days at the farm it felt as if Rainy and Frenchy were right there, in my room, on either side of me on the bed. As I lay listening to the rain on the roof I heard Frenchy whispering in my ear, *sound of the rain be better than a thousand mothers.* Rainy liked to stay inside, where it was warm and dry. *I be so sweet I go outside I dissolve like a sugar cube, the rain wet my head.*

One morning I woke suddenly, in that hour between black night and bright dawn, and saw the clock had stopped ticking during the hours I'd slept away. I had been dreaming I lay in a coma surrounded by strangers trying to decide whether to unplug me from a life-support system. A sign above my head (one I could read because I had separated from my body and felt as if I were a spirit floating loosely beneath my own skin) said, "Visitors to the dying must use the pay phone at the end of the hall where the smoking room used to be". I wanted to call Vernal, but whenever I tried to pull the tubes out of my arms a nurse, who looked like Jodie Lootine, pushed me back on the bed.

The morning after I arrived in Desaguadero, and every morning for the next four days, a small group of midwives led me and others who had been "slain in the spirit," to the borrachio tree where the *curandero* sat to perform his healings. Every day the Lord for the Body broke a raw egg over Angel's forehead, to prevent *Caída de Mollera,* and then sprinkled cobwebs, used to stanch wounds, into the yoke. The *curandero* believed that because my baby was very beautiful he suffered from many *mal de ojo* ailments. When a child is beautiful people will admire him and not touch him, and this, the *curandero* insisted, would project negative forces into my boy's heart.

Once we had participated in the *curandisimo* Angel and I would be walked to the chapel in the centre of town where a famous folk saint was said to have been buried. Some women rolled with their infants in the dirt, others crawled on their knees, in imitation of the suffering of Christ. The chapel, at the end of the Camino de Penitencia, was crammed full of *momentos* — desiccated body parts, ones that had been removed through amputation or excision, in jars — a collection of fetuses in different stages of growth, and the shards of broken glass that the saint had used to perform his surgeries. Outside the church was a great pool of water where people bathed, laving themselves with the muddy water known to have miraculous healing properties.

I lay with Aged Orange stretched out on my chest, scratching him under his greying chin, combing bits of fur from his back with my fingernails, afraid to move because he seemed so peaceful there. He made me think of the Chinese emperor's cat who had fallen asleep inside the sleeve of his master's kimono, how the Emperor had had the sleeve cut off rather than disturb the sleeping deity.

After a while — when Aged Orange sprang from the bed for no apparent reason, as cats will do — I got up and opened the curtains that Vernal had closed. As Rainy used to say, whenever she caught me looking out the window in the chow hall at the Facility, "You got some place better you thinkin to go?" Most prisoners didn't bother to look out any windows because we were no longer part of the outside world. Besides, all you could see was the Hill, where the unclaimed bodies of executed women were laid to rest. Something else I'd been warned: women who had been considered escape risks were buried in leg-irons.

I opened the window to breathe the fresh air. (Vernal had removed the lilies, I noted with relief, and replaced them with a bouquet of pumpkin-coloured chrysanthemums.) The sun stole through the trees and spilled onto the blue-black rocks below where not so long ago the creek had overflowed its banks, and then receded, leaving twigs and dead branches of spruce and hemlock that had snapped off, in the rush of watery silk. I thought of my friends: Rainy, whose idea of nature was something that happened in beer commercials, and Frenchy for whom "outside" meant the place you had to go to get to the car.

I could hear the distraught bird again, calling from the trees, *Ohhhhhhhhhhh ohhhhhhhh* and another one, answering him, *Aaaaahhh Aaaaahhh.* I tried to shut out the noise by closing the window and turning on the radio: a woman said every night she had been forced to kneel at the foot of her bed, and pray for her mom and dad, her brothers and sisters, and the gun lobby. The radio dial had been turned from *Weather or Not* to *God Listens.*

Puzzled, I turned it off, dressed myself, and went to make my bed. That's when I found the wet patch in the spot where Aged Orange usually slept, next to me. He had disappeared for the moment but I vowed that when I found him I would make him sleep on the floor. Then I went to my bedroom door and reached for the knob with none of the hesitation I'd felt the first time I'd had to face the challenge of opening a door that someone was not going to lock behind me.

Vernal met me at the foot of the stairs. "You should have woken me," I said.

"I've been letting you sleep. I figured you must have needed it." I said I'd been sleeping my life away for the last twelve years, now all I wanted to do was wake up and live.

The kitchen, a bright spacious room with a solid yellow cedar table in the middle, was a mixture of welcoming smells. Vernal had made coffee, real coffee, not the kind guards spit in if they're having a bad day, but the kind that clears your head, like the high altitudes in which it is grown. He had set a place for me at the table: orange juice the colour of California poppies, half an onion bagel spread with peanut butter and jam, and a bowl of Fruit Loops. He had tried to make pancakes but had tripled the baking soda to make them rise, and they hadn't turned out as he'd hoped they would. I laughed and said it was hard not to admire someone who, even though he is a catastrophe when it comes to reading a recipe or substituting ingredients, refuses to stop trying.

I could smell lemon furniture polish, too. Vernal had always insisted his house be spotlessly clean, and had regularly disinfected his work space, the tables or shelves, on which his clutter was piled. When we were first married I used to tease him that he was the easiest of men to please — one who wished for nothing more than that his toilet bowl be clean enough to eat out of.

Vernal's idea of living simply included a collection of gadgets that promised to make living simply easier — a Dancing Can Opener that gyrated in time to the coffee grinder, an automatic ice-crusher. His most recent acquisition was a toaster that branded slices of toast with the day's weather forecast — a sun, clouds, or raindrops — a prototype to show how Internet technology can be used in the average home. He hadn't had a chance to use it yet. He first had to replace his computer.

I didn't need a toaster to see what kind of day it was, but I didn't want to hurt his feelings by being critical of his latest toy. I heard the squalling of crows and mentioned the screaming birds I'd heard in the trees; Vernal explained that the former owner had raised peacocks, but because he hadn't always been around to look after them, they'd "gone native", terrorizing the flower garden, flying up at dusk to roost in the cedars, well out of the way of predators, such as dogs and raccoons.

His predecessor believed peacocks to be symbols of immortality. "He thought they were too godly to mate in the usual sense, but when the peahen drinks the tears of her mate, conception takes place. He couldn't have been more wrong," Vernal said; he had taken to using earplugs at night. In the mating season that he hoped would be over shortly, the rattle of their tails could be as noisy as a room full of skeletons playing dice.

Their leader — a white peacock — would one day be supplanted by a young challenger, in a ritual fight to the death. "The white one is always the most vocal, especially when there's a moon," Vernal said. "You're particularly vulnerable upstairs. They can keep you awake all night with their . . . and when they stop, it seems *too* quiet and then you start missing them."

I said the cries didn't bother me. As long as I knew the bird wasn't injured, or dying of loneliness at the top of a fir tree, I would sleep.

I caught myself before asking Vernal's permission, and stepped out through the patio door into the daylight. He had taken up gardening with a vengeance. His decorative planters were filled with bitter-smelling marigolds, fire engine red geraniums interspersed with chrysanthemums and purply blue heliotrope. The latter gave off the scent of baby powder that made me think of Grace again with her crack-addicted surrogate child.

The sun was coming up, hard. I went back inside. Vernal said he was afraid the peacocks were becoming drug addicts — he'd seen them nibbling on the opium poppies that grew wild all over the property, and then stumbling around with heroin-honeymoon eyes. He was considering putting them on a methadone program for the winter because the cry of a peacock going through withdrawal would probably wake the dead. "Worse than their mating call, if you can imagine," he said.

I slid the door closed behind me. "Do you still take both in your coffee?" he asked.

"Black, please." I'd never taken it any other way, but why should Vernal remember now, when he hadn't ever remembered during our marriage?

"If it isn't too much trouble," I added, staring at my distorted face in the stainless steel vastness of Vernal's prototype toaster. I was beginning to feel like a house guest, all these pleasantries.

Vernal, I noticed, still kept his newspapers stacked neatly on the kitchen table: another habit that hadn't changed. When we'd lived together he would sit and drink his first two cups of coffee and read me anything he thought I ought to know.

Vernal said he was the only person on the island who actually read newspapers; most people used them to light their fires. He took the lid off the sugar bowl and waved it in front of my face. "Hmmmm, empty already. I filled it just last night." I didn't respond, as I went through a month's worth of papers Vernal had saved. I had imagined my story would have made headlines since the day I walked away from the prison van and boarded a plane. Newspapers have a way of sensationalizing prison escapes: "Killer Mom Flees Custody." "Authorities Say Escaped Murderer Back in Canada." "Canada Mum on Extradition Where Death Penalty Involved." "Armed and Female: No Child Safe While Killer Mom at Large." But nowhere did I find the smallest mention of my prison break. Instead I found myself confronted by a photograph of my seatmate from LAX, who'd been arrested and charged with conspiracy to import three tonnes of cocaine into the country. I looked up to show Vernal.

"Small world, isn't it?" he said. "He retained me as counsel a couple of days ago. They don't have much of a case against him. All circumstantial evidence except for what he had strapped to his body — for his personal use, of course.

"That's not all you missed out on," Vernal said. He went into his study and brought me the one paper he said he wasn't going to burn. I stared at the headline. "Terrorist Attacks Claim Thousands." While I had slept six commercial airliners had exploded in mid-air, within twenty minutes of one another, over "the targeted attractions" of Hollywood, Las Vegas, Disneyland, the Vatican, the Eiffel Tower, and the Pyramids of Giza.

"Unreal," Vernal said, as he spread a tortilla with ketchup then topped it off with a dollop of mayonnaise and folded it in half. For a moment I thought he meant the tortilla sandwich. "For the first time since I've been coming to the island, I wish I had a television."

I sat contemplating the headline, trying to picture the claimed souls. Wherever there is death we speak of it "claiming" us, a reminder that the Grim Reaper, from the beginning of our lives, has a stake in our destiny.

"There was a suicide bomber on board each of those flights. Each one supposedly had a grenade in her vagina," Vernal said. "A group called the Army of Roses has claimed responsibility. It's an extremist faction that encourages women to commit *Jihad Fardi*, or "personal initiative attacks.""

He bit into his tortilla and got mayonnaise on his moustache. "This kind of experience isn't encoded in our collective genetic makeup," he said, wiping the mayonnaise away. "What could have prepared us for something like this?"

Our care and treatment counsellor used to tell us stories, giving us, in each of them, an *exemplum*, a little sermon that preaches by example. In a good story the experience is primary, not the message, and the message — whatever it was she believed she was trying to communicate — was usually lost on us. One of her favourite cautionary tales was about what happened to a frog if you dropped it in a pan of room temper-ature water and heated the water to a boil. The frog floated half-awake, like she was taking a lovely bath — nothing in her experience led her to believe she was in danger — her eyes slowly sliding shut. If, however, you plunged the frog into a pot of boiling water, she would try to jump out. Instinctively she knew that the hot water meant death.

Rainy and Frenchy and I figured that either way the frog was toast. I wondered if, back at the Facility, she was repeating the frog sermon now, comparing what happened to the cooked frog to what happened to those doomed souls inside the jet planes.

I set the newspapers aside. My serendipitous escape had been pre-empted by America declaring war on terror.

PART THREE

Dead children do not give us memories, they give us dreams.
— Thomas Lynch, *The Undertaking*

I HAD BEEN AT THE FARM A little over a month, when Vernal said he thought a change of scenery would do me good. He made waffles, spread them with peanut butter and set my plate down on the paper I was reading, obscuring the thoughtfully pious faces of four of the women martyrs, *shahidas* in the Army of Roses, not one of whom had lived to blow out the candles on her thirtieth birthday cake. In a perverse way I knew I should be grateful to the terrorists. They had taken the heat off me.

The photographs of the looters at the crash sites made me think of the last riot at the Facility that had been caused by peanut butter — those individual portions that come sealed in matchbox-size containers. It is hard now to explain the relevance of what occured, from a bigger-picture perspective, but in prison an unalterable daily routine was what spared many of us from going insane. To wake up and go to the chow hall only to find the single-serving packs of peanut butter, jams and jellies were smaller than the ones we were accustomed to — it was an undermining of morale. If you couldn't count on a small thing like a portion of peanut butter staying the same, what *could* you count on? That same day the girls started ripping their toilets out of their walls causing massive flooding. The riot squad moved in and soon we were all on our knees, retching and blinded.

I didn't want to upset Vernal any more than I did simply by living under the same roof — a reminder of how hard he'd tried, how much he'd failed — but I couldn't eat the waffles. The peanut butter made me smell tear gas and want to throw up.

Vernal said I looked unusually pale and suggested we take our coffee outside to the pergola the former owner had built as a place for meditation on the edge of a berm. In a moment of tender loveliness, I saw a blue heron standing among the lily pads; he took flight as we approached, his slender lines a haiku inside feathers.

"That's the villain who eats my goldfish," Vernal said, and the moment died.

We sat together, not speaking, looking up at different parts of the sky, as if seeking direction. I thought of something Frenchy had said, wisely, in group one day. "It never be a good mistake — be alone wid someone you shouldn't have loved."

I can't say I shouldn't have loved Vernal to begin with — who ever gets love right the first time? — but we both held onto grief because it was all we had left of our love. I was afraid, if I let my grief go, there would be nothing left of us.

The sun, as if newly out of bandages, shone weakly from behind bouldery clouds. I felt, in the tearing of the wind, the trees waiting for winter to strip them. Vernal said he'd tried meditating in his spare time, but hadn't been able to sit still long enough. "I'm hoping they'll invent a drug to help me meditate," he said, half seriously, as he felt around inside his jean jacket and pulled out a baggy full of bud, and rolled a joint.

He lit it, inhaled, and smoked half of it before offering it to me. "Toke?" he said, through his teeth, so the smoke couldn't escape.

I shook my head. "I thought you'd stopped." I looked away, up into the sky, an aching blue over my head.

"I have. This is just . . . it's medicinal. Helps me relax. Helps me . . . appreciate the natural world better."

Vernal nudged me and pointed back across the creek towards the meadow. "Some people spend their whole lives looking for their own personal space. All you have to do is die and you get more space than you know what to do with." Vernal often began to speak enigmatically when he got high, another habit that I had found irritating when we'd lived together.

But I caught myself worrying about him again, thinking back to the hopeless days of our early marriage when I used to take his cigarettes out into the garden and break them, one by one, as if this simple act of caring would be enough to help him break a lifelong habit.

The sign at the Christian vegetable stand now made the Lord sound like an abusive father who comes home from a bad day at work and starts taking it out on his kids: "Don't Make Me Come Down There". A headless rabbit lay stretched out across the top of the sign warning against trespassing, loitering, or soliciting. "He shoots cats, dogs, anything that moves, the son of a bitch," said Vernal. "He's one of those Right to Silencers — but he thinks it means he has the right to use a silencer on his gun."

We did a wash at the King Koin Launderette and shopped for the new clothes I needed at Natural Lee's — a rain jacket that fit properly, jeans, work socks, three T-shirts, and two left-footed gumboots. I asked about the likelihood of buying a matching pair in the future. "It's what we get," the clerk said.

We had one minor skirmish in the grocery store: Vernal insisted we needed a bag of sugar and more Fruit Loops. He accused me of being a cereal thief, of sneaking downstairs in the middle of the night to feed my addiction. I protested — I'd never had a sweet tooth — but none of my protestations were going to change Vernal's mind.

He had one item left on our list — a woven willow coffin. I said I would price one while he went to a noon hour meeting.

At first I thought the door to Down to Earth was locked but it turned out to be, like my dresser drawers at home, merely swollen. There appeared to be no one behind the counter in the dark, serious shop smelling strongly of incense.

I stood, looking over the stock: the pottery coffin; the one made of papier-mâché; waterproof, biodegradable, sound-proof, earthquake-proof coffins in all shapes — tapered, rectangular, or teardrop. The saddest of all were the coffins stacked to one side, pint-sized and painted a bare white, as if white was the most innocuous, the colour least likely to excite strong emotions.

"I can help you." A statement, not a question. A man, wearing an ill-fitting suit, a black shirt and an incongruous tie with dollar signs and dice all over it, stood beside me — I hadn't even heard him creep up on me. I glanced at his eyes, the green of freshly squeezed limes. I told him I was thinking of buying a Chrysalis.

"That will be for yourself." His voice sounded hoarse, broken and interrupted as though being transmitted on faulty wires.

"No. Yes. I mean, for storage."

"You don't need to explain," the man sighed. "No one ever comes in here saying they want a coffin because they are going to die. We might die at any moment, yet we all live as if we plan to be here forever. My job, you get good at reading futures."

"It would be a useful thing to know," I said.

He went on, undeterred. "This is your lucky day, those bad babies just went on sale." He must have felt the subtle change that passed through my body at the word "babies". "You catch insensitivity, working here," he said, backpedalling. "Someone kicks the bucket, it's just another day. Business as usual, if you see what I mean."

I did. What I'd learned in my moments of deepest grief was that the world, which had turned into a nightmare for me, was the same ordinary world for everyone else. I had also learned this: the grieving don't forget their grief simply for someone else's sake.

He pointed to where the woven willow coffins were stacked, neon-red price tags hanging from their handles, giving them a cheap, discounted look. "Two for one sale," he said; his eyes had become cloudy, like beach glass, as though a fog were trapped inside. "One size fits all." I couldn't look at him straight because I felt as if I might step into his eyes and become lost in the fog that was wisping its way into my head.

"People come in here all the time. They say, 'Life is passing me by.' I tell them, 'You don't want to make the same mistake with death'. Did you want these bad babies . . . my bad . . . you want those units delivered or will you be picking them up in the hearse?"

I remembered Vernal saying everyone here knew everybody else's business. I said I'd stop by for the coffins later, grabbed my parcels and left.

Ceese & Son had reopened for business — a sign in the window read, "Grand Opening Free Coffee Balloons for the Kids" as if it were a factory outlet selling unpainted furniture.

I crossed the road to the Snipe hoping to see Hooker Moon's red truck pulling up outside, but when that didn't happen I wandered over to the cemetery, a stony shrubbery of grave-stones that sloped towards the sea, behind the Church of the Holy Brew. I had to ask myself why I had let Hooker — a man I'd never met and only seen once — fill so many of my waking, and dreaming, hours. *He's the one they wrote the song about, "Bad Moon Rising".*

The graveyard was undergoing a facelift. During the winter high tides, a sign informed, parts of the graveyard were awash, and the dead were being evacuated and moved to higher ground: "Your Tax Dollars at Work: Another Project for a Growing BC". I acquainted myself with some of the town's permanent residents. In the pioneer quarter I found the Shakespeare clan (including a William who had died at birth), the extended Ceese family, and a plot of Bend's. A tusked bronze boar, "Erected by His Wife" squatted impudently in the centre of Orbit Bend's grave: visitors, perhaps hoping to increase their sexual prowess, had rubbed shiny the tusked boar's testicles. I was tempted to reach out and rub them myself, they looked that trusting.

The world had changed in many ways since I'd gone to prison, but one thing that hadn't changed was graveyards. They were still sombre places and, like Vernal said, full of sober men and women. A granite slab with your name, birth-hyphen-death date, and someone else's idea — "Rest in Peace" — of how you should spend eternity.

I strolled on beneath the dark conifers, then stopped before a grave decorated with crushed beer cans that had been arranged into the shape of a cross. Someone, a girlfriend perhaps, had placed Mickey and Minnie Mouse figurines in amongst the cans, a strand of dried seaweed binding them together at the neck.

I was contemplating the tides, the graves in danger of washing out to sea, when I came upon the most woeful part of the graveyard. There were few trees here whose root systems might disturb the restless sleep of those who died before they were old enough to know the meaning of the word grief.

I walked without purpose, then sat in the shadows between a grave containing the ashes of Mary Joseph's five children who had been "lost in a fire", and the memorial to Crystil Sam's three sons, drowned at sea. Other women had lost far more than I had lost — though I remembered a slogan from the one NA meeting I'd attended in jail: "a teaspoon of pain, a cup of pain, it's all the same". Losing three children or more equalled, to me, a cup of pain. Losing one child, in comparison, a teaspoonful. But that teaspoon could be as full or as empty as the world.

There's this to think about: if I hadn't had Angel, I could have lived my life without ever wanting anything enough to hurt over. What if We Never Wanted Anything Enough to Hurt Over? I'd written this in big letters — to remind myself in case I ever started to forget — and stuck it on the wall in front of the table in my cell where I used to sit everyday to write letters. Rainy asked me what the words said and when I told her she asked if she could use those words for her twins, who shared the same grave, an unmarked one. Her excuse was she had never been able to think of anything important enough to have carved in stone and even if she could have thought of something, she wouldn't have been able to afford it.

I told her to quit her snivelling, she wasn't the first poor person on earth to bury her kids. That sounds cruel, the way I talk about it now, but I had just got to the part in *Beloved* where Seth selects a gravestone for her baby. She wants her baby's name chiselled on it; the engraver says "you give me ten minutes, I'll do it for free."

All she gets for ten minutes is "Beloved". If she could have stood it for longer, up against the dawn-coloured stones sprinkled with chips of stars, the engraver's young son looking on; if she could have given him ten minutes more she would have earned the two words she so desperately desired for her child, "Dearly Beloved".

Rainy thought "Dearly Beloved" sounded lame, and not how she felt. She liked "What if We Never Wanted Anything Enough to Hurt Over?" She just hoped she had enough cash so she wouldn't have to double up on the engraver and his crew to pay for that many words. She said this the night before she was executed.

The most heartbreaking tomb, the one that Vernal found me kneeling beside, was built like a granite bunk bed, with an angel-baby surrounded by carved animals who looked as if they had turned to stone the moment his eyelids closed for the last time. A stuffed teddy bear held a handful of red and yellow balloons that hung limply puckered from their strings. I tried to remember, as I knelt in the sweet, uncut grass at the edge of the bed — the stone sheets had been tucked in so tight there would have been no escape from that final sleep — how capable of emotion I, too, had been once.

I've heard that, when a limb dies and is amputated, a person can still feel pain in the body part they've lost. When you lose your child that phantom limb is the whole world trying to reach out and wrap you in its grief. You do not want to outlive your children. This is the only thing I am sure of, the one thing I know.

≶ ≶ ≶

That night Angel appeared in my room, sitting at the foot of my bed, the heaviness of his presence tugging me from a troubled dream. He looked hungry, and he sucked his thumb as if he could draw sustenance from it. While I watched he began pulling out his eyelashes, too, the way he'd done in my dreams ever since I lost him. He would dip the eyelashes into something sweet — honey or molasses — then suck the sweetness from them while I watched, helplessly: the dream always ended before I could reach him to feed him. *Sorrow is nourishment forever.*

In the jungle town where I'd taken Angel to the *curandero*, the women believed that when a child dies his soul becomes a drop of dew in a hummingbird's eye, one that wells up, like a tear, then wanders the world looking for a woman who has lost a baby and wants to have another of her own. The *curandero* advised expectant mothers to drink water that had been boiled with gold jewelry in it and wear *perfume chuparrosa* — hummingbird perfume — to drive men wild and cause them to remain faithful.

I sat up in bed and whispered my baby's name. My quilt slipped to the floor and a moment later Angel was gone. On my dresser that looked sepulchral in the dreamy light, the water jug and the vase had turned into two severed heads — Rainy, her hair matted with blood, and Frenchy with her eyes rolled upward. And then, as quietly as they had come, they vanished into a wall drenched with moisture, and the air filled with the mist of their leaving. The heads became a jug and a vase again, and I was left with no one.

I lay for the longest time, then got out of bed, wrapped myself in a blanket, and hobbled to the window. I always slept with the window open but now, again, it had been closed. I rubbed a spot in the dampness — even my windows were weeping — and for a moment the clouds parted, and the silver face of the moon swam out, casting a pallid glow off my dripping walls.

When I heard the radio come on, I didn't turn around, but stood staring out at the darkness. "Women in Paradise are so beautiful that a man will be able to see the very marrow of their bones through the flesh on their legs," I heard a voice say, words that conjured up Rainy, so thin her bones looked like they would cut right through her baby doll pyjamas, to break free of her skin. Rainy with her no-colour eyes, because she'd cried all the colour out of them the day she was born. "The women in Paradise have neither buttocks nor anus created as these parts were for the elimination of faeces — and there's nothing of that nature in Paradise." I thought of Frenchy, with her one missing finger ("nine fingers gets me a discount at the manicurist's") and the birthmark on her cheek, white and heart-shaped, like a beauty mark in reverse.

I went back to bed, turned off the radio, and fell asleep as it began to get light. I dreamed of a dark blue sea with babies rolling in the waves, being tossed ashore, weightless, into my arms that could neither hold them, nor let them go.

§ § §

It was the rattling of a peacock's tail that woke me. I felt an old uneasiness coming over me, settling on my chest and then pressing deeper. Vernal had carried the two willow coffins upstairs for me; I climbed out of bed and arranged them along the adjoining bare walls, then put my new clothes away. I dressed and, after opening the window again to let the room air, went downstairs.

We drank our coffee, fierce and black, then Vernal found a half-smoked joint in his pocket, lit it, and took a toke. He opened the fridge, and brought out the fillet of sole he had thawed for our lunch. Vernal had learned how to make a piece of fish go further by poaching it in a can of Campbell's alphabet soup, a dish that had made him famous in legal circles when a group of friends, including a judge, petitioned that he be tried for crimes against humanity.

"Add in some spices, get this dish up on its feet," he said. I wanted to add *and running out the door;* short of lowering one's naked foot into the bottom of a slimy pond I found it hard to imagine a more depressing experience.

I sipped my coffee, making little canyons in the sugar bowl with a spoon.

"I worry about you sometimes," Vernal said. I often caught him these days looking at me sideways as if he suddenly realized he knew nothing about me at all. I wanted to say to him what I knew to be true: we are all unknowable, aren't we? But now — his eyes touched, for a moment, with an old kindness — he confessed he had been worrying about going back to work, too, about leaving me alone at the farm. He'd been racking his brain, he said, trying to think who he could ask to come and stay with me, so I wouldn't have to fend for myself.

I said I liked the idea of spending time alone, after thirteen years of not having had a moment to myself. He finished the joint and looked at me again, closely. "I know what you're thinking. You're thinking I've got an ulterior motive."

I said, "How do you know what I think."

He said, "How do you know what I know?"

I took my coffee to the sink and poured it down the drain, then went back upstairs feeling that vague uneasiness coming over me again, as if I'd caught a fragment of a shadow lurking just beyond the edges of my sight.

My room was now filled with a musty, humus-like scent intermingled with Bounce. I heard Kurt Cobain singing "Jesus Don't Want Me For a Sunbeam" even though I had left the radio off. There were flies everywhere. The window I had opened wide had been shut, and a wind had infiltrated my room like a malevolent spirit, upsetting the vase. I picked Angel's photograph out of the spilled water, and dried it off on my sleeve.

Aged Orange sat upright on my bed like a cartoon cat, his head rotating as he watched a fly circumnavigate the room. I drew the curtains and opened the window to get rid of the cloying smell that reminded me of Frenchy when she came back to the range after they failed to kill her the first two times, from the firing squad, then the gallows. The morning of your "date" you were given a change of clothing, a clean orange jumpsuit. Even though our keepers insisted it had been "freshly laundered", it was bound to retain traces of the last girl who'd worn it to her execution. The smell of Bounce hung around for as long as a week afterwards.

My copy of Beloved lay on the floor beside my bed. I only had one chapter, that last chapter, left to read and I had been savouring it: every time I had picked up the book I'd put it down again, as if I could postpone the bitter-sweet pang of disappointment that came with endings of any kind. I used the book to squash a fly the size of a blackberry that had landed on Angel's photograph, then went back downstairs for a fly swatter or an aerosol can of Raid.

Vernal said the sun must have enticed the flies from the cracks. He rummaged through the cupboard under the sink until he found what he said I needed — a device that let you suck up insects from a comfortable distance without having to risk making contact.

I didn't comment, but "from a comfortable distance without having to risk making contact" struck me as how we had spent much of our married life. When I was on the Row he had written to say he had finally taken my advice and started seeing a psychiatrist. He quit after the first session, claiming he didn't need to pay $150 an hour to be reminded he had trouble getting close to people.

I went back upstairs carrying the cordless insect vacuum, but by the time I reached my room the flies had disappeared.

Aged Orange had become even more agitated in my absence. I tuned in to *Radio Orca*, and sat next to him on the bed. I stroked him until he calmed down to the sounds of humpback whales singing in the depths, and waited. Waited for a sign that life after death wasn't just something invented by those left behind trying to be hopeful.

After a while I got up and went into the bathroom. Here my mirror had been taken down and put back again, the reflecting side facing the wall. My toothbrush lay beside the sink, and my hairbrush, webbed with black hair that wasn't my own. My box of tampons had been opened and left on the edge of the bathtub so that when I picked it up the contents spilled onto the floor. I left it there (I didn't turn the mirror around, either), rinsed my toothbrush, and went back downstairs. Rainy had still not got it through her head that I didn't like sharing my toothbrush — with anyone.

One morning Vernal announced he was going to drive up to the Yaka Wind village of Old Mystic to ask Grace Moon to come and keep me company when he went back to work in Vancouver which, he said, he couldn't put off doing forever. "She'd be closer to the ferry and to the airport, if her baby decides to come earlier than expected," he said. When he put it that way, it was hard for me to object. He asked me to come for the ride.

The road to the north wound under tall, keening poplars shedding their last gold leaves. Vernal drove more slowly than usual, as if competing with the proliferation of roadside shrines for sobriety. White crosses festooned with yellow ribbons, photographs of kids in their rented grad gowns, scraps of poetry duct-taped to telephone poles, and messages from friends: Have a Good One, You Go Girl, See Ya Around Bud. A few had bunches of dead carnations in glass jars green with dried algae, but mostly what we passed was an abundance of artificial flowers, in faded pinks and blues, which gave the memorials a kind of Value Village aura that made them even more sad.

"I acted for one of these kids, a couple of years ago," Vernal said. "He used to drive up to Old Mystic to do his drinking. He ran over a young girl, I forget her name, Charleen-something. His father bought him a faster car when he got acquitted, presumably so he could get out of town quicker next time. When he drove off a cliff a year after the accident, there were some people who thought he had it coming."

The Bend straightened out and the crosses died out, too. For a stretch there was little evidence of human life or its inevitable end, only solitude crowded with loneliness. It started raining as we climbed Garbage Dump Hill — what the locals called it, Vernal said. When we got to the top I saw the sign — "Mystic Landfill: Keep Our Dump Clean" — nailed to a tree at the start of a dirt track leading into the forest.

"The original dump was on the sea side of the road," Vernal said, pointing to the edge of a cliff that fell seven hundred feet to a rocky shore. "That's where the first settlers — I don't mean the natives — used to bring their trash. Pretty practical lot, when you think about it. They figured if you tossed your tins and bottles over the cliff the tide would take them away. That was back when "environment" was the hard word on a spelling test."

We drove on, descending to where the Bend followed the coastline north, then veered inland. The vegetation thinned the further from the sea we drove until we reached a clear-cut on Vernal's side, and on mine a sheer rock face with netting to keep debris from falling on the road. "Whoaaaa," Vernal said, swerving so that the cliff came close enough for me to kiss. I covered my head with my arms.

"Buck. Two point. Nearly a *dead* buck," Vernal said. I told him I'd watch the road for him if he would watch his driving, and at that moment the sun burst, like a fireball almost blinding me, from behind a muzzy cloud.

Vernal slowed, put the hearse in neutral, let his window down, and pointed to the top of the rock cliff where a white and blue plaster statue of the Virgin gazed down on us, her hands folded in prayer.

"Native Honour Site," Vernal said. He said you could read the name of everyone who had died in an accident since the road had gone through. "The Yaka Wind people don't go in for that individual shrine business. If you get killed on the road they don't want to commemorate the spot. He paused, squinting into the sun. "Rain always slacks off around this place," he said.

I watched a gang of crows slice through the air, then land up ahead, not far from where a man stood, as if he had been waiting for us to come along. I hadn't seen him at first because he blended so well with the terrain.

Vernal put the hearse in gear and inched forward. I saw the hook sticking out of the man's sleeve.

"What's *he* doing here?" Vernal said. He didn't sound pleased.

He braked, then accelerated again, as if he had felt the subtle change in heat that had passed through my body.

"We can't just leave him," I said.

Vernal pumped the brakes until we came to a stop a little way up the road from where Hooker stood, and leaned on the horn. I looked over my shoulder, watching Hooker walking towards us with his distinctive, rolling gait. The crows scattered, then regrouped further ahead. I opened the door and Hooker leaned in, said "back in a minute," then disappeared into the bush.

"Unreal," said Vernal, shaking his head, and shutting off the engine, when the minute had stretched into five. A quarter of an hour later Hooker reappeared from the trees with a green garbage bag.

"If you've got body parts in there, I don't want to know," Vernal said, as I moved over so Hooker could slip in beside me. His hair, smelling of wood smoke, brushed my face.

"Roadkill, that's all." Hooker nudged me: a furry paw poked out of the bag he'd placed on the seat between his legs, and I looked away. "Most people won't even bother picking it up anymore. Game warden catches you, you pay that new roadkill tax."

Vernal shook his head. "Who thinks up these things?" He glanced at the garbage bag, then asked Hooker what happened to the pickup he'd been driving the last time we'd seen him in the Port of Mystic.

"Tide got her. We were clam digging and my sister she hit a soft spot. I told her, 'Keep your eyes peeled for soft spots', but she never listens."

Hooker didn't sound too perturbed by his loss. He nudged me again, smiling so quickly that when it was over I wasn't sure I'd seen it at all.

We hadn't driven more than a quarter of a mile before the rain began hammering the hearse again. For a while no one spoke, then Hooker said he'd caught a ride to the Honour Site earlier in the day to visit two of his cousins, Brad and Sugar, who'd died on their way home from an AA Meeting. "They were too smart, those two. Everybody knew they were going somewhere."

Vernal asked Hooker if life had quieted down in the village since the film crew had left. Hooker shook his head and said it didn't even feel like home anymore; he wondered why he bothered hanging around. Vernal explained, for my benefit, that the band council had been paid a lot of money to let a Hollywood producer use the village as a location. They were making a movie about Vikings, but had come in August so had to import tons of Styrofoam to look like snow and transform the village into a Viking settlement. The Styrofoam had broken up in a storm and now the beaches were covered with snowballs that weren't going to melt.

"They covered the poles in front of our longhouse with dragon masks and shit. They even fucked up our church," Hooker said.

One night he and a few of his friends had been partying, and the film crew had come to shut them down. Complained they were making too much noise; the crew was trying to shoot a Viking ship full of Viking berserkers stoked with mead landing on the beach. "We weren't supposed to complain about *that*," Hooker said. "We couldn't even pass out, not until *they* raped and killed everyone and went to bed."

Hooker reached across me and took my left arm in his hand. He grinned at my frog bracelet, turned it around to examine it. "Nice carving," he said, "nice and deep."

The frog was his *naha's*, his mother's crest, he said, the crest of a secret society that in the old days belonged only to women. "She told me — you put a frog on your head. If it stays on top it means you'll have a long life. If it jumps off right away, it means . . . " he looked at me as if trying to decide whether it was safe to continue.

I took my bracelet off — I don't know why I did this — and put it on my head. Hooker laughed when it fell off and rolled away from me on the floor.

" . . . it means someone *else* is going to die," he continued. And then he said most white people thought they were crazy to believe in things like that.

I looked up at him and met his eyes. He looked back down at my bracelet. He said he had been making jewellery himself for the past few years, but that you gained too much weight sitting still. He had recently started to work in wood, bigger pieces where you had to move around more.

Vernal, as if sensing the mutual attraction, asked where Hooker wanted to be let out. "My *naha's* place'll do. She's off island until next week some time, but Gracie'll be there. I've been looking for my dog since yesterday. I figure he might have stopped in to visit Gracie and them for a bit."

Vernal said we had come to pay Grace a visit, too. "How's she making out?"

Hooker drew the flat of his hand across his throat. "You know how she gets," he said.

§ § §

The further north we drove, the harder the rain fell. By the time we reached the village it was bouncing off the road and going back up.

Vernal pulled in at the first house we came to, one with antlers hanging above the entrance, and strips of salmon drying on a clothesline. We followed Hooker into a mudroom where a hollowed out log — the start of a canoe — took up most of the space. On a table made of rough planks balanced on top of a stack of old *Reader's Digest* magazines lay a mask Hooker said he had been working on — a welcoming gift for Gracie's baby. "Wood keeps splitting on me," Hooker said. I saw where the moon's face had been severed by a crack in the grain.

I heard laughter or crying — I couldn't tell which — coming from inside the house, on the other side of a yellow cedar door carved with Raven stealing the light from the sky. Vernal said we should go, he didn't want to intrude, but at that moment Gracie pushed open the door and stood, naked — except for her three gold bracelets — and hugely pregnant, in front of us. She seemed unaware of her nakedness and made no attempt to cover herself. Her cheeks were flushed, and she hadn't brushed her hair, which made her look as if she'd just come back from running against the wind, or having lazy afternoon sex. Vernal began to apologize, said we were in the area, hadn't meant to intrude, but Grace seemed to be in her own world, one it would have been difficult, if not impossible, to intrude upon.

"Come on in, come," she said, smiling at the cracked moon mask Hooker held in his hands, her brown eyes flecked like crumbled honey. She looked pleased to see him, but Hooker's eyes had gone black. He glanced at Vernal, then at me. "Seen Toop?" he said, refusing to look at his sister.

"I sure miss that dog. He never visits me anymore," Grace said.

Vernal and I followed Hooker inside, hesitantly. A teapot and a matching set of cups and saucers sat next to a bowl of sugar with silver tongs on a table that looked as if it had been laid for afternoon tea with the late Queen Mum. The cups were thin and veined, heady with Victorian roses. Grace leaned forward to remove a syringe from a water glass.

Al, who was not wearing any clothes either, sat hunched over the table, getting ready to fix. I tried not to look at him, my eyes moving around the kitchen instead, stopping at the handcrafted sign over the electric stove saying, "Welcome Friends".

Grace said she'd just made tea, and asked if anyone else would like a cup. Vernal tried not to look at Grace's body while Hooker focused somewhere beyond the "i" in "Friends" dotted with a bullet hole.

"I made tea?" Grace repeated, making it sound more like a question this time. "Don't anyone go. Please?"

Hooker cleared a space on a couch — the maroon cushions, once dark as pig's blood, faded to pink except for a few places around the upholstery studs — and told us we might as well sit. I squeezed onto the couch between Vernal and a pile of *Bride* magazines. A coffee table had another syringe and a length of rubber tubing in the middle of it, and a pamphlet from Social Services on how to breast feed your baby.

I saw, out of the corner of my eye, Baby-Think-It-Over, lying twisted in a corner, wires spilling from his gutted body, a pillow covering his head. All his lights, it was evident, had gone out. Grace, who no longer wore the giant key around her neck, kept glancing at Hooker, then smiling anxiously across the table at Al.

Al scowled, then lowered his eyes into his lap. Both his hands, one holding a hypodermic needle, disappeared under the table.

Grace looked at him, hopefully. "You all right, hon?" I had been too distracted at first by Grace's nakedness to notice her resemblance to her brother. Even though her skin was paler than his, she had all Hooker's dark, uneasy restlessness, and something else besides. She draped a blanket over Al's shoulders and asked Vernal what he took in his tea.

"Just sugar, please," Vernal said.

"One lump or two?" Grace asked.

Al sat with his hands under the table staring numbly through the window. Grace asked him, for the second time, if he was feeling okay. "If you keep worrying about shit you'll fuck up my high," Al said.

Al had more track marks than Grace had scars on her arms. Vernal asked Grace how the baby was doing and Grace said he'd been doing a lot of sleeping lately. She showed us the Moses basket she'd been weaving for him, from cedar bark cut into strips, soaked, boiled and beaten. "It's harder to find the bark I need now because — where are all the cedar trees? They're gone, all logged off. Miles and miles of nothing."

Out of the corner of my eye I saw Al raise his teacup to his lips with one hand and then, as if he had decided swallowing wasn't worth the effort, or he resented the attention Gracie was paying to the rest of us, spit out the tea and let the cup drop to the table. Even as the hot liquid scalded him, he didn't lose his stunned expression.

When Al and Gracie started fighting, Hooker said he was leaving, he didn't want to get Al's kind of blood on him. Grace began shouting that all Hooker had ever done was ruin her life. She said Al only needed unconditional love. "You can't kill our love, Hooker," she cried. "You can't even kill it with all your hate." Vernal went to comfort her but — I'd been watching Al's face — I pulled him away.

Vernal and Hooker walked ahead of me back to the hearse.

"She's high, she didn't know what she was saying," I heard Vernal say.

"What that Al needs is an unconditional bullet in the head," Hooker said.

§ § §

The rain had let up and the sun broke through again, the way it had at the Honour Site. Vernal's mood had darkened since he'd set eyes on Grace. On the plus side, though, he hadn't invited her to come and stay with me at the farm.

Hooker said he had to stop at the Uncle's to see if his dog had ended up there, and told Vernal where to pull in. He got out, said "right back," and Vernal and I waited in the hearse until he returned, alone, five minutes later. "No dog. I'm not worried — wherever I end up, Toop always finds his way back to me," he said. Vernal exhaled, as if he'd been holding his breath the whole time Hooker had been gone.

We drove north through the village, past the fucked-up church draped in black tarpaulins held in place by scorched timbers, with "Painkiler" sprayed across the door, past a solitary memorial pole that stood ten feet from the tide line on the gravel beach covered with Styrofoam snowballs. Vernal made another stop at Matt's Yaka-Way, the only store in the village that sold tax-exempt gas and cigarettes for anyone with a Status Card, and gave away free coffee and packages of flavoured condoms to everyone else. Most of the shelves had been given over to objects associated with killing, in particular fishing and hunting. I helped myself to "gratuitous" coffee while Vernal gassed up.

When we were on our way again, Hooker said he'd get out at Dead End Road. "They call it that because it ends at the graveyard, eh?" He gave me another quick smile. "I like it there. It's where you'll find all the people I get along with best." We left him, roadkill in hand, then drove back the way we'd come, through the village.

The sun dropped behind the rain wall into the sea as we passed the lone totem pole. I asked Vernal why it had been raised so close to the tide line and Vernal said from what he knew of the case a judge had awarded Lawlor Moon's wife custody of their only daughter, so Lawlor bought her a colouring book and some new Magic Markers and took his daughter to the beach. "He drowned her because he didn't want anyone else raising her. Then he took his own life." Vernal said the memorial pole had been raised on the spot where the Magic Marker pens had been found scattered amongst the stones.

Further on I watched a fat, white tourist dog being humped on the road by a three-legged skinny dog half its size.

"I had a teacher who used to say nature thrives in mongrels," Vernal said, honking at the dogs, then giving up and driving around them. "It's called hybrid vigour — if you want to create the strongest healthiest offspring you should mate with someone whose strengths are different from your own."

As we left the village behind Vernal tried to tell me why he felt responsible for Grace, how much he was to blame for her circumstances. He told me he had met Grace when he

GIVEN

first came to the island and had encouraged her to move to Vancouver, to get into modelling, to make a life for herself. She made the move and then, walking home after an audition, in daylight, she had been raped. "You've seen the scars . . . her wrists, her throat. She tried to commit suicide after that. On more than one occasion."

Vernal seemed comfortable talking to me as long as we were in transit. Driving was an ideal time for intimacy, because it forced him to keep his eyes on the road, and he didn't have to look at me.

He said Grace started doing heroin again when she found out she was carrying the child of a rapist and because she kept failing at killing herself. She had promised him she was flying straight, because of the child, but he realized she'd been high again today when we'd arrived at the house, even though she tried to hide the fact, unlike Al, who had to fix in his penis, where he still had one vein left that hadn't collapsed.

As Vernal spoke I noticed the paper bag that had rolled out from under the seat. I opened it and saw a 26er of Silent Sam and a bottle of homemade wine.

"Hooker must have forgotten this," I said, almost too quickly, tucking the bag back where it had come from. It had to be Hooker's — Vernal would never, even in his worst moments, drink homemade wine. I suppose I should have thought it strange that Vernal didn't ask what was in the bag, but this was symptomatic of our entire marriage. Any marriage, come to think of it. You learned to accept things, as if they had never happened.

We drove home down the east coast road, so that I would be able to say it was official: I'd gone round the Bend. I questioned Vernal about Hooker — how he had lost his hand.

Vernal said everyone on the island had a story. Some said he had been born without it, others that his hand had been wizened at birth and later dropped off. There was speculation that the injury happened in his teenage years, a rumour involving a homemade grenade and a car-bombing campaign.

"That's not all he lost," Vernal said, keeping his eyes on the road straight ahead. Some people swore he'd gone to Vancouver and injected so much cocaine into his urethra that he got a hard-on for three days, then gangrene set it. "He's supposed to have left the hospital minus five fingers, and his dick."

Vernal must have heard my small exhalation. He said he didn't want to talk about Hooker anymore, he wanted to talk about *us*. Neither of us spoke until Vernal asked me if I thought I might ever come to love him again, the way I once did. I said I had already used up a lot of my mind thinking about the way things had been; I tried not to think about the future.

"I just keep wishing there was something I could do. To make you feel, you know, *better,*" he said.

Vernal had always tried to protect me from myself, from my own melancholia. I believe he was jealous of my moods, because they belonged to me, I owned them. It had been easier for him to control my ups and downs as long as there had been cocaine, but eventually the drugs, and what was left of our marriage, had run out. Vernal took my hand and said he was sorry. For what, I could only imagine. Our shared history of sorrow?

The east coast drive was uneventful, no Honour Site, no dangerous curves, shrines or garbage dumps. No hitchhikers, either. Back at the farm I poured the homemade wine down the drain and stashed the bottle of vodka under my clothes at the bottom of a Chrysalis, then sat for what seemed like hours, staring at the patterns the rain made inching down the glass, seeing nothing beyond the pane. When I thought of Hooker's mouth, his lips, his melting eyes, all the songs of lovesick devotion I'd ever heard came back to me then in one confused medley.

Part of me wished I could love Vernal again, but love, I knew, never agrees to share your attention with anyone.

Vernal put off returning to work until the last week of October, when he had to make his first appearance for Deacon Maplethorpe. He arranged to take the ferry to the mainland and fly home a week later.

The current slogan at the Christian vegetable stand read, "I Brake For Jesus", and reminded Vernal that the hearse's brake shoes needed adjusting, and he asked me to book an appointment at Chubb's. When we reached the ferry landing I let Vernal out, blew him a kiss goodbye, and drove back to town where I stopped by the Snipe to grab a coffee before going shopping.

"What's the difference between erotic sex and kinky sex?" asked Marg, before I'd taken a seat.

"Erotic sex you use a feather, kinky sex you use the whole chicken," she said, when I told her I didn't know. I glanced over at the board. Today's Special was Philosophical Chicken.

"Basically it's your chicken curry with your hardboiled eggs in it," Marg explained, as a couple of sorry-looking tourists bundled in out of the rain.

"They must have Christmas here, at least," I heard the woman say, looking mournfully at the permanent-fixture tree.

"It's supposed to make you ask, which came first, the chicken or the egg?" Marg said; I eyed the couple dressed identically in yellow slickers with yellow gumboots and hats to match. The woman carried a child bundled up in a bright blue tarp.

"It makes you think, don't it?" Marg answered.

The woman looked at Marg and asked if she was open. I could hear the frustration in her voice. Marg jerked her head towards the sign in the window but the woman said she had learned on this island that "Open" could mean anything. Marg, who always brightened at the prospect of new victims, said this was as close to being open as she was ever going to get. The man took off his rain hat and shook his head, spraying a halo of water. "We finally got that rain," Marg added.

The two huddled together as far away from the door (open, as always, to let the flies out) as they could, looking as if they expected to be served. I overheard the man say no one had ever heard of the word *mañana* on this island, "because people here don't understand that kind of urgency." The child began to fuss.

"A baby, eh?" said Marg, as the woman got out a bottle to make formula.

"He's almost three and he's still on the bottle," the woman said.

"Who isn't?" Marg replied. "Every guy on this island's weaned himself off his wife's tit onto the bottle." I took a sip of my coffee that tasted like tea. Marg asked if we knew why Jesus crossed the road, and the man in the yellow slicker said, "to get to the other god damned side where it wasn't god damned raining?"

His wife nudged him. "Take it easy," she said.

Anyone who knew Marg would have answered her question with a simple "I don't know", even if they did. It was just easier.

"He was nailed to a chicken," Marg said.

The couple looked more despondent by the minute. The man asked Marg for the directions to the town where "that movie" had been shot. His wife said he hoped to photograph native islanders in their natural habitat.

Before Marg could think of a reply, I told them they should stay on the Bend, the only road you could take, that it was a half hour drive, unless you got lost. The man said, "what do you have to do to get a drink around here?" and his wife told him to take it easy, again, that as he could see nothing was exactly speedo. "When in Rome, do as the Romans do."

"Any chance of getting a hot drink, something to warm us up?" she asked Marg, trying to sound as if it made no difference to her one way or the other.

"I got vodka," said Marg. "You want something stronger, you get it up at the Brew." She waved her hand at the window in what could have been any direction. "The church on the left as you're leaving town?" She looked at her watch. "You'd better haul ass up there though. They close at noon — for an hour. Most everything around here does."

The couple discussed what to do and decided they'd stay and have regular coffee and a couple of the muffins, solid as doorknobs, that sat on the counter besides the TIPS jar, and a note saying "Help Put Talene Thru Collage."

"They'll have to be to go," Marg said. "We close over the lunch hour, same's everybody else." She paused when she saw the blank looks. "For *lunch*," she added, shaking her head, as if to say some people had to have *everything* spelled out for them.

❧ ❧ ❧

Dis here little pig jet ta market,
Dis here little pig be layin back in da cut,
Dis here little pig had roasted beef,
Dis here little pig had jack shit,
Dis here little pig said, "Yo! Yo!
Ah can't find ma muhfo way home!

I had hesitated before the meat counter at Natural Lee's when I heard Rainy reciting her favourite nursery rhyme. I stepped back and she appeared, standing between me and an overkill of chicken. Her whole body, surrounded by a fine red mist, had collapsed, like her veins. She looked like a ghost whose body had been sucked inside out. Her head had become horribly misshapen, and she had six fat syringes jammed into her neck, as if to keep her brain connected to the rest of her body. She had pierced her eyebrows with so many silver rings she looked like a walking shower curtain rod. Her once brown skin was now the colour of burnt toast, and she was crying, thick brown tears that stank of vinegar as they trickled out of her eyeballs. Blood oozed from her neck where the needles pierced her skin.

When she turned to face me her eyes remained fixed in their sockets, the way a doll's eyes do, then Frenchy materialized next to her. She had an elongated neck, and her wiry black hair, which she'd been proud of because it blunted the matron's scissors each time they forced her to get a haircut, had been burned off. Frenchy's birthmark, floating like a cumulus cloud across her cheek, (she called it her "ugly spot") had been charred until it had become almost the same colour as the rest of her skin. If you looked hard enough you could still see the shadow of it, the way you sometimes glimpsed the new moon holding the old moon in her arms.

A boy — hard to tell his age because of the hood of blood covering his face — had his arms cinched around her leg; wherever Frenchy walked she dragged him behind her. He was covered, from head to toe, in blood, and a feeding frenzy of flies. *This be the HE* Frenchy said, picking a bag of Fritos from a display, and tucking it under her shirt. When she spoke her bottom lip spilled down over her chin exposing her gums, teeth, and her tongue that she could no longer control.

I decided not to buy chicken after all and wheeled my buggy into a ransacked SALE aisle. Frenchy hobbled beside me, talking non-stop as if we were two old mothers whose lives had taken different directions, coming together over the last of the year's school supplies and Halloween novelty items, and the difficulties we had both faced raising children.

This how it be when your kids die first, Frenchy said. *When it your turn they come back and hang widju.*

I pushed my buggy towards the produce section, trying to guess what else Frenchy might filch — possibly the *Ghostbusters* lunch kit, dented on one side, or the box of Crayolas that had been opened and returned, for Rainy, who liked to draw. The damaged boy trailed after her, wanting everything he saw and striking himself in the face each time Frenchy told him *no*. Getting your dead kid back to raise for the whole of eternity, Frenchy said, was the worst part about being dead; the best part was you never had to be in a hurry. You could take your time getting anywhere because you'd already reached your goal. Being dead meant you got to enjoy the things you'd never had time for while you were too busy living your life.

PART FOUR

That's what ghosts are . . . spirits living inside you. Your eye is like a movie projector, shining them out.
— Darcey Steinke, *Jesus Saves*

LIVING WITH RAINY AND FRENCHY ON THE Row had been, in comparison, easy: we had separate cells so we weren't on top of one another, and we didn't have to share a bathroom. Now Rainy had become afraid of the dark, and insisted the lamp be left on beside my bed at night, as if light were enough to ward off loneliness. *Dark creep me out,* she said, *make my head stand on end.*

Frenchy, on the other hand, with her see-in-the-dark eyes, shrank from any kind of light. When I tried to compromise by switching off my bedside lamp and lighting a candle instead, Frenchy said the sound of the flame hurt her ears, and drew away from me into one of the room's dark corners. She could barely tolerate daylight. During the days she took to wearing my aviator shades that she had coloured over with a black Crayola to further prevent any vestiges of light from seeping in, but if she woke in the night and blew out the candle beside my bed Rainy would wake, too, and start shrieking. (Back on the Row Frenchy used to call Rainy a human tuning fork. When she struck a high note hard enough, she could break bulletproof glass.)

Their presence, every minute of the night and day at the farm, was yet another test — a daily reminder of what Vernal had said when he decided to tell me he'd had a vasectomy. He couldn't bear the idea of having children because all they would ever be able to fulfill in him would be his worst fears. He said that with Brutus and me in the house his life had started to feel like an overcrowded lifeboat, and he couldn't make room for anyone more. After a while I felt him begin to push the rest of the world out — first his friends, then his family, then everyone he'd ever loved, and finally, even me. "There's only room in the lifeboat of your life for one person," he told me. "You have to choose yourself."

I discovered later that Vernal had stolen this from a novel he'd been reading, the way he got most of his feelings, second-hand, through characters in books, but this was Vernal's power — to save himself — and also one of our irreconcilable differences. (After I gave birth, Angel had called forth my own capacity to love: that was *his* power. I would no longer choose myself, to save myself, that is. I went down and the sea swallowed me. But each time I came up for air I saw Angel waving to me from the shore. It was the sight of him, even as he grew more distant every day, that kept me from ever letting go, from all-the-way drowning.)

Rainy named my room the Apocalypse Now Suite, after the staccato beat of the ceiling fan that sounded like a helicopter coming down from the skies. She spent much of her time slipping between the wall and my dresser to try and do her hair on the other side of the mirror. *When you dead,* she said, *don't matter what side of the mirror you lookin on. Both be the same shade of nuttin.*

Even without a reflection Rainy managed to style her hair in whatever shape took her fancy — her favourite being a helicopter with moving rotors. With her dead twins a red mist swirling around her I expected to see her rise, like a medevac chopper along the edge of the South China Sea, scooping

up Frenchy where she sat beside her boy on the banks of the
Perfume River trying to breathe life back into him.

What you doing? Frenchy would ask.

My hair? Rainy would say.

But Frenchy and Rainy had, in most ways, stopped paying
attention to the way they looked, and especially to matters
of personal hygiene. Even from a distance I could smell on
them the odour of death. Only people who have never smelled
death, in the flesh, would say it smells sweet.

Rainy admitted she'd been the one who'd switched the radio
to *God Listens* every time I'd left the room. She'd taken the
mirror in the bathroom down, too, hoping to find herself on
the other side, and then hadn't been able to remember how to
put it back up again.

It had been Frenchy who had closed the window when I
went downstairs: she said the sound of water rushing over the
stones in the creek hurt her ears. On TV you could turn the
volume down, but here there was nothing she could do but
use a couple of tampons to block out the roar. (She confessed
to having opened my tampons without asking, and borrowing
a few.)

When we had first arrived on the farm, she said, she
had enjoyed hearing the creek, but after a while the sound
changed — the noise of the water rushing around the stones
kept her awake at night. Instead of hearing the lullaby of
the water over stones, right away in tune with it Frenchy's
mind would begin to replay the judge addressing the jury, or
handing down her death sentence. Frenchy wanted my help
to move the rocks in the stream. If we could just alter their
pattern, the way the stones were arranged on the bottom of

the creek bed, she felt she could get them to change their tune. Frenchy had always believed that by transforming the world around her she would find peace. (In prison it had been a train that kept her awake. She got so obsessed she took legal action against the railroad company, claiming they were deliberately harassing her. When the train passed the prison at 2:16 every afternoon, it whistled and woke her up.)

My friends kept odd hours, preferring to sleep during the day. Sometimes, late at night, Rainy would creep downstairs and bring back a sugar fix from the kitchen. Other times she would begin endlessly sweeping.

Twice I had been awakened in the night to the *fshhhh fshhhhh fshhhhh* sound of her sweeping moonlight from the walls. Rainy had earned her name because at one time shopping and crying had been her hobbies. Now it was crying and sweeping. *Take the "s" out of sweep and weep's all you got left,* Frenchy said. *You be cryin and weepin both at the same time, yo.*

I weep all I want, Rainy replied. *Weepin bring me closer to God.*

Aged Orange had been banished from my room the day my friends had moved in. Frenchy claimed her boy was allergic to cats — if he were exposed to their fur his body would break out in hives and he'd look like he'd been sunbathing naked when a bomb went off in a strawberry patch. Aged Orange was demoted to being an outside cat and spent much of his time clinging like a monkey to the screen doors of the patio, ever hopeful that I would relent and let him in.

I soon discovered the real cause of Aged Orange's banishment — the white rat with red eyes who lived in the lining of the HE's long black waistcoat and lived on whatever fell from his mouth as he tried to eat.

"Why does it have to be a *rat?*" I asked Frenchy, exasperated.

You catch one and don't gatt his ass — you got a friend fo life, Frenchy replied, kissing the rodent on his greasy lips.

Despite his youthful appearance, the HE was a sickly boy. Pus oozed from the sides of his head where the bugs had chewed off his ears when his mother had left him to die on the riverbank. He slept standing up, one blind eye open, and from the way he sometimes behaved, slapping his head against his open palm, first one side, then the other, I wondered if the bugs has infested his brain. (On Tranquilandia a runaway slave was punished by having his ears stuffed with carnivorous insects and sealed shut with wax.)

He wanted the windows covered, day and night, and closed the curtains whenever he could. He lit incense and placed the Qur'an on the bedside table that he had moved to the wall of my room facing east, the wall he would face daily for the five prayers.

A smelly, bloody discharge issued from both his nostrils and he sniffed constantly, making a *glock-glock-glock* sound in his throat, and blowing his nose, over and over again, into his red-and-white checkered *kaffiyeh*. He sounded like a cat trying to cough up a massive hairball.

The day Frenchy took the time to scrub more than just the surface of blood off her boy's face I could see God had tested him more severely than he had tested the rest of us. I saw the place where her bullet had struck between his eyes, severing his optical nerve and lodging itself above his nose. She couldn't be convinced that she had left her son blind. He saw, she insisted, what the rest of us couldn't see. Her boy saw with the eyes of the heart.

The HE was responsible for the fly infestation in my room. Not only were the flies drawn to the blood he left behind every time he moved, but when the HE's hair got too unruly Frenchy tried to slick it down with a daub of butter that she also used to polish his boots. The butter attracted the flies, and they stuck to the HE's body as if he were a living twist of flypaper; only once when a fly landed on him did I see something come loose inside him, as if the boy's brain had finally got word that the body it lived in had been badly hurt, and he tried to smash off what was left of his face, and broke my water jug in the process.

The HE, anyone could see, was still angry at having been shot by his mother and left to die. Frenchy said she'd seen her boy manifest himself in a thousand different violent ways. *It be what the angry dead do,* she said. Rainy was of the opinion that Frenchy's boy ought to do a few therapy sessions around his murder issues.

Boys who had been made by hate, I learned, didn't want to be unmade. In the ten years or more the HE had been dead, he had been fighting more than just his own battles.

After Frenchy shot her boy and left him by the river, he'd been reborn. He hadn't been a natural reborn killer, he had had to work hard to make the name he had earned for himself. I asked Frenchy if being shot in the bank robbery hadn't changed his mind about shooting other people. *You stop eating ham sandwiches just cause Mama Cass choke herself on one?* Frenchy said.

The HE spent his teenage years toughening himself up, driving splinters under his fingernails then lighting them on fire, killing time by lying in a burlap sack full of biting ants, in the hot sun. He had joined the army and been sent, along with 10,000 other children, into the line of fire and across minefields. The children were deployed so that their bodies would explode all the mines (the donkeys were "too stubborn" to do it), and clear the way for the soldiers who came after.

Each child wore a plastic key around his neck, the key that would open the gates to Paradise once he had died a martyr's death. At one time the keys had been made of iron, but iron had become too expensive and too many of them were needed.

Before stepping onto a minefield Frenchy's boy would wrap himself in his desert-sand-coloured blanket (the one on which his dog slept at night) so that his body parts wouldn't fly in all directions after a mine had been detonated. When the dust finally settled, after the *ker-boom* of a detonation, he never saw anything more of the other children who'd been at his side. Maybe a scrap of burned flesh or a shard of bone lying around. That was all.

Day after day the HE detonated mines, wrapped in his blanket; he got up each new morning and set out across the minefields, willing and eager to die over and over again. He blew up so often and so spectacularly that he was given the name *shahid as-said,* the happy martyr, one of God's Chosen, the HE, the Holy Explosion. By the time his mine-jumping days came to an end he was left with as many pieces of shrapnel in his body as he had bones.

When the human wave of children had swarmed the land and won the day, The HE began his training as a soldier. He was made to dig his own grave and was buried alive, next to a corpse, for days. He learned how to handle grenades and machine guns. While many of the other children didn't survive the first few days — they suffocated in the earth, or threw the grenades too late and blew themselves up — it was the dog test that was hardest for Frenchy's boy. He loved dogs and would sooner poke out his own eyes than have to watch one be mistreated in any way.

His handlers hauled him out of bed one morning and drove his dog — the one he'd shared his blanket with — across the parade ground, and shot him. They shot to wound, then ordered the HE to slit his throat. When he refused he was given a rucksack full of river stones that he had to run with on his back, until he collapsed. He lay in the sun, dying all over again, a different kind of death, and the hurt dog limped over and lay down beside him and licked his face. Frenchy said her boy dug a grave for his dog, put its body in the rucksack, and made a cairn out of the river stones. He buried his heart, that day, too, under those stones, knowing a broken heart is an open heart and he couldn't risk ending up like his dog, bleeding and licking his master's hand for the rest of his afterlife on earth.

The next day he woke up ready to kill dogs.

Rainy's twins spent their first days at the farm in a red mist, hovering around their mother's head, wailing whenever the rat poked his head out of the HE's shirt, reaching a pitch they only could have inherited from their mother, one that caused the windows in my room, and the bathroom mirror, to crack. Rainy added to the problem by ignoring their terror, complaining because we didn't have TV — the only reality she knew that could save her from her life — reminiscing about the bad old days back on the Row where we all watched "westruns" every Friday night, and the first time she saw a vision of the "Version" Mary in her bowl of microwave popcorn.

Then, early Sunday morning, the twins, who had been fed on anger, who had sucked it in with their mother's milk for the short six weeks of their lives, manifested themselves before my eyes, as Twin Terrorists. I was lying in bed listening to *Radio Peace and Love* when their transformation took place. They appeared out of their fine red mist, covered from head to toe in voluminous white robes. They wore white veils, too, that concealed their heads, so that only their burnt-almond eyes were visible to the world.

As far as terrorists went, the twins were fairly low maintenance. They prayed for two hours a day, standing, stooping, and kneeling in devotion, and spent most of their free time — the way some girls obsess about their first menstrual period — talking about strapping on their first explosive belt loaded with nails and screws to make the damage from the blast more deadly.

Rainy was distraught when she saw what her twins had become. *You take a huge rip off of yo bong and be smoke and coughin and homies be dyin from how much smoke and coughin there be,* that *be a suicide bonger,* she said. She didn't approve of children being used as human killing machines. In her religion the power over human life — including the right to take it away — belonged exclusively to God.

Frenchy tried to explain to Rainy how "sacricide" bombers didn't think of themselves as killers of innocent people, but as being on call for a holy cause. *Muhfo walk in, shout jihad! put the truth back in killin, his body be da bomb.* All you needed, she said, were nails, an explosive, a battery, a switch, a short bit of cable, a couple of chemicals, and a sturdy belt with large pockets. *That and be pumped to sacricide yo self.*

Rainy thought about this. *What he get hisself? Seventy-two-year-old version chillax wid in Paradise?*

Now when the HE began going *glock-glock-glock* I realized what it meant: he was getting ready to detonate, to relieve the pressure building up inside his head. The only way Frenchy could distract him from blowing us all to kingdom come was by naming off sniper rifles — *Remington, Beretta, Mauser, Savage, Parker-Hale, Sig-Sauer, Dragunov, Steyr* — like some kind of deranged child's lullaby.

I got out of bed and rummaged through the coffin where I'd hidden Hooker's bottle of vodka, opened it and took a swig. Rainy said *pass that bottle, road sister* but Frenchy stopped her. *You been dead too long, girl. Don't start wid that now.*

Rainy had always said she could drink any man under the table if she wasn't already under the table with him to begin with. But she never got drunk — she was too angry for that. The booze would always vanish into some black pit in her soul.

I put the bottle under my pillow where Rainy couldn't get at it, and lay back down on the bed. She stretched out beside me, smelling worse than something dead that had been exhumed. I told her if she was going to stay in my room she had to start washing at least once a week. And I said I didn't want her, with those needles sticking out of her veins, always cozying up to me on the bed.

Rainy, who once told me she thought her heart was located in her neck, replied that the needles were there for a good reason — to keep her heart from falling out. Then she began to cry, the viscous tears stuttering down her cheeks. Rainy had the ability to work up a tsunami of tears that would send you scrambling for drier ground. In the broken heart of her life she was like the bottomless well grown-ups warned their children to stay away from.

Crying was the one thing she had left that could get my attention. Her tears were brown and pungent smelling; they leaked from her eyeballs and all her joints. Whoever had made Rainy over had done a terrible job.

I got a facecloth from under the bathroom sink, ran hot water into a bowl, and added a squirt of liquid soap to get rid of the vinegar smell. I hoped I wouldn't catch Rainy's crying disease — I'd kept my tears on the inside since I'd lost my son, and I and wanted it to stay that that way. "You got to hide things to keep love, coverin' up, puttin' everything on the outside and crying in yo oatmeal on the inside," Frenchy, when we became friends, had explained.

I gave Rainy a towel and told her to dry her face and especially her neck to stop the needles from rusting any further. I said I was going downstairs; Frenchy complained I was no fun to be with anymore, all I did was read books and sleep ever since we had come to this house. Rainy had smeared the brown fluid all over her face with the towel so that it looked worse than ever.

Beyond my window the sky had turned the colour of old gravestones. I left the room when Rainy began reciting "Tree Bline Mice" to the HE's rat, as if it were a fundamental morality lesson, and the twins started shrieking in stereo and jumped up on my bed, hiking their long skirts up over their knees. I closed the door behind me, wishing I could lock it and lose the key. Knowing, at the same time, losing my two friends and their dead kids who'd come back to get the mothering they'd missed, wasn't an option.

Tree bline mice,
tree bline mice.
Dem suckers be runnin!
Dem suckers be runnin!

Dey all run atta dis white man wife,
She done whacked dare tail wid a fuckin knift.
Whassup, you ever see anything dat bad in yo life,
As tree bline mice?

❧ ❧ ❧

Rainy and Frenchy had spent years of their lives arguing about God, and being executed had only further entrenched them in their positions.

God exist, why he walk on by? Frenchy said. She figured God must be playing a big joke on people like Rainy who went around praying he would answer their prayers. *You think prayin's gon save you? God gon gatt yo ass one day, same's the rest of us.*

Rainy, who sat on the floor, bent double, biting her toenails, wasn't fazed. *God just be doin his job,* she said, *policin the hood.*

Frenchy got up from where she'd been sitting and curled up next to Rainy on the floor.

What colour you figure God be? she persevered, as Rainy spat out another toenail. I told her to pick it up, but she ignored me.

I figure God be white and fat, weigh more than a second-hand Cadillac, Frenchy continued.

Rainy looked up, and narrowed her eyes. *You barkin up the wrong dog,* she said, colouring what was left of her toenails Mauvelous with a Crayola from the box Frenchy had lifted. *Me, I figure everythin in this world be 'xactly the colour it stupposed to be.* She emptied the Crayolas into her lap, picked Burnt Sienna and began drawing a portrait of herself, and her twins, emerging from a pale brown mist, on the wall.

You got a broken brain, Frenchy said. *It always been broke. Your daddy give you a money shot right in the soft spot before you pop out. You certified retarded, he get that extra money welfare gives people with dumbass kids.*

Rainy stuck out her bottom lip. *You not the smartest crayon in the box, yo own self,* she said, selecting Lima-Been-Green for her twin's hair. *'Sides that, Holy Spit-it be the only father I got to look up at. Ain't nobody smoke his ass on Nintendo.*

I listened to them argue and thought of our care and treatment counsellor who used to say, to Rainy and Frenchy, "You two, you bicker-nicker-natter. Like two peas and pods."

Frenchy kept on at her. *God tough, like a $2 fry-steak maybe? What you think? God made of steel? Like yo mama's dildo?*

Rainy shook her head. It sounded as if a bag of nails and bolts and other shrapnel the HE picked from his body had been dropped into a metal bucket and kicked across a pit of pointed rocks.

Ain't got no mama. My mama dead like a doorknob, Rainy said. She sucked in her lower lip, scribbling over the drawing she'd just made with a fistful of jarring colours, obliterating herself and her twins. Frenchy said it was time her twins got names, like George Bush or Osama bin Laden.

Them tags been already used, Rainy fired back. Rainy had refused to name her twins, from the moment she gave birth to them and saw how they were joined. When you named someone it made them harder to kill, and she hadn't wanted to get attached.

§ § §

That Rainy and Frenchy had decided to come along for the wild ride I was on, hadn't struck me as strange. I wasn't surprised when my mother tried to make contact with me, either.

Once a month I had been allowed to make a phone call from the Facility. Most times when I called home my mother seemed to remember who I was, but occasionally she would apologize and ask me to tell her again where I had been for so many years, and why I had never come to see her, why, especially, hadn't I come when my father had been ill and asking for me. I reminded her, as gently as I could, that they didn't issue day passes from Death Row, not even to attend funerals. Their rationale? "You knew your father was old and would probably die one day. You should have thought about that *before* you committed your crime."

"I don't know from one day to the next whether I'll even have a place to live," my mother had said, the last time I'd called. "Vernal's got the house up for sale. I suppose he didn't mention it?"

"He told me he doesn't expect it to sell," I'd said, quickly. "Not anytime soon. I know he's happy to have you living in the house, Mother."

"Vernal wouldn't know what it's like to be a burden on anyone," my mother sighed. "He doesn't even call. Unless he wants something — last time it was the car. I told him the tires needed rotating and if he took it and something happened to him, your father and I would never be able to forgive ourselves. You know how your father feels about lending his car; he'd rather lend his toothbrush. At least if something happens to a toothbrush, it's replaceable."

My father had been dead for six years. I didn't think he'd mind lending his car *or* his toothbrush under the circumstances.

I never got to say goodbye to my mother. She died two weeks before I was permitted a call to let her know I was being transferred and that if my new trial went according to my lawyer's plan, I would be coming home to take care of her.

Now with Vernal out of the house, the phone calls began: the first came when I was getting ready for bed, and by the time I got downstairs to answer it, the caller had hung up. The second call came a little earlier, around nine o'clock on

Tuesday evening. But while I heard nothing but laboured breathing over the line, I could hear a familiar impatient grinding at the edges of my own words.

"Mother, it's me. I know you're there. Please talk to me."

She didn't speak, and I began picking at the dry skin around my fingernails, then biting, tearing the skin off in shreds, with my teeth. I'd picked up Frenchy's flesh-eating habit — the way she kept trying to consume herself, bit by bit, before the world swallowed her whole — when we were in prison. Frenchy used to say she wished she could have been something normal, like an alcoholic or a heroin addict, because then she would have had Twelve Step programs like AA.

"Mother?" I repeated, emptily. Two of my fingers were bleeding and I was working on the third. I had half-hoped, in that way in which we never stop being our mother's child, that she might ask how *I* was getting along, but that was selfish of me, I knew.

Be patient, I told myself. Be kind. I remembered the last words I'd heard my father say: "Hasn't she hurt us enough?" How much is *enough*? How much more could I do?

ട ട ട

Rainy and Frenchy were still at it when I went back upstairs, the sound of their bones rustling like insect wings through the darkening room. Frenchy wanted to know who I'd been talking to, and why I was bleeding like a nailed-to-the-cross Jesus.

I climbed into bed and drew the covers over me. The HE, who had been trained to feel at home in a coffin, had made up a bed for himself in one of the Chrysalises; the Twin Terrorists had taken possession of the other that they'd moved as far away from the HE and his white rat as possible. Rainy wouldn't go near them — she believed they were "attempting fate". *Coffins be for dirt napping, best believe.* Gooey brown tears began oozing from the corners of her eyes, and around the needles in her neck, whenever she saw her twins lying in repose. The HE had found my blow dryer; he turned it on, shooting hot air into Rainy's face until she started to melt. Then he turned it off and tossed it onto the floor, where it lay clicking as it cooled.

I closed my eyes. Rainy, her face a bloated mass of wet darkness crawled in beside me. She whimpered like a small animal and I wanted to put my arms around her but was afraid I'd get jabbed by the needles. Frenchy got under the covers on my other side. She said Rainy and I had all the blankets, and Rainy said *she* didn't get any pillow; Frenchy said Rainy didn't need a pillow because her neck was full of spikes so she couldn't lay her head down anyway.

You dissin me? I be doin aight, Rainy said. *You try holdin yo neck up, walk round like a pincushion.*

I lay in the middle, growing more awake by the minute. I realized I'd have to go and sleep downstairs on the couch, that perhaps this was what they were hoping for, that I would vacate the bed so they could lie in it, side by side, and bicker-nicker-nacker all night. *Two peas and pods.* I made a motion to get up, but Frenchy reached over to hug me with her helplessly out-of-control arms.

Don't go, she said. *Chill here wid us.* I wasn't used to hearing such tenderness coming from Frenchy's sloppy mouth.

I lay awake between them until they fell asleep, listening to the cry of the peacocks, and beyond, in the forest, the cedars speaking in tongues, the giant spruce trees creaking like old planks. Overhead the buzz of a jet drilled in the reminder there was nowhere, finally, you could go to be alone. Not even up there close to heaven, where flight attendants were moving through the cabin distributing complimentary headsets for the movie about to begin. And suddenly I felt a tremor, a series of tremors, in my heart, as if it wanted to share with me the secret of how it went on beating while being locked inside a place of inescapable darkness, alone.

§ § §

On Tuesday morning I drove to Mystic to do laundry and pick up more cereal and a bag of sugar at Natural Lee's. I was leaving the market when I saw Grace Moon and Al coming out of the liquor store.

Al carried a six-pack under each arm. When I stopped to say hello to Grace and ask how she was doing, Al answered for her. "She's doing good, got me on a new health kick," he said, nudging her in the belly with the six-pack's sharp edge. Grace blushed and wrapped her arms around her body, as if by doing so she could hold herself, and her baby, together.

I started to ask Grace about her brother, but at the mention of Hooker's name Al's eyes flared as if I had struck a fistful of matches behind them. I said I had to run, I was on my way to the airport, which was true, and that I'd catch up with them later, which was a lie. If I never laid eyes on Al again it would be too soon.

I got to the airport early — Vernal's flight wasn't due in until 10:15. I waited in the arrivals area that smelled of freshly baked bread. Two island entrepreneurs had opened a coffee and baked goods stand called All Your Kneads in a quiet corner of the anything-but-busy terminal. When the plane still hadn't arrived by eleven forty-five, I ate a bowl of Happy As a Clam Chowder and two pieces of bread still baking-hot from the oven, then ordered an organic shade-grown-bean latte. I took a sip and thought, for a moment, something was wrong with it. It didn't taste like tea.

Vernal was uncharacteristically quiet when he got off his flight at twelve-thirty. The rain-slick road gleamed a royal grey-blue and, as we drove, Vernal, for once, didn't point things out to me — the small white dog in a red raincoat poking along the ditch, a matted teddy bear impaled on a stick — before I'd had a chance to notice them myself. I asked him if anything was wrong, if something was bothering him. "It's nothing," he said. "It's everything. It's killing me."

I knew what this meant. If Vernal wanted a drink, he would find any reason to have one. In the past I had always known, without even being anywhere in his vicinity, when he was about to fall off the wagon. Vernal said I was the only person he knew who could smell the thought of vodka over the telephone.

Back at the farm Vernal fixed himself a small lunch of aspirin and ice cream. The Walled Off had finally sold, he said, to a wealthy Asian couple who had arrived to close the deal in a black limousine that took up most of the driveway. If he'd seemed upset when he got off the plane, he said, it was because he'd forgotten my mother's ashes.

My mother had requested that she be scattered in the garden where she could go on being useful, fertilizing the flowers for others to enjoy. Since the house had been sold, Vernal didn't think the garden a suitable depository and had set the urn on the kitchen counter, in a container, but at the last minute they had slipped his mind and he'd left in a taxi without them. He had called his house-sitter and asked him to put the urn in the freezer until he could get back to the mainland to empty out the house.

"I don't think Mother needs freezing," I said, feeling protective, suddenly. "Ashes don't come with a Best Before date."

"I'm sorry," Vernal said. "I'm doing the best I can. I'm sorry."

I heard the soft rattle of the dustpan and the thump of the wooden broom handle against the wall above my head. When Vernal lay down to take a nap on the couch, I went upstairs and found Rainy sweeping my room, which was unusual because she most often swept in the middle of the night. She and Frenchy had stayed up all day, awake and waiting, expectantly, for news from the outside world. They wanted to know everything I had seen and heard in town.

I told them I'd stopped to buy groceries and that I'd run into Grace and Al outside the liquor store. It was Rainy's indignant opinion that Al had no right leading Grace, in her condition, into temptation.

Rainy claimed she always knew the difference between bad and wrong. At least she had a pretty clear idea about what was *wrong*. Wrong was what had happened to her when she was a kid.

Rainy's father had been a man who believed in beating the gentle Christ into his unruly children. Her brothers got the full force of his anger but when he beat Rainy he kept a Bible under his arm so as not to administer the lashes too heavily. *Ain't no makeup thick enough to cover yo father's fist kisses, either,* Rainy was fond of saying.

Because she wet the bed every night, Rainy had been forced to eat soap and recite the alphabet endlessly — the reason, Frenchy figured, she never learned to read or write. Her father, convinced that she was too lazy to get up and walk as far as the outhouse, sewed up her *chocha*. Rainy peed through the stitches in her sleep, and that made him so mad he beat her with the toaster cord and made her stand in his bedroom doorway, until dawn, in a half-packed suitcase. Some nights she said it felt as if her heart had got away on her, quit her body for good.

Frenchy figured the reason Rainy kept doing it in her sleep was because peeing wouldn't have hurt so much when she was unconscious. (I felt guilty over how I had treated Aged Orange when I remembered this. To think I had accused him of incontinence!)

Every night at the Facility, Rainy wet the bed. Every morning she changed her sheets, and every night before going to sleep she kneeled at the foot of her cot and prayed for God to help her make it through at least one night dry. *Help me to grow up,* she prayed. *Help this foolishass pissin baby.*

Muh Nigga, Dat Be in Heaven,
Chillin Be Thy Name, Yo.
You be sayin' it; I be doin' it
In dis hood and in Yo's . . .

Cut me some slack
So's I be doin' it to dem dat diss me
And keep dem muhfo's away
Cuz you always be da Man.

ও ও ও

Vernal stood by the stove, tiny white feathers floating all around him. "He can't say he wasn't warned," he said, when he looked up and saw me staring at the albino peacock he'd just finished plucking. I watched as he dropped the bird into the stockpot on the stove, then gathered the elegant tail feathers into a bouquet and arranged them in a vase. My mother believed having peacock feathers in the house was bad luck, that they brought troublesome spirits inside, but Vernal had never been superstitious.

He leaned over the pot to sniff the broth, and added more salt. Behind the vase I saw the shot glass and the bottle of whiskey. He must have seen the worry on my face.

His lips had that soaked overnight look. I asked him if he didn't think about the future, about what was going to happen to him if he continued to drink.

Vernal said he didn't expect to live forever. "That's as far ahead as I'm looking." Whiskey didn't make you drunk, he said, just brought you to a higher level of lucidity.

He said he was sorry. He had been concerned about me, which was part of it — having to leave me alone at the farm. He was afraid something might happen to me. He picked up the shot glass and held it in his hands as if it contained the rest of his life, then emptied it in the sink.

I looked away as the room filled with things left stubbornly unsaid. I couldn't bring myself to say he was mistaken, that Vernal was ringed by doubts far bigger than my plight. The landscape of living together never changed. It rolled on and on until it became indistinguishable from the horizon.

I heard a car pull up in front of the mounting block. Vernal said he was going to attend an evening AA meeting at the Brew, and had asked a friend to stop by to give him a ride. He pushed the pot to the back of the stove where it would simmer until the fire went out.

I followed him to the front door, where I stood watching him try to manoeuvre his shoes onto his feet.

"Don't wait up," he said, adding, "I'll see you in the *mañana*," as he had always done, in the old days. He reached down to kiss my cheek, but stopped at a comfortable distance without having to risk making contact before his lips touched my face.

I sat for a long time at the kitchen table, staring somewhere beyond the white peacock simmering on the edge of the stove.

The next morning Vernal was not where I expected him to be, passed out on the green leather couch. I ate a bowlful of cereal, then left the house. The Christian vegetable man had posted his thought du jour: "Jesus Didn't Know My Alcoholic Father".

I parked in front of the church, and stepped inside in time to catch Vernal ordering a last double single malt from a man who looked like a cross between Friar Tuck and Popeye.

Vernal looked tiredly guilty. "I'm sorry," he said, "this isn't going to become a habit. I've been having a nice little relapse, that's all."

Vernal told me he hadn't made it home because he had arrived at the Brew halfway through Holy Hour, when the drinks were two for one, and then his ride had left halfway through the AA meeting that followed. Vernal introduced me to "his saviour," Father Tunney, who had given him a bed for the night. When Father Tunney blushed, even his neck turned red.

"What's your poison, Missus?" he said. He made "poison" sound like "pie-zin," and when I didn't answer right away he went back to staring mournfully out the window where the rain fell like a curtain between the church and the town.

The wall behind the counter was plastered with placards about the haplessness of the drinking life: "Religions change; beer and wine remain"; "A Hangover is the Wrath of Grapes."

Vernal handed me the Holy Brew Wet List. "Here's a good one to wake up with," he said, pointing to a drink called God's Blessing. I said I'd always thought Irish Coffee was a contradiction in terms. Why bother to get drunk and sober up at the same time? I took a seat on a bar stool and said I'd like a cup of tea.

Father Tunney agreed with me. "She's got a fair point." He pronounced "point" "pint," and said I'd given him a new purpose in life, to find where the teapot was hiding.

I said I didn't want to put him to any trouble, and Father Tunney said, "no trouble at all, not at all." He'd be back in the time it took a crab to reach its destination even walking sideways, he would just have to conduct a small search of the kitchen where the teapot had last been seen trying to conceal itself behind a multitude of sins that he'd been meaning to remove from the premises.

He came back, eventually, empty-handed. "There's all the whiskey your heart could desire, but not a drop of tea at all. It was on my list, didn't I forgot to pick it up last time I was over to the store . . . "

"Not to worry," I replied, cutting him off before he had a chance to use any more words. "I'll have a glass of water instead."

"T'will rust your insides, so," Father Tunney said, which I took to mean water was not his poison of choice. He winked at me, one eye disappearing in the fat folds of his skin.

Vernal kept half-rising from his stool at the bar, then sitting back down again. He could maintain this air of being just about to leave, I knew from years of experience, throughout a whole night's drinking. I watched him try to put back a stack of credit cards that had spilled from his wallet next to a jar of pickled eggs. Then he chugalugged his drink, and asked me to wait for him. His noon-hour meeting was about to begin in the church basement; he was in charge of making the coffee there and he would personally bring me a cup. I'd asked for tea, but since when did Vernal listen?

Father Tunney watched him go, shaking his head as if he could read the tangled thoughts going every which-way through my mind. "What whiskey won't cure they say there's no cure for, so. Your man there, he has a great strength for the weakness."

I sat contemplating Vernal's on-again off-again funeral with the glass. I felt so desperate I even thought of asking the half-cut Father Tunney for advice, but my train of thought was broken by the sound of the church doors banging open.

"We're closed," said Father Tunney. "'Tis no place here for a bag-eyed inebriate such as yourself." His expression abruptly changed; I turned on my seat to see who had lifted his spirits.

"Come on in, son, you're very welcome. I thought you might be one of them film crew fellas. They practically drank the place dry."

I watched Hooker Moon, in slow motion, walking towards me. He stopped in front of the stool that Vernal had just vacated.

"This seat taken?"

I shook my head, then nodded. "Vernal's gone to get me a coffee. There's a noon hour meeting . . . downstairs."

Hooker gave me a conspiratorial look. "I used to bring this one bad friend of mine here. He'd run out of coffee at home, I'd tell him, 'come to AA, partner. They always serve coffee at those meetings downstairs.'"

Father Tunney asked Hooker if he was having the usual, and when Hooker nodded, opened a Diet Pepsi and poured it into a glass. Hooker lowered his lips to the rim and ran his tongue around the edge. His tongue was pink, like cyclamen. Then, as if to prove he could do with one hand everything I could do, he handcuffed the stem of the glass with the hook, and snapped it shut.

I asked Father Tunney for more water.

"I'm supposed to be closed at noon," Father Tunney said. "You're a fine lot of sinners, coming in here and ordering me about." He stopped, and placed his hand on Hooker's shoulder. "There's been another bereavement. I've the funeral to conduct in an hour's time." He said this in the same weary tone he'd used when telling me he would have to search the kitchen, hoping to find the teapot behind a multitude of sins.

"Better make it a double, then," Hooker said, nodding at my empty glass.

"That's right," said Father Tunney. "I'll leave you two to your madness. Lock the door behind you on your way out, will you? If you leave, that is, before I get back."

I took a sip of my water, and then another, but I couldn't taste anything. Vernal still hadn't returned with my coffee.

Hooker was watching me. I felt my face growing hot.

He asked me if I would join him at a table. He'd never liked sitting on stools at the counter, it made him feel like one of those deadbeats who propped up the bar.

"You don't drink," I said. It wasn't a question. I remembered the bottles I had found in the hearse, thinking how sometimes when a light comes on it's for the darkest possible reason. I'd been fooled, once again. Or, as I had done enough times in the past, fooled myself.

"Not anymore," he said. "Not for about seven years lately. Gave it up. Nothing better to do, I guess."

A change came over Hooker's face. "I'm not going to lie to you. You only lie to the police or to your girlfriend. The Uncle boots, and your old man he asked me to get him some hard stuff so I did. The Uncle threw in that parsnip wine as an extra. Most of the time he can't even give it away, but he's proud of it."

He sensed my agitation and stopped, then lowered his voice, fixing his eyes on his hook as he spoke. "Sometimes you have to do the worst thing, the worst thing you know how to do. It's the only way, sometimes, you can get free from yourself."

I wasn't sure what he was talking about — the fact that Vernal was drinking again, or that he, Hooker, had procured the booze, but Hooker had moved on to another subject. He was telling me how lucky it was that his mother had died where she did and they'd been able to bury her before the ground turned too cold.

"Your mother passed away?" I said, shocked by his matter-of-fact voice. "When? When did that happen?"

"Friday night, coming home from getting her hair done. She'd stopped over at the Uncle's to pick up some pie dish Agnes never returned. She got all the way home, stepped out of the taxi and bingo! Seized up."

Hooker could come from nowhere with a nonchalance that punched your breath out.

I touched my bracelet, as if trying to cover the frog's face so it couldn't look at me. "I'm sorry," I said. *If it stays on top it means you'll have a long life. If it jumps off right away, it means someone else is going to die.* I felt suddenly like a murderer.

"Sorry for what? You didn't kill anyone," Hooker said, shrugging it off. "It's pretty hard to care about a dead person you never met before."

He closed his eyes and leaned back in his chair, pushing it out from under the table so I could see his whole body. I liked it when he had his eyes closed because I could stare at his lips, his cheekbones, his nose, his perfect skin, his hook; it was as if, looking at him, my eyes had been opened to a different kind of beauty.

"The way I figure it, if you choose a new life you must not have had time for the old one anymore," Hooker said. "It just didn't take her as long as most people to figure that out."

He spoke with his eyes closed, as if he knew I was studying him and wanted to give me time. "We buried her yesterday. That's what she would have wanted — get her money's worth out of the new hairdo." I couldn't tell if he was kidding.

He stopped and rubbed his hands across his belly, opened his eyes and laughed at me. "I'm just having fun with you," he said. "My *naha's* never been afraid of what will happen to her in the afterlife." He said his mother had attended the church before it burned down, but since the church didn't approve of their traditional ways they'd held the funeral service Monday afternoon in the community hall with the ladies making tea and sandwiches and Father Tunney officiating.

The real send-off, Hooker said, was tomorrow night, something he called the Feast for Hungry Souls but in his typical fashion didn't try and explain. "Come on up to the village. I'm inviting you."

My eyes had settled on the yellow toothbrush around his neck. I tried not to let myself look at the rest of him, to explore further than where his white shirt, missing the top three buttons, opened to expose a V of smooth brown flesh.

But my eyes travelled down to his cobra-skin belt and, for a moment, rested between his legs. "When should I come?" I asked. I folded my hands on the table, feeling awkward again.

"Whenever you're ready, that'll be good. Just show up. When you make too many plans it interferes with the way things are meant to turn out on their own." He paused. "Go to the Uncle's place. Agnes will tell you where to find me. I'd tell you myself except I don't plan that far ahead."

Hooker still hadn't opened his eyes, but I knew, by the dance going on in the corners of his mouth, he was laughing at me.

"You'd think you'd gone handicapped on me, the way you keep staring." And then, more gently, "Never be embarrassed by something you like."

When it came time for the AA meeting to start and Vernal still hadn't come back with my coffee, Hooker and I went looking for him. The downstairs meeting room was empty but the doors opening onto the graveyard were ajar. A crowd had gathered around a recently excavated plot in the pioneer section, and when we went to investigate we found Vernal, his limbs jutting at odd angles from his body, at the bottom of a grave. A man with ill-fitting teeth said that before anyone tried jumping in to help him out we ought to get a medical opinion. I whispered to Hooker that Vernal didn't believe in doctors. Hooker said when you fall drunk into an empty grave it doesn't matter what you believe any more.

When Father Tunney returned from his lunch and discovered the entire AA meeting outside, coffees in hand, clustered around the grave, he tried to take charge, sending Hooker to borrow a ladder from Marg at the Snipe and the man with the bad teeth to fetch Dr. Bucket from the walk-in clinic.

Dr. Bucket said this was the first time he'd had to administer a painkiller in a grave. Vernal groaned and said all he needed was a drink. The doctor said he could use one, too, then lectured Vernal on the art of drinking as much as you could without embarrassing yourself in front of other people. But this was not the moment to imbibe, he said; the polite thing to do would be to get Vernal out of the grave before the grave's rightful occupant showed up. Vernal would have to be medevaced to St. Jude's in Vancouver because they didn't have the facilities on the island to cope with anything serious. Vernal had broken his hip, one of his arms and an ankle. Dr. Bucket felt Vernal was lucky he hadn't sustained any mortal injuries, that God looks after drunks and babies. "Let me put it another way," he said, when he had climbed out of the grave to give us his considered opinion. "The only thing he's not going to be doing is a whole lot of ballroom dancing over the next couple of months."

"No sober man dances, unless he happens to be mad," said Father Tunney, "as you would know if you had been reading your Cicero lately."

It took most of the afternoon to get Vernal out of the grave and onto a stretcher one of the AA members procured from the clinic. The funeral that had been scheduled for two o'clock, and over which Father Tunney was to have been presiding, had to be postponed.

Half-a-dozen alcoholics, as solemn as pallbearers, hefted Vernal from the graveyard into the hearse. All six insisted on accompanying us to the airport. Before he was carried out to the plane, Vernal told me to look for his wallet in his pants pocket — I'd find a couple of hundred in change and he wasn't going to need spending money where he was going, anyway.

"You're going to be fine, you're not going to hell. Not this weekend, anyway," I said, adding that I doubted the devil would want to be saddled with an invalid; he'd have to get better, first.

"Don't," Vernal said, screwing up his face to keep from laughing. "You're torturing me. It hurts."

I held his hand and told him I would come to the mainland as soon as I'd made arrangements. I would stay at the Walled Off, sort through what was left of my mother's possessions and clean the place out. I felt guilty as I spoke; I knew myself well enough to know that "making arrangements" was my way of buying time to rendezvous with the bad Hooker Moon. Time to do the worst thing, the very worst — a chance to free myself from the place where, despite my recent escape, I still remained imprisoned.

I stood in the parking lot, watching Vernal's plane take off and slip behind scumbled clouds, then drove back to the farm. I was on my way upstairs to tell Rainy and Frenchy about Vernal's fall when I heard the phone ring.

She sounded out of breath, as if she had sprinted in from outside.

"Mother?" I wanted to tell her what had happened to Vernal, that I was coming to the mainland to stay at the Walled Off, but out of the silence I heard her cough, and then put the phone down to light a cigarette. I had an image of her from my childhood, sitting in the summer garden late at night, lighting each gasper from the butt of her last, flicking the glowing end into the dark. "It's not the coughin' that carries you off, it's the coffin they carry you off in," my father would say whenever she lit up.

I heard her inhale, then let out a deep breath, as if expelling the last remnants of the person she'd been. I knew what she would say back to my father, too. "I love the feeling of smoke filling my lungs. There's nothing quite like it."

I began picking at the skin around my fingernails that had had time to heal since our last communication. I wanted to go upstairs, crawl into bed and rock myself, gently, to still my heart and my mind and everything deep inside me racing away in darkness. I wanted to hang up the phone and walk outside into the severely sunny evening and lie down in the long grass and listen to nothing more than the sound of the worms turning in the earth. I tried not to sigh, but it came out that way. I curled my hand into a fist, to stop myself from picking, and when she refused to speak to me, hung up and went upstairs.

A couple being interviewed on *God Listens* claimed they'd found Jesus while selecting cold cuts at the Winn Dixie Superstore in Miami Beach, that His light shone down on them over the shaved ham.

I seen the light once. It hurt my eyes, Frenchy said, as I pulled my duffel bag out from under the bed so I could start packing. Rainy asked where I was going and I told them about Vernal's accident, that I would be going to the mainland to clean out my mother's house, but first I was going up to take a trip up to Old Mystic on Thursday evening.

I saw horror twisting at Rainy's eyes in their oozing sockets, and then she started sniffling. *You not plannin on takin us widju?*

I shook my head. *You always bouncin,* Rainy said, in an accusatory tone, and turned her back on me, the sour smell of her filling the room. I could feel the cold coming from her body. *How you gon keep us here? You gon shut us in a box and nail down the lid?*

She pursed her lips at the HE, lying on his back in his coffin, going *glock-glock-glock* and stroking his rat. The Twin Terrorists sat in their Chrysalis, on the other side of the room, fantasizing — the way some women spent hours poring over bridal magazines for the right train — about their wedding with eternity. I hadn't given any thought to what would become of my friends without me at the farm. I felt the shock coming from Frenchy's eyes, even from behind the blacked-out lenses of my Eternals.

"You have each other," I said. "You can keep each other company."

Frenchy insisted the house was haunted, there were too many ghosts. Rainy cried and pleaded with me not to leave them alone. She'd thought death would be a cure for loneliness, but it had only made her feel worse.

We come back to chill widju. What you think, you just walk away? Frenchy said, looking at my eyes, not into them.

Jello salad tilt both ways, girl, Rainy said; she seized my duffel bag, opened it, climbed in and stood in it by the door. The sight of her wiping away parts of her face, loosened by the deluge of her tears, wore me down. I told my friends if they promised to stay at the farm while I went to Old Mystic tomorrow evening they could come with me to the mainland.

PART FIVE

*You can grieve your heart out and in the end you are
still what you were. All your grief hasn't changed a thing.*
— Charles Frazier, *Cold Mountain*

BEFORE I LEFT THE FARM I CALLED the hospital in Vancouver. When I finally got through to Vernal, he sounded sober. He had a private room, with a phone and a TV. The only thing missing, he said, was a mini-bar.

I drove to Old Mystic, worrying about Vernal; everywhere I looked I was reminded of the trip we'd made to the north end of the island together. And when, on the outskirts of the village I saw a black pig rooting in a field of dead goldenrod, I heard Rainy in my ear, reciting nursery rhymes:

> *Dis here little pig jet ta market,*
> *Dis here little pig be layin bac in da cut . . .*

Passing a pink tricycle that had been left, twisted out of shape, by the side of the road, I thought of Frenchy, after her father had cut off her finger. She had wrapped it in a paper towel and stolen a tricycle from a neighbour's yard to ride to the hospital, where they wouldn't let her in.

I parked in front of the Uncle's house and sat for a while, watching great cloud-wagons being pulled out to sea by the wind. Hope complicates your life; this much, I knew, and nothing could make me start desiring my husband again, the same way I couldn't stop thinking about Hooker Moon.

I got out and walked up the crushed shell path to the front door. After I had knocked three or four times and had turned to leave, a tiny woman with a crumpled face opened the door. In the half-light of the hallway, her body looked like a boulder shaped by a century of storms.

"Come in, come in," she said, ushering my inside. "I thought it was a *koko-stick* the way you knocked. *Ha ha ha to hell with you.* That's how it sounded: *ha ha ha to hell with all of you.*" Her voice was clear and quick, but sad underneath. "A *koko-stick*," she repeated, seeing my questioning look. "That's what we call the woodpecker in our language."

I guessed she must be Agnes. She knew without asking who I was looking for, and said her nephew was up at his cabin, but insisted I come in and meet her brother. The way he was carrying on since their sister had passed, she said, I might not get another chance.

The Uncle lay in bed, attached to a respirator, drinking from a Tweety Bird cup, holding a paper bag in his other hand, a Sears Christmas catalogue open on his lap. A poorly recorded tape of drumming and chanting issued from a tape deck surrounded by an array of pills and empty Drambuie bottles on top of the TV. The Uncle bore a resemblance to both Agnes and Hooker, though his black hair was specked with silver, braided and tied together by a shoelace. He reached for my hand and pulled me down on the bed. He was, I could tell, a handsome man under all the wreckage.

"The old goat," Agnes sniffed. "If he steals a kiss, count your teeth afterwards."

She made as if to tuck in the sheets at the bottom of her brother's bed. He wouldn't let go of my hand and fixed me with watery eyes, as if trying to fathom who I was. I looked around the room at the wallpaper with dimple-cheeked cherubs pressing their chubby bottoms up against one another — and down at the Christmas Wish Book, opened at a page of women in white underwear.

The Uncle made a dismissive gesture, as if he could guess my thoughts. His voice was faltering, weak; he said he was too old to be reading the kinds of girly magazines that showed you everything girls had to offer but nothing of what they felt.

I shifted my body as he continued to grip my hand, tried pulling me close again, and leaned into my ear to speak. Then he began coughing, as if the effort of speech was too much for him.

He let go of me, closed his eyes, and let the paper bag slip from his hands. "When's that Agnes going to bring my lunch?" he said, as if she wasn't there. I rescued the bag and set it on top of the television, upsetting the bottles of pills.

"They're all empty anyway," said Agnes. "He doesn't remember, but he already ate two hours ago."

I backed out of the Uncle's room and he opened his eyes again. "Bend over and touch your toes and I'll show you where the wild goose goes," he said, starting a coughing fit at the same time.

"The old wolf," Agnes said, shaking her head and closing the door behind us. She laughed as I pretended to count my teeth, and showed me into the cluttered kitchen where she was pickling sea lion flippers, next to three loaves of bread on the counter, rising in pans. Agnes had covered the softly swollen loaves with a dishtowel to keep them warm as they rose.

She gave me directions to Hooker's cabin: north through the village all the way to the end of Dead End Road. She said I could park where the sign said not to, and take the well-marked trail around the graveyard, or I could cut through the graveyard and save myself some wear and tear. She told me to watch out for *lumaloos*, and that once I made it through the graveyard it would be easy enough to find the path that led to her nephew's place.

I set off through the village, saw a wisp of cloud spiralling into the sky over the dome of the Catholic church, as if a spirit were taking leave of a body. I passed Matt's Yaka-Way, and swung left onto Dead End Road. When the road ran out I parked and took the shortcut through the graveyard that was nothing but sucking mud and wound under the twisted apple trees — ghostly presences in a place that lacked all colour other than gradations of gloom.

The trees, though leafless, still had small, golden apples hanging on to the branches that were weighed down by grey hanks of moss. I stopped before a mound of black earth — a new grave piled high with fresh, wet flowers — in a part of the graveyard inhabited by Moons: William Moon, 1937–1985 (there was an empty Bombay gin bottle on his grave labelled "Wholey Water Do Not Consume" next to his wife, Violet) and a string of relations. Lawlor Moon lay side by side with his drowned daughter. Her grave looked like the floor of a hastily abandoned playroom — a headless doll, a scattering of faded Magic Markers. The markers appeared to have been, once upon a time, stuck into the earth, describing a circle around her plot, as if she were being admonished — the way children are told not to colour outside the lines — not to stray from the confines of her final resting place.

At the base of one gnarled apple tree, as close as you could get without disturbing its roots, I spied a small, untended grave. I felt as if my heart had rounded a corner and bumped into a lost part of myself. I kneeled, brushed aside the rotting-apple scented grass, and read the words I'd spent the last twelve years of my life praying I would never have to see:

Baby: Born and Died.

An angel lost his wing
Crooked he did fly.

I fled, stumbling between rows of older graves, with their almost rubbed-out names, until I reached the far side of the orchard. I wept as I ran, seeing Angel with only one wing flying up from me, flying crooked out of my heart. In the dim light under a thick canopy of hemlocks, I found the path.

The trees — pushy, spiky, ill-tempered spruce with needles that felt as friendly as barbed wire — made the forest seem more forbidding. A single small fern caught my eye, undulating playfully even though there was no breeze. Having risen from the walking-dead I had believed I could walk away from my past. Instead I had come full circle, as if the loneliness from which I'd fled was the only place I had left to go.

In the House of the Dead at the Clínica Desaguadero I remembered the many candles burning, a strong chemical smell, and a cloying scent of flowers. An Italian oil painting — a saint having his intestines slowly unwound from his body on a reel — hung, crookedly, as if no one had looked at it long enough to take the time to right it, below an old Spanish proverb meticulously penned in italic script: "God Does Not Send Anything We Can't Bear".

The *curandero* had taken my arm, trying to keep me on my feet, as he led me down the hall into a spacious high-ceilinged room with rows of marble tables in the centre of it. A nauseating wave of cold air hit my face; I recognized now the chemical smell of the embalming fluid.

Angel lay on his back in an open coffin made of some endangered wood the *curandero's* assistant said they reserved for *los angelitos*. I looked down at him, in that final room, with orchid blades cutting shadows across the grim slabs, his quiet face, and the cotton wool in his nostrils like puffs of breath. I remember closing my eyes for a long time, and opening them, and turning my head to one side to see a wreath of crucifix orchids in the middle of which a pair of baby boots sprouted miniature wings. Clipped to one of the wings in metal lettering, the one word: Angel.

My teeth started to rattle, my body shook, my legs crumpled from under me and I collapsed onto the floor. I fought to control the spinning sensation in my body; I fought to breathe. With each small breath I took I felt as if my own intestines were being unwound on a reel, the tears icing over in my eyes before they had time to drop, like pebbles of frozen rain, into my hair and face.

The last thing I remember was asking the *curandero* for a blanket — a thin sheet wasn't good enough — to keep my *angelito* warm. As if he were still alive. Because if ever I allowed myself to believe Angel was dead, I knew there'd be nothing more that could happen to me.

Gradually the trees thinned out and the dominant conifers were replaced by the rebel alder, whose hold on life was more tenuous. The trail wound down through salmonberry, huckleberry bushes and salal, and ended abruptly, just as I tasted the smoke in the air that rose from Hooker's chimney, and streeled towards the sea. His cabin sat in a clearing halfway to the end of the point. A raven the size of a flight bag crouched on the edge of the roof as if preparing to ambush me.

I made a noise to try to shoo him away, and a dog began barking inside the house. The raven hopped further up the roof, almost to the peak, where he sat tall and erect with his bill angled up, his throat hackles puffed out, and his wings spread broadly to the side, making himself even bigger than he had first appeared. I knocked on the door, and the barking became more frenzied.

"It's open," Hooker called out. "Come on in. Don't worry about Toop. He barks at nothing."

I was more worried about the raven than Hooker's mutt. I approached the door, and opened it a crack. "Sit!" I heard Hooker order, but it was the opportunity his dog had been waiting for. He got his nose in the crack and forced the door all the way open; if I hadn't jumped to one side he would have run right over me, three legs and all. When he looked back at me over his shoulder I saw he carried a shoe in his teeth.

Hooker lay on a mattress in the middle of the floor propped up on one elbow. His hair was pulled back into a ponytail and he was naked except for a pair of jeans, faded around the crotch. His belt was undone.

"He has to bury everything," Hooker said, as if that explained why his dog had been in such a hurry to knock me over, "just so he can dig it up again. He likes to chew on things after they're nice and ripe. He's got caches all over."

I asked how his dog had lost his leg, as I closed the door behind me.

"Guy I got him from amputated it off to slow him down. You might as well try and stop the sun coming up in the morning."

I said I had rarely seen the sun come up on this island. I figured it was afraid to come out because it might drown.

"You've got a point there. Anyways, Toop keeps me out of trouble a lot of the time." He yawned, and stretched. I tried hard to keep my eyes off his body. "Keeps me in line."

Hooker told me to come on in and take a seat. I looked around but could see nothing to sit on. A driftwood slab piled with shells, bullet cartridges, dishes, and a bowl of fruit served as a table, and a large steel barrel that had been converted into a woodstove squatted on a platform of flat rocks.

"My old man built this place," Hooker said. "Gracie and I were born here . . . though I tried to put it off as long as possible. I could see my old man's fists at the end of the tunnel, waiting to pound on me."

He paused as if waiting for me to comment. "After two days he got tired of waiting and he reached up inside my *naha* and grabbed hold of one of my arms. He thought he could force me out."

I didn't know what to say and moved towards the heat of the stove, in front of which lay a heap of running shoes, all different sizes, the same kind Hooker's dog had carried in his mouth. They looked as if they had been sentenced to a dozen life cycles in a washing machine with a grudge.

"Cat got your tongue?" Hooker said.

I was saved from having to try and answer by the sound of a *thunk* on the roof, as if Toop might have been plucked up by an eagle and dropped from a height. I'd watched birds let go of their victims — clams and mussels, mostly — from the sky, to dash their brains out on the sharp rocks below, but Hooker didn't look concerned.

He raised his eyes to the ceiling. "That would be Charlie. You probably met him on the way in. He's letting me know it's chow time." I listened to the sound of wings beating, and the discussion that followed, one that Hooker appeared to understand.

"He and Ralph are at my feeder, up on the roof. I keep it supplied with roadkills. I like to have ravens around, they're better than any watchdog you'll find . . . even Toop. If I'm not home they won't let anyone near the house. And I like to watch them eat."

He reached out, picked a big red apple from the bowl and polished it on his thigh. "I like to watch *people* eat, too," he said, taking a bite of the apple, then tossing it to me. He had juice on his chin, and didn't bother wiping it away. I caught the apple, and set it on the driftwood table.

"Come over here," Hooker said, quietly, "and help me do up my belt. It's one thing I have a bad time doing myself." His trousers were unzipped and I could see he wasn't wearing any underwear. My throat felt like I had a roll of quarters stuck in it.

I walked over to where Hooker sat on the edge of the mattress with his legs stretched out, and squatted between his knees; he didn't even need to hold in his breath while I zipped up his fly. His skin felt hot where my hands touched it. The draft coming from under the door made the fine hairs on his arms horripilate.

"You cold?" he asked. His hair tickled the back of my neck, my mouth was inches away from one of his nipples. I sat back on my heels, shivering.

"I could put more wood on the fire. I don't get much company so I usually stay in bed. It's always warm under the covers."

He got up, bent over a pile of laundry on the floor and searched for something to wear. "My old man used to talk down at my *naha* for not picking up after him. These are mostly his clothes. The only thing I got left of him. Besides this . . . ." He held out his hook.

He pulled a black T-shirt over his head, opened the stove door, and fanned away the smoke that belched out. He looked at me and laughed as the smoke rose to the ceiling, spread flat against the boards and hung there, grey and featureless, like a version of the actual sky.

Hooker said his mother lay on this mattress, in this same room, in labour for three days. On the fourth day his father hiked into town to fetch Agnes. "He told her I was stubborn. He says to Auntie, 'The kid's not even born yet and already he's a pain in the butt'.

"When they got back Auntie seen my arm sticking out from between my *naha's* legs, rubbed raw and that from where the old man had spent so much time tugging on it." Hooker said Agnes massaged his arm — he still remembered the feeling — how she stroked the inert limb with her index finger. She told him, years later, she thought he was gone and that all she could try and do was to save his mother. But when she began to stroke his tiny hand, she said, it suddenly closed, clutching her finger, refusing to let go. Agnes got to work. "Long story short, she saved my hide," Hooker said. "That's pretty well it. What time's it getting to be, anyways?"

He looked at me and smiled, a slow half-dance of a smile. I stood with the emptiness of the room between us, feeling as if I had lost my nerve even for speech. "I don't even know why I am telling you this," he said. "It only makes you old, when you hear bad things like that."

"You care about him. He's your father," I said.

"He was a mean bastard who hurt the people who were stupid enough to love him. Why should I bother to care? By now he's probably dead."

I wanted to say, if the dead live on in us for any reason, it is to force us into remembering. But Rainy said, in group one day, "The truth is a bully we all pretend to like just so we don't get singled out and picked on," and nobody could come up with anything better than that.

"I'm just having fun with you, anyways," he said. "Jus' kiddin' around."

Hooker wadded up a newspaper and laid a tipi of kindling on top of it. "You ever had a kid of your own?" he asked, striking a match. He looked up at my face as he spoke, fanning away the smoke.

He sat down again, his eyes moving from my face to the fire, and back again, generating their own heat. I wanted to tell Hooker about my son, but Angel was a secret I wasn't ready to share, as much as it hurt keeping it to myself.

"You're beautiful when you're sad," Hooker said. "Anyone ever tell you that?"

I turned away, frowning. Hooker cocked his head, looked at me sideways. "I'm jus' kiddin' you. If you're good at something, that's beauty," he added, quickly. "That's all I meant. You're good at looking sad. It's a compliment?"

He always seemed to get the better of me. He was quick, an expert at feeling me out. He had a way of looking at me, too, that made me feel I was standing before him, dressed in a white cotton bra and French-cut briefs, like a model in the Christmas Wish Book. I folded my arms across my breasts.

He walked over to the door, then turned to look at me over his shoulders. "You're easy to like," he said. "I think I like you more than might be good for either of us."

This time he didn't add, "Jus' kiddin'."

Hooker led the way through the darkening woods, away from the sound of the pebbles on the beach being drawn back into the sea. Toop, who had reappeared with a worried 'W' on his forehead the moment Hooker whistled for him, limped beside his master, his large wing-like ears sticking straight out on either side of his head. Every so often he stopped to mark his territory on a tree root that snaked across the trail.

Hooker said he had taken this path so many times he could walk it blindfolded, and that he knew the surrounding woods just as well. When he was a boy his mother had sent him into the forest to learn the secret of seeing into shadows, and find his animal guide.

"No animal I ever found was crazy enough to take on the job of looking out for me. Except for Toop, who looks after me all the time, don't you, little guy?"

Toop cocked his head to one side, the same way Hooker did when he was about to say, "jus' kiddin'." There was something else unusual about Hooker's three-legged friend: I looked closer at his face — he had one blue eye, one brown. "A dog with one blue eye, they say he can see the wind," Hooker said, when he saw me staring. Toop lifted his head, sniffed the air, and blinked. "He knows what we're talking about, too. Don't you, buddy?"

We had reached the end of the trail when a slaughter of crows lifted up from the trees and swept across the sky, as one entity, like iron filings, magnetized, over the inlet. I covered my head, as if they might sweep me up with them; Hooker laughed and said that was nothing, there were so many birds here in the old days that when they took off from the inlet the sky went black over the graveyard.

Up ahead I could see the spectral white dabs of the gravestones floating beyond the trees and had started towards them when I heard a branch snap in the bushes. "What's that?" I whispered.

Hooker grinned at me over his shoulder. "Could be a *lumaloo*. A person like you, who asks too many questions."

In the Yaka Wind language, he explained, *lum* meant spirits, *memaloos* meant dead. *Lumaloos* were the spirits of the dead who lived, mostly, in the ancient apple trees growing in the graveyard. Hooker's mother had told him the story of a girl who'd been killed by an enemy tribe during her wedding ceremony: the mother cut off her daughter's hair and spread it on the limbs of the apple tree they buried her under, with apple seeds in her cheeks. Her hair blew from tree to tree, turning grey with the years, an enduring tribute to those who died in love.

"Even the moss has a story, eh?" Hooker said. "My *naha* told me once, "you have to risk your life to get love.""

I stooped to pick up a windfall, but Hooker took it from my hand.

No one ever touched the apples that grew in their graveyard, he said. "You wouldn't want to eat one. Once you get a taste for flesh you become a *Tsiatko*, a badass who prowls the graveyard at night looking for *kahkwa mimoluse* — the restless ones — spirits who won't stay still in their beds."

Toop, who had been sitting quietly at Hooker's side, jumped straight up in the air, his tail a stiff excited feather. He bolted ahead into the graveyard.

"What does it mean when he does *that?*" I asked.

Hooker lip-pointed to the fern I'd seen dancing by itself on my way to his cabin. It hadn't stopped.

"That's a *lesash,* Hooker said, "an angel, a dead gone soul. You can feel him blowing down your neck sometimes. They say the wind's his breath."

₧ ₧ ₧

I don't know why I was surprised to find the hearse where I'd parked it less than an hour ago, but when I was with Hooker, time, as I had known it, even in my years on the Row, ceased to exist. Hooker's presence allowed me to reset my mind and my body to a time that had nothing to do with clocks and everything to do with a dreamlike sense of events flowing together.

He climbed into the hearse; Toop jumped over him and sat up straight behind the wheel on the driver's seat.

"He got a valid license?" I asked.

Hooker chuckled and said good thing there were no cops on the island, as he bundled Toop in his arms and set him on the floor at his feet.

He directed me past the church then left up the hill, filling in Toop on the protocol as we drove. "No scratching, no begging," he said, wagging a finger in his dog's face. "No humping, not even any sniffing butt. Stay close to me or you'll get us all kicked out. Got it?"

The wingtips of Toop's ears dipped in agreement, and he stayed at Hooker's heels as we elbowed through the crowd outside the Community Hall. I didn't recognize anyone, at first, except Agnes, who greeted us at the door. She addressed Hooker as Stloos, and said Gracie had arrived earlier on.

"Alone?" Hooker asked, and she nodded.

Hooker asked me to keep an eye on Toop, said "right back," and disappeared through the doors, back the way we came. Toop sat at my feet with a long-suffering expression on his face, his ears somewhere between half-mast and the ground.

Agnes told me to take a plate, and motioned for me to join her in the line. "Fill your canoe," she said, "don't hold back. You're eating for my sister, too, so she doesn't leave this world on an empty belly." I stood next to her as we filed past the tables heaped with platters of smoked sea lion, halibut cheeks, braided seal organs, slabs of venison meat, herring roe on dried seaweed, and chicken salad sandwiches. It felt strange to be at such a lavish going-away party for someone I'd never met.

Ahead of us in line the Uncle held court in a wheelchair, trying to goose every woman who stopped to offer condolences. "Happy New Year," he called out — his voice sounding even more tenuous than it had a few short hours ago — when he swivelled in his chair and saw me standing with his sister. "If your right leg is Christmas and your left leg is New Year's, can I come between the holidays?"

Agnes raised her eyebrows, and shook her head. "He never forgets a pretty face."

Grace Moon — I saw the hair first, the thick red corkscrews, red like the heroin-blood mix — stood behind him. Grace was even thinner than the last time I'd seen her, outside the liquor store, her tawny eyes full of the same fear I'd seen frozen in them since the day we met. She wasn't wearing her bracelets, either. They would have slid right off her popsicle-stick arms.

Agnes stuck out her bottom lip. Her voice never seemed far from weeping. "She'd be doing better if they would mind their own businesses. Leave her alone to have Baby. A few years ago these people came to the village saying God sent them to adopt our kids. In their religion a man can have many wives; my brother wanted to get adopted, too, when he heard that. After they left the island, a new bunch, a bunch of social workers came. Everyone thinking they know best about how other people should live."

When Toop spotted Grace he bounded across the room to try and knock her over. I chased after him but he ducked between the Uncle's legs and I decided he could stay there.

"I'm sorry for your loss," I said, when Grace reached to hug me. Her body felt empty, despite being big with child. "It has to be a shock ... "

Grace finished my sentence for me, " . . . when your *naha* dies. You're right, I wasn't expecting it. I didn't think she was the type."

We both tried to laugh, a little nervously. Grace parked the Uncle's wheelchair beside the dessert table, and poured a drink from a paper bag into his cup. "He keeps his bottle in a bag so he won't have to see how much he's got left," Grace said.

At that moment I spied a vat of what looked like my favourite dessert, chocolate mousse. I took an extra scoop; Grace nodded approvingly as she spooned rancid-smelling oolichan grease over the mousse that turned out to be whipped seal meat. Some traditional food was an acquired taste, she said, and she was glad to see I wasn't picky like some of the visitors on the film crew who'd been invited to a potlatch and ate nothing but white bread sandwiches. Grace had loaded a plate for the Uncle — I noticed she took nothing for herself — and wheeled him to his place at the head table in front of a plywood altar, with two candlesticks, a bouquet of silk calla lilies and a devotional print of Jesus with rouged lips and soap opera eyes, — a concession, I assumed, to Father Tunney's faith. She asked why Vernal hadn't come to the feast with me and I told her about the accident in the grave, how I worried about him.

"You worry too much," Gracie said, her voice full of teasing. "You got too much eagle in you. You need more raven."

I looked around the room, saw Agnes at the front door again, but couldn't find Hooker. "He said he'd be right back," I told Grace. She shot me a smile, half-dressed as a look of concern, but with a warning tossed in. Hooker's idea of "right back" could mean anything from five minutes to forever, she reminded me. You never knew where you stood with him.

I asked what Al was up to tonight knowing, before I asked the question, I shouldn't have. Her smile collapsed. Grace said he had gone into hiding after Hooker ordered him out of the house because Al had taken a splitting axe to Baby-Think-It-Over. "My brother thinks we'll have to buy a replacement doll for Social Services."

She lifted her chin and I could see the scars across her throat, the emptiness in her eyes growing even darker. "Hooker doesn't trust anyone who tries to get close to me. Anyone who loves me, he tries to drive them away." Her voice had become hollow and suddenly frail. "It gets lonely around here. I thought Al would help, but he didn't."

I tried to change the subject and asked Grace if she had picked out a name for her baby, then regretted that question, too. One of the first things I was told, after Angel died and I wanted to take him home, was that I needed to give him a name. He had to be issued a *Partida de defunción* if I wanted to take him out of the country, to be buried in a place closer to home.

Burying my child in the ground, anywhere on this earth, felt far from home. "You must give him a name," an official scolded me. "We cannot issue a *certificado* without a name. There can be no death, otherwise. ¿*Entiendes?*"

I only remember leaving his office that day, looking around me as if seeing, for the first time, the earth's needless beauty. I felt the kind of brokenness wild grass must feel after a scythe has passed through it.

Grace said the name didn't matter, as long as he was alive — and every day she could feel his heartbeat inside her like a tiny moth's. "My *naha* told me, 'If you don't suffer with your pain, then you haven't learned anything about yourself. Only by suffering can you learn to forgive.'" Grace had even been able to forgive her "fly-by-night" rapist who had given her a gift, though this baby had been a difficult gift to accept. He was due on Christmas Day, and Grace was planning on doing her drying out at the same time, in hospital. "Hooker doesn't think I can quit. He doesn't think I know how to be a good mother." She blew her nose into a handkerchief embroidered with tiny knots of flowers. I looked away so she wouldn't have to pretend she wasn't crying.

I wanted to say who among us is good enough to be anybody's mother? The official in the City of Orchids said that a baby with no name was like a motherless child, that right from the start my baby never stood a chance. When you didn't name a baby, have him baptised before he was six weeks old, other women — women who had no children of their own — would try to steal his soul. The official, I could tell, believed this is what had happened to my baby. In his delusive way he held me responsible for my baby's death, and I'd been afraid, ever since, the blame would find a way to stick to me. That's what blame did.

ᔕ ᔕ ᔕ

When Lavinia had been fed, so much so that she would never feel hunger in the spirit world, and all her relations had risen, one by one, to stand in front of the altar and tell stories about her life, The Uncle said the Lord's Prayer in his language. Grace translated for me.

Nesika papa klaksta mitlite kopa saghalie,
"Our Father who dwells on high . . . "
Potlatch konaway sun nesika muckamuck,
"Give us all days our food . . . "
Pe kopet-kumtux konaway nesika mesachie.
"And stop remembering all our sins . . . "

At this point she stopped, took my hand and placed it on her belly, a gesture that made me feel bound to her, the way a mother is bound to her child, by things she cannot know.

"He's got something going for him. He's an old spirit, this baby," she said.

Kloshe kahkwa, the Uncle said, and everyone else repeated. *Amen.*

The Uncle asked that we remember Lavinia in silence, and while I sat with my head bowed I thought of my Angel, how he had had something going for him, too. It made people reach for him, as if they hoped his way of being in this world would rub off on them. I pictured Angel watching me with round eyes that seemed to say *don't ever stop believing in the goodness of this world.* I had felt, even as I had stood holding him in my arms, that he was the one holding me.

Kloshe kahkwa. Amen. As we said the words over again Hooker slipped into the empty chair next to me, a doggy bag of leftovers for Toop in his hands. *Kloshe kahkwa,* he said, as if he had been there all along.

After the speeches most of the men disappeared to drink the Uncle's whiskey and play Texas Hold'em while the women stayed behind and finished the last of the coffee, washed dishes, and reminisced about Lavinia's life. Hooker spoke briefly to Agnes, in their language, as we left. There seemed to be no question in his mind that I would go home with him — nobody in their right mind went round the Bend in the middle of the night, he said — but he was distracted and edgy as we walked out to the parking lot and drove back down Dead End Road.

We started across the graveyard, the moon casting a peckled shimmer on the headstones. Toop stayed close to me, so close I kept tripping over him. Hooker said it was "just *lumaloos*" in the shadows, that dogs were more in touch with the spirit world, more sensitive than humans when it came to contact with ghosts.

As if he could sense my own restless spirit Hooker stopped when we came to the place, slightly off the path, where I'd found the newborn's grave. He told me the baby had been born the same day his auntie's *kloshe* — her beloved's — fishing boat sank in a storm. "She went loopy after that. She couldn't feed her baby, and then he got sick. When he died she carried his body, everywhere, on her back. She got sent off-island. They only let her come home a couple of years ago."

Hooker's voice seemed to come from a well of loneliness, as he talked about how when you think you have lost something it is usually still with you. Baby Born and Died. And Agnes Moon, gone loopy from grief.

Not even the moon's light was powerful enough to penetrate the dense forest on the far side of the graveyard. "Think about it. There's nowhere as black as inside your own body," Hooker said, stopping on the trail for me to catch up. When we got to the cabin Hooker couldn't find his flashlight or the candles. He must have felt me shivering again. "You go ahead and jump under the covers. Toop will warm you up. You roll around, try to catch the fleas that jump off him, it'll get you hot."

Hooker had a way of putting things. I groped for the mattress and crawled under the sleeping bag that doubled as a quilt, and felt Toop burrow down beside me. I heard the sound of newspaper being crumpled, and the snap of kindling, and Hooker striking a match. The match flared and the room, for a moment, filled with promising light.

"What you thinking?" Hooker's voice sounded low and throaty in the dark.

"Nothing," I said, but too quickly.

The fire sputtered and went out. I could smell smoke.

"I read minds, you know," he said, striking another match and looking in my direction.

"Then you tell *me* what I'm thinking." Time to call his bluff.

"A smoky cabin, a full belly, and a flea-filled bed. You're thinking it doesn't get better than that."

The fire began to crackle and he closed the door to keep more smoke from escaping into the room. "Or maybe you're thinking you wished I'd brought that deer sausage home from the feast because you could use a snack."

I propped myself up on my side. "Not even close," I said.

"You're thinking you wished I'd brought onions to fry up with the sausage and that."

"You're getting cooler."

"Liver. Deer liver and sausage. That's what you'd like."

"Cold," I said.

I waited, but heard nothing except for the spit and hiss of the fire trying to take off. "Well?" I said. Hooker had disappeared into a shadowy corner of the room where he poured water from a plastic bottle into an empty Mason jar. I heard him cleaning his teeth.

"I'm going outside. To go *cheegan*. You can borrow my toothbrush if you don't mind getting my germs"

It was the second-most romantic proposal I'd received this night. I heard him open the door and step out into the darkness. I didn't ask if he needed help with his belt or with his zipper. Toop sighed, and began licking himself.

"You still dressed?" Hooker said, when he returned, with the stub of a candle burning in a clamshell. "You planning on making a quick getaway, or what?"

"Where would I go?" Toop had settled down again with his head resting on the pillow beside me.

Hooker took the elastic out of his ponytail and let his hair fall loose around his shoulders. He took off his shirt, his belt and his boots. He undid the zipper on his jeans, toying with me, like a cat with the night's meat in his gums.

He placed the candle on a windowsill and crawled under the covers, still wearing his jeans. Toop lay between us, snoring quietly. I tried to suppress a giggle.

"What you laughing about?" Hooker sounded tired.

"At Toop, your bodyguard. He's fallen asleep on the job." I reached over and petted Toop's sleeping body.

"Believe me, he'd wake up if he had to," Hooker said.

I watched a pair of moths, the colour of button mushrooms, bounce out of the darkness, drawn to the candle's light. I wanted to touch Hooker, too, but something made me hesitate. "What did your auntie call you?" I said quietly. "When we got to the hall?"

"Stloos. That's the name I was given when I was born. It means Sweet Hands."

I reached across Toop's body and my hand came to rest on his hook. I pulled my hand away, then, feeling self-conscious, put it back.

"Can you feel anything when I touch your hook?"

"What do you think?" Hooker said.

I thought there was nothing I could do or say that would come out right.

"I can feel you touching me, and it feels good," Hooker said after a bit.

ᕟ ᕟ ᕟ

I woke to the insomniac cry of a seabird, and rose out of my sleep to catch the last light of the gibbous moon before it sunk into the surf breaking on the reefs. Hooker was gone — outside to go *cheegan* or to fetch wood: the reason didn't matter, the bed felt emptier than the world. The sleeping bag had been tugged off me in the night and I pulled it back on, though the room was warm — Hooker had finally got the fire to cooperate before he'd left. A kelp-smelling breeze washed in through an open window facing the sea, and a kind of lazy peacefulness settled over me.

It seemed I had been away from the farm for weeks, that it had been months since I'd driven Vernal to the airport. I closed my eyes again; next time I woke it was to the nosey smell of garlic frying in butter, but when I opened my eyes the room began whirling away from me, as if I were entering a weightless dream.

I cried out, terrified by the sensation of having nothing to hang on to, free falling towards the earth that was moving away from me even faster than I could fall. Hooker came running in from outside and knelt beside me on the mattress. "You probably opened your eyes too fast," he said when I tried to explain what had happened.

"How can you open your eyes *too fast?*" I asked. Hooker said he would demonstrate; he closed my eyes with his fingers and told me to count to ten. When I got to seven his lips touched mine, and opened slightly, tentatively: not so much a kiss but a hint that he might like to taste more of me.

A soft heat seeped through my skin. I stopped counting, but kept my eyes closed; I didn't want to scare him away, or change the mood in the room. His lips tasted of salt, and of the wind, and I could smell the wildness in him, something elemental, as of fire, storm, and the fluctuant sea.

He took my face in his hands. We were so close it was as if he were breathing for me — I couldn't tell where his breath stopped and mine began. Toop gave a wounded, pay-attention-to-me kind of bark, and Hooker pulled away. I opened my eyes and felt dizzy again, this time for a different reason.

"You taking advantage of me?" I said, smiling with my eyes.

"I hope so." Hooker kissed Toop, too — who drooled — then wrestled his dog to the ground. "I had an ulterior motive, though," he said, laughing. "Toop wants breakfast — I thought maybe you could feed him while I finish fixing ours."

I asked what my reward would be (I would rather have gone back to bed and kissed him all morning long) and he said he might take me to the beach with him, later, to see the wreck of his red pickup before it disappeared in the winter storms. A north wind had got up in the night, which meant it would be a good day for beachcombing, and I could help Toop find the left-footed running shoe he knew was out there somewhere, riding the swells, waiting to be washed onto the shore for him. When Toop heard his name he fetched a shoe from the pile of waterlogged runners stiffening in front of the woodstove, and dropped it in front of me.

A container ship from Japan had broken up in a high sea, Hooker explained, and the runners, after being tossed around by the waves and knocked against the rocks, had washed up along the beach. "Toop finds them for me. All right feet so far. I need a ten-and-a-half left. To go with the right. Same's I need a left hand, come to think of it."

Hooker passed me a blue enamel pan of warm water to wash in, and a roll of toilet paper to dry myself. I got out of bed, still fully dressed, splashed the sleep from my eyes, and rinsed my face, being careful to avoid the area around my mouth. I wanted the taste of Hooker Moon on my lips for as long as possible.

When I had finished I called Toop, who was standing by his bowl, waiting, and spooned some leftover seal organs mixed with halibut cheeks into his dish. Toop looked at it, then went and stood by the door, his tail between his legs. When Hooker let him out I heard him throwing up in the bushes. "What's the matter, don't like barfaroni?" Hooker asked when he slunk back inside. Hooker looked at me and shook his head, passing me the bag of sandwiches he'd brought home from the feast. "This is the only thing Toop eats. Chicken salad sandwiches."

"I hope he'll forgive me." I arranged the sandwiches in Toop's dish, but he stood, looking at it, his ears sticking straight out on either side. Hooker shook his head. "Not like that. I'll show you."

He took out his hunting knife, bent down, and began slicing. Toop nearly decapitated me with his tail when Hooker stood back to show me his handiwork. "Chicken salad sandwiches with the crusts cut off. You wouldn't think from looking at him he'd be such a picky eater."

I sat watching Toop eat as sunlight stabbed through the gaps in the weathered planks on the windowless side of the cabin. "I'm making breakfast," Hooker said. "You like Indian food? Mussels and seaweed and shit like that?"

Hooker, and his way with words. He removed the garlic from the butter then set to work steaming the mussels he had picked off the beds at low tide while I was still dreaming.

"I'll try anything once," I said, but then had to admit that wasn't true. I had heeded all the warnings about paralytic shellfish poisoning I'd seen posted along coastal beaches, how one bite of a contaminated bivalve could kill you before you had time to spit it out.

"How do you know they're safe?" I asked.

"You worry too much," he said, shaking his head and laughing at me. "Worry's going to kill a person quicker than anything you eat off the beach."

On Tranquilandia they had a saying: "Don't worry, at least not until they start shooting. And even then you shouldn't worry. Don't start worrying until they hit you, because then they might catch you."

"If you're seriously worried," Hooker said, "touch one to your lips. If your lips start to tingle, that's a warning sign."

My lips had tingled when Hooker's lips had touched them. I had been fairly certain, falling asleep last night, we weren't meant to be lovers, but this morning after that almost-kiss, I felt there might be a faint hope clause at the end of the tunnel of love. Hope was one thing I'd taught myself it was best to live without, though I'd heard it said there is more hope on Death Row than in any place of similar size in the world. To me, hope had become another phase to grow out of, like wetting the bed, like picking at the skin around your fingernails until you bled.

Hooker set up a table outside so we could watch the ravens eat. We ate with our fingers, sitting on a couple of chunks of wood he used as chopping blocks, dazed by the fiery orange of the mussels, purple inkiness of the seaweed, and the fragrance of alder from the fire. A barge of mist floated through the trees towards the sea, and dragonflies, iridescent blue, darted back and forth as if they were stitching up the air.

I looked up at the sky, flecked with bright ticks of cloud, then down at the stream where a dragonfly landed on top of another, and two pairs of wings became one in a whirring over the red-brown water.

"I can see why you stay here," I said. "It feels . . . it's like the rest of the world hasn't caught up to this place yet."

Hooker licked his fingers and looked past my eyes to the beach. "I like it out here because not too much is happening," he said, after a while. "I've got this personal feeling so many things aren't meant to be happening to us so much of the time. We're not built for it."

It was true, I thought, that in many ways my life had been much simpler at the Facility. There I'd had only Rainy and Frenchy to feel responsible for, and the rest of eternity to contemplate. Every day had seemed important because each act was, potentially, the last act of our lives. We used to say we lived in the last place on earth a woman could feel safe — a maximum security penitentiary. The only threat to our security was that of our pending execution.

Hooker boiled more water and brewed Labrador Tea. Neither of us felt the need to talk. Once the ravens got used to me they flew down and began tearing at the chunks of sea lion meat Hooker had brought home from the feast. "Ravens find roadkill, they act like eagles," Hooker said.

After rinsing our dishes in a bucket of sea water we set off across the point — over the beds of blue-violet mussel shells waiting for the tide to come in — that separated Hooker's bay from the white sand beach. Hooker whistled for Toop who had disappeared into the foam covering the sand from the high tide mark to the sea's edge.

I left Hooker and walked through tangled mounds of kelp, across a series of old weathered planks from a ship that had broken up in a storm, out to where the sea met the sand, and jogged through the knee-deep foam, letting my shoes get soaked, the foam stick to my clothes, my face, my hair as the sun played hide-and-seek behind a blustery cloud. I emerged from the foam onto a clean stretch of sand and saw how the sea absorbed all the little streams that trickled down the beach as if they couldn't wait to become part of something bigger, while the ocean went its own way, breaking up on the shore, pulling itself back together, breaking up on the beach again.

I heard Hooker shout, and when I looked up saw him crouch down a small distance from the carcass of a sea lion half-buried in the sand. A conspiracy of ravens hunched over their find, taking the occasional nip out of its flesh, as if they were testing it to see if it tingled on their beaks.

I rubbed my hands together and stamped my feet. The wind off the sea had a chill in it, the first bite of winter. At that moment I saw a solitary raven plummet out of the sky into the foam, and rise up again, his black head white.

The trickster raven dive-bombed his brothers, who were still hopping around the carcass; they flew off leaving him to feast, until the foam on his head began to disappear and they recognized him as one of their own — not a bald eagle, after all — and chased him away. Hooker shouted at me to hold my breath and plug my nose as he moved closer to the sea lion, and the ravens flew up before us, and wheeled back towards the surf.

I turned around, letting out my breath, and saw Toop, in the distance, a new find, a shoe, in his mouth, running so fast his back foot overtook his front feet, chasing sandpipers up and down the sand. Further down the beach I could make out the metal frame of Hooker's red pickup lying on its side, half-sunk into the sand, already a permanent part of the landscape. "I'm going for a run," I called to Hooker, "up to your truck and back."

I ran, wishing I could make Angel return the way Rainy and Frenchy had come back from the dead, so that he would know how it felt to run against the wind, to hear the wild music of the world, to stumble from his dreams and hear the trees speaking in tongues, to taste rainwater on his tongue.

I was halfway to the wreck when I found the shoe. Dry, almost weightless, no longer than my lifeline, it fit in the palm of my hand. It was the same brand as all the others Toop had brought home, but unlike the ones heaped in front of Hooker's woodstove, this one had scarcely been damaged. It was small enough to have been spared, to have been cradled across the surface of the waves.

In this world there is an unending supply of sorrow, and the heart has always to make room for more. I grasped the shoe to my body, trying to make it disappear the way I'd tried to make love disappear in the years I'd been separated from Angel. I'd always imagined that, given time, my love for my boy would lessen, so that the closer I got to the end of my life, the less I would remember it. I don't know what I expected love to do — maybe curl up and die the way I'd seen people do.

I looked back; I could see Hooker, his hair the same blue-black as the mussel shells he'd steamed open that morning; he had taken off his shirt and tied it around his waist. In his hands I could the blood-red strips he'd cut from the sea lion's bloated sides.

I felt the wind blowing through me, and a soft rain coming down as I started back, turning the shoe — left or right I couldn't tell which — in my hands, as if it were some hopeful relic the sea had coughed up, trusting I would find it, knowing it had come home. It was perfect in every way but one. The logo, which appeared to have been Boss Angeloss, had almost disappeared. All I could make out was the ghost of an impression, the word Angel, and I knew — a message had been sent to me, written by the wind.

I hardly remember the walk back up the beach and over the point to Hooker's cabin. I do know the rain stopped for a while and the sun peeked out and that I felt, once again, like a ghost inhabiting my own body. I watched Hooker stock his birdfeeder and we stood together in the doorway as the ravens descended one at a time, and then flew up with pieces of bright crimson meat in their beaks.

Toop flopped down beside the woodstove, licking the salt from the waterlogged runner between his paws. I buried the baby shoe deep in my jacket pocket and stretched out on the bed. Hooker woke me, later, with a cup of nettle tea and some fry-bread he'd made while I'd slept. I thought about the mussels he'd picked that morning, trussed together with hair-like bonds, and looking at Hooker, then, a thin layer of trust began to form, like a scab, over my heart. I wanted to tell him about my son, show him the shoe I'd found on the beach — a shoe the same size as the ceramic impression — the "cherished sole" footprint the *curandero's* assistant had made for me the day I'd left Desaguadero — as if it were further proof of my child's existence beyond the grave. But Hooker said back in a minute and left to go outside.

I sat on the floor by the open window, sipping my tea. I had no idea of the time — impossible to tell time when the sky loomed grey and vague — only that the tide had come up and started out again since we'd risen earlier in the day. When Hooker returned he said a storm was coming in.

He had begun to look edgy again, the way he'd looked the night before leaving the community hall, and after a while he came and crouched next to me, and asked if he could trust me, if I considered him a friend. I thought this an odd question, since we had just spent the night in the same bed, even if nothing had happened, in the traditional sense of the words *nothing* and *happened.*

"Of course I'm your friend."

"Can I *trust* you?" Hooker wasn't going to let me hedge on the wheel. "I'm not asking you to trust *me.* I'm asking if I can trust *you.* If you are that good a friend.

At the Facility we had a saying: *A friend helps you move; a good friend helps you move a body.*

"It depends on how you define good," I said.

Hooker said he had a favour to ask; he wanted me to drive him to Gracie's. I said I'd take him anywhere, though given a choice I would have opted to stay in his cabin, closing my eyes and practising opening them slowly to look at him lying half-naked on his bed. "When you fall in love you have to stupefy yourself and become blind otherwise love would never happen," Vernal used to say, after I'd left him to live on my own. "When you wake up, and open your eyes, that's where love stops."

But my desire for Hooker had almost transcended love. Almost. My desire now was to crawl inside his skin and live there, behind his eyes, to feel his heart beating away in the hot darkness.

Hooker kept glancing at the sky as we left the cabin and started up the trail followed by Toop with his pointy ears drooping as if he took the unsettled weather personally. By the time we reached the graveyard the clouds in the west had turned a lurid red. "Cloud gets that much blood in it, means we're going to have a real humdinger," Hooker said, swatting at a fly that buzzed his face. There were flies everywhere. I knew what this meant.

Toop snapped at a bluebottle and gave me a puzzled look, as Rainy materialized, sitting on a decomposing nurse log that had become host to a colony of hemlock and spruce seedlings. Her twins, who had manifested themselves back into their fine red mist, and Frenchy, still wearing my shades, appeared beside her. The HE clung to his mother's leg. His face, I saw, had become one suppurating wound, and a breeding ground for maggots.

My friends had promised to stay at the farm, and I gave them a look to say as much. *You promise you be home this morning, yo own self,* Frenchy said. *We get tired of waitin.*

Rainy held her whole body clenched, even her eyes. *We figure we hitch a ride home in yo dead-wagon,* she said, as I opened the door on the driver's side. She and Frenchy pushed their way in, pulling their offspring after them. They draped themselves across the front seat; I told them, under my breath, they had to ride in the back.

Rainy took a hard look at Hooker, and whistled. *He be the lookingest guy I ever seen,* she said, her voice gone all congested. *He be a statue in a park, no one spray paint over him, best believe.*

The HE had begun picking at the pieces of shrapnel trapped under his skin, going *glock-glock-glock* as he tried to clear his nose. Frenchy massaged her boy's shoulders and listed off sniper rifles: *Barret M82, Barret M90, Barret M95, Barret M99, Nechem NTW-20,* until his breathing returned to normal and he went limp in her arms.

Toop had to be picked up and lifted into the hearse, where he cowered low to the floor, trembling. Rainy perched between the rollers in the back, hissing like a cat, to further terrify him;

I gave her an irritated *shhhhhh* as I took off my jacket and tossed it over her head.

"You talking to *lumaloos* now?" Hooker asked, as he got in the passenger's side. He glanced over his shoulder and narrowed his eyes. I remembered what he'd told me, about learning the secret of seeing into shadows, and wondered what he knew.

❧ ❧ ❧

Talcum pole creep me out. Make my head stand on end, Rainy said, as we drove past Lawlor Moon's memorial pole. Every time she spoke, Toop growled. "Something's spooking him," Hooker said, as his dog jumped into his lap and sat up, ears pricked forward, as if he were trying to ignore what was going on behind him by concentrating on the road.

The hearse, the road, even the black clouds were awash in an ocean of cochineal. The sea itself, and the few boats left in the bay that hadn't headed for shelter looked as if they had been bathed in Al's tainted blood. As I drove I wanted to reach into my pocket to make sure the tiny fragile shoe was still there. I pictured slipping my child's foot into it, the way he would curl his turned-in toes and I'd have to tickle his sole to make him straighten them out again.

As I pulled in at Gracie's house, the sky opened up and let loose a downpour. Hooker told me to back up against the mudroom door, then got out, telling Toop to stay close. I ordered Rainy and Frenchy to wait for me, and followed Hooker into the carving shed. He said, "right back," then went into the house, and this time he kept his word, returning at once with garbage bags, a rope and a gas can. "I guess it's dark enough," he said. "Let's do it."

He led the way through the carving shed to a door that opened at the front of the house, facing the water, onto what

Hooker called their appliance garden. The ghost of a bathtub overflowed with empty bottles, and a cook stove bloomed corrosively.

The refrigerator lay on its back, white, closed-coffin-like. I understood, in that instant, what Rainy meant when she said, "one door closes, another bangs shut." Some part of me didn't want Hooker to open the fridge door because I knew it was going to close off, bang shut, a part of me, of us, of what Hooker and I might have become.

"I need your help," Hooker said. Toop sniffed the air, panting, making excited yipping sounds. I sat down on a toilet that had mushrooms sprouting from the mossy bowl. "We need to get him out of here."

For one naïve moment I thought he meant Toop, but then as he opened the fridge door I saw the hand, a human hand, poking out of the fridge. I remembered, then, what my son's father said to me in the big yard at Mountjoy, shortly before he was shot down in the botched escape attempt and the *contrabandistas* flew me away to Tranquilandia: "It is much easier to kill a man than it is to make love to a woman. There's no risk in killing. Bang. He's dead. You go on living."

Had I, I wondered, fallen into the sweet hands of a killer? Hooker hadn't looked to me like someone who would kill, but what does the kind of man who kills look like?

"What happened to him?" I asked, somewhat naïvely.

"Best part of him run down his old man's leg." Hooker answered.

I could see the whole body now. From where I sat, a distance away in the near-darkness, I saw he was naked, except for a pair of running shoes that were too big for him and made him look clownish. I wondered if Al had been naked at his moment of death, if he'd stripped down to fix in the only useable vein he had left, or if Hooker had stripped him of any whiff of dignity he might have possessed.

Hooker sounded matter-of-fact. "Last night, when I left the hall. He'd OD'ed. I dragged him out here because I didn't want Gracie having to deal with it. Just because his life's over, doesn't mean hers has to be."

Even when we harden, we each turn to stone in our separate ways. I had wanted to feel sorry for Al the first time we'd met, and now I found myself trying *not* to feel sorry for the cold skin-and-bones body of a man I'd never warmed to in life.

"I need your help," Hooker repeated. I slid off the cold toilet and walked over to where he knelt, stuffing Al's head in a garbage bag and tying the rope around his throat. He took hold of Al's torso; I grabbed the ankles, recoiling, at once, at the feel of Al's skin.

"Keep hanging with me . . . you and me, we could go places," he said.

"Like where? The electric chair?" Helping a friend move a body no doubt made me an accessory to murder. Hooker seemed irked when I hesitated, before taking Al's legs in my hands. I said what did he expect me to do, I'd never lifted a body out of a refrigerator before.

Al was heavier than I'd imagined a dead body to be (I'd always wondered why it took six pallbearers to carry a coffin to its grave) and one of his shoes came off as we carried him through the doorway into the carving shed. I dropped the legs to the ground again. Hooker said "not much further to go," and stooped to retrieve the shoe.

He pushed the mudroom door open with his foot, then unlatched the back of the hearse so we could slide Al in. *What you going to do now, dumpster his dead ass?* Frenchy asked?

Rainy told the twins they'd better not touch or she'd hold their hands flat on a hot stove element with an egg lifter until they learned some respect. Frenchy admonished her. *Threatenin your kids wid a good burnin, that be way-killer not cool.*

Al's other shoe fell off as we set him down between the rollers. Toop swooped it up and limped off into the bushes, his ears sticking straight out on either side of his head, as if he were about to lift off above the trees.

"There's something unnormal about that dog," Hooker said.

§ § §

Vernal had a client once who hunted down a renowned Nazi war criminal and, when he found him, put a bullet between his eyes. "There is no evil in reducing life to other, more enduring forms," Vernal said, in his most famous address to a jury. "Homicide, in this case, was not a sin. It was, I submit, a necessary resistance against an ossified form of existence."

He stole those lines from another book, of course, but he said no one ever went to prison for failing to be original. I got Toop back in the car, using Al's other shoe as a lure. Hooker seemed to relax once we were on our way and had left the village behind. He even joked that we ought to stick the "On Appointment" sign in the window. I wasn't in the mood.

I didn't speak or take my eyes off the road after that. Hooker made small talk, about the sea lion and other creatures washing up dead on the beach, "an albatross, couple of eagles, a ton of seals," and wondered if it had anything to do with the eerie weather conditions. The only dead thing Hooker didn't seem concerned with was the body in the back.

We flew by the Yaka Wind Honour Site. The cloud cover had lifted and when we passed the first of the roadside shrines, the wreaths jumped out in our headlights.

The sky stayed clear for a while longer, even as we got to the top of Garbage Dump Hill, as if the moon, the stars, and the planets had all conspired with Hooker to give him light in darkness. He told me to pull over when we got to the lay-by. I killed the motor, and sat staring straight out over the ocean. Hooker was quiet for a while, then asked me if I knew how to tell the planets from stars: I said "no idea", my mind elsewhere, on more urgent matters, like not getting arrested. "By their reflections in the water," Hooker said. "A planet makes a straight line. A star's reflection dances. See, up there? Take a look."

It wasn't the moment for an astronomy lesson. Hooker reached over and put his good hand on my arm, in a motion halfway on its journey to being a caress. "All the shit we're made of? It comes from those dying stars. We're made out of stars, you and me."

When I didn't respond he turned his head towards the side window and looked out over the water again. "Something bugging you?"

I stared at my hands and began picking at the little bits of skin coming away around my nails. Hooker let out a deep breath. Toop looked at me, the worried 'W' between his eyes, and then over at Hooker, as if trying to decide which of us needed him most. "Go on, out you get," I said, looking at Hooker and nudging Toop out the door.

Hooker asked for my help again, getting the body out and hauling it as far as the "Keep Our Dump Clean" sign. He went back for the gas can. "Don't worry, I always clean up after myself," he said.

I left him by the side of the road, stooped over Al's body like one of the dark birds at his feeder.

৶ ৶ ৶

Rainy and Frenchy climbed onto the front seat beside me. Rainy curled up with her head in my lap, and Frenchy rolled down her window so she could stick her head outside.

Them stars up there? she said, pointing out over the sea where Hooker had shown me the dancing reflections. *They be in the sky same night I be born?* Frenchy, I knew, had been born in a mental hospital, where you couldn't see any stars. They'd loosened her mother's straightjacket to help her bear down.

"Same stars, same sky," I said.

How come you figure there be so many stars up there? she continued.

Rainy made a hissing noise between her teeth. *God figure he put them there so we have light out after dark.*

Frenchy said she'd always wondered why God created light in the first place, before he made anything that had eyes.

"Don't start," I said. I could hear the helplessness in my voice.

Why you don't drop us by the side of the ditch and we bail ourselves on home . . . Rainy said, her voice trailing pitifully off. By this time we were pulling into our driveway.

Too late to bail, girl, Frenchy said. *We be in Paradise now. Ain't nowhere left to go.*

Paradise be a whole lot more like paradise, it got TV, said Rainy.

Frenchy had never cared much about TV. *I don't miss it,* she said as I manoeuvred the hearse into the barn. *You ever seen a baby spit up on TV?*

What that stupposed to mean? Rainy asked.

You ever see a fat black girl win a beauty contest on TV?

Rainy blinked and wiped away part of her face. *Nobody be fat on TV.*

What I sayin. No one on TV be actual. They got a problem, they solve it by talkin, not by smackin or shootin each other in the head.

I told them I needed to be left alone, but privacy wasn't a concept either Rainy or Frenchy understood; they had begun to view our friendship as a kind of medicine they couldn't live without. They followed me into the house, then upstairs, sticking to me like peanut butter to the gums, refusing to be quiet, and interpreting my need for silence as evidence of a troubled mind. I sat on the bed without taking my coat off, reached into my pocket and felt around for the shoe I'd found on the beach. It brought me closer to Angel, present always in his absence, teetering on the unseen edge of every moment.

I drew a bath and sat soaking, my thoughts returning, also, to the night I'd spent with Hooker Moon, our trek up the beach this morning, and Al's body, naked except for a pair of shoes. I thought of this, too: the foot that had fit the baby shoe meant for an angel — that foot would grow to one day fit a shoe the size Al had lost.

Rainy came and sat beside me while I soaked in the tepid water. *Shoe fit, we find another one just like it,* she said, eventually.

PART SIX

To discover the true enemy, the holy war, the good fight, shift your eyes.
— Sam Keen, *Face of the Enemy*

THE WIND RAGED ALL NIGHT AND THE rain blew in torrents across the land. I woke in the morning with the same sense of vertigo I'd experienced in the airport the day of my escape, and again waking in Hooker's cabin on Kliminawhit.

In my dream I'd been driving down a highway in an unfamiliar country. I turned at a sign saying, "Dead End Road Please D i e Slowly", (the 'r' and the 'v' in Drive whited out), and lured by VACANCY flashing on and off in blue neon, checked in for the night at the Cause of Death Motel.

The manager, wearing a three-piece pinstriped suit with an incongruous tie — blood red with dollar signs, dice and martini glasses splashed all over it — asked if I would care to join him in a bowl of vodka soup and said he didn't mind smoking in the room "long as you don't burn the house down." The hands on his watch ticked counter-clockwise. I could feel his smile on the back of my head. A six-pack of beer, Death Lite, sat on the counter next to a stack of invoices stamped "Overdue."

"Help me," I tried to whisper.

The manager lit a cigarette, and sucked the smoke in through teeth that were stained as yellow as his moustache. I pushed the smoke away with my hand, and tried to communicate, by using sign language, that I needed a place to hide.

"Everybody wants help, usually when it's too late," the manager said. He preferred doing business with the dead because with them there were no obligations, even though they could be a joyless lot. "A corpse can shed tears for hours after death, but most can't manage a smile."

He looked at me again, to see if I smiled, but my face stayed closed like a fist. "You just visiting?" he said.

I said I didn't know anymore. I hated that circumstances could take away your life without even killing you.

Beneath the warm and mannered smile, his eyes seemed to ask, "What about your death is going to be memorable?" "People want most what they pretend to hate," he said, with a dreamy lack of emphasis. He poked out his cigarette on the back of his hand, then passed me a leaflet that he said might help me make up my mind. "There's this to think about," he said. "During your lifetime you take 500 million breaths. Where would you most like to be when you breathe your last?" He reached for a bottle of beer opened it with his teeth, and poured it into a champagne flute. When I took it from him, his fingers were colder than the chilled stem of the glass.

"To the dead and the undead," he said. "Our unholy alliance."

I drank the flat, tasteless beer, and glanced over the pamphlet. I could choose the Black Room if I wanted privacy, the medicine cabinet in the bathroom being stocked with every kind of narcotic, measured out in lethal doses, or the Green Room where a chair had been placed in the centre of the floor in front of a TV screen, and a rope, with a noose at one end, dangled from a beam. In the Red Room it got messier.

I left the leaflet on the counter and walked down what seemed like an endless hall with a door at the end of it. The door was ajar. In my dream I started spinning as I entered the White

Room, where Angel lay strapped to a mortuary slab. A circular saw hung from the ceiling. Each time I took a breath, the saw that sounded like the cry of a peacock was lowered, so slowly it would take a lifetime — 500 million breaths — before it would sever the spine of my beloved who had, only moments ago, been born. I don't remember how I got there, but I found myself back outside, sitting in the hearse, On Appointment in the window. Above the sign "Cause of Death Motel", the word SORRY had replaced the neon VACANCY. I opened one eye and saw Rainy standing over me, chewing the ends of her dead hair. *Time warp fast when you having fun,* she said, trying to blink. She caught one eyeball mid-cheek, and popped it back in its socket.

I lay without moving until the dizziness passed. Frenchy insisted on serving me breakfast in bed: a limp salad, a diet Pepsi, and a dill pickle. I tried to eat the pickle until Frenchy complained the crunching hurt her ears and she'd run out of vampire's tea-bags (her name for the tampons) to block out the noise.

Over the next few days the storm showed no sign of abating. The house swayed and creaked in the wind and the rain drove at the windows, blinding them. Whenever a gust shook the house, the twins began wailing in surround sound and the HE made the *rat-tat-tat* sound of a machine gun followed by the pinging of bullets hitting rocks. When he couldn't get Frenchy's attention he buried himself in his coffin, going *glock-glock-glock*, until she scooped up her damaged boy and rocked him in her arms, soothing him with her inexhaustible stock of sniper rifles. Rainy tried to drown out the wind by reciting nursery rhymes:

Yo! Yo! Ebony sheep
Got me some wool?
Yo muhfo, you muhfo . . .

Muh, one of the twins bleated, as Rainy stopped to take a breath and the wind whipped the roof so hard a row of shakes was torn loose, bouncing off our windows on their way to the ground.

She just say what I think she say? Frenchy asked, letting the HE fall from her arms onto the floor. *She just say her first half word!*

Say Muh, best believe, Rainy said. I'd never thought I would hear Rainy sounding like such a proud mother.

Rainy told us she had something else to brag about: she was about to become a grandmother. I studied the twins closely. Their bellies under their all-enveloping robes had swollen in unison, from zero to nine months, almost overnight.

On the seventh day the wind died though the rain continued to fall all through the weekend. I booked a space on the next scheduled sailing of the *Island Spirit,* which had been sitting at the dock for ten days due to gale-force winds in the straits.

To make ready for the journey the HE dressed in a white, musk-smelling robe and wrapped his face in a checkered red-and-white *kaffiyeh* to conceal his features. He wore a key as big as the care key Gracie had worn to activate Baby-Think-It-Over, on a chain around his neck. The rat, sensing the twin's hatred of him, stayed hidden inside the HE's robe.

Rainy did up her hair in a bongolock with a built-in zipper that opened to reveal a foot-long python. Say Muh (the name had stuck) lay in her coffin dressed in a floor-length skirt and long-sleeved blouse embroidered with the slogan, I Have Special Permission to Enter Heaven, but her no-name sister was nowhere to be seen. Rainy figured she had manifested herself into the python for the trip. *Be what the angry dead do.*

"Women suicide bombers are especially desirable because, like stealth bombers, they are much less detectable. Women more easily conceal bombs under their clothes, passing themselves off as pregnant." I listened to *Radio Peace and Love* as it faded in and out while I scrubbed the back of the hearse, where Al's body had taken its last ride, then slid one of the woven willow coffins onto the rollers — the HE and the twins, in their various manifestations, would have to share. I filled the space on either side of the rollers with pillows for Rainy and Frenchy. Rainy said she felt seasick already, remembering the last voyage we took, when they'd been stuck below deck in the dead-wagon. Rainy said when Frenchy'd told her we'd be going to an island in the Pacific she'd envisioned spending eternity under a palm tree drinking piña coladas, not under a "Chrimas" tree growing moss. I left a week's supply of food in the barn for Aged Orange, though I suspected the raccoons would eat what the peacocks didn't steal first.

"Drive Carefully: It Is Not Only a Car That Can be Recalled by Its Maker", read the sign at the Christian vegetable stand, reminding me I was supposed to have made an appointment at Chubb's to have a brake job.

We boarded the *Spirit* after a short wait at the ferry terminal where we had to thread our way through a crowd of protesters calling themselves the Right to Turkey Lifers, whose cause it was to raise turkey-consciousness in the weeks leading up to Christmas. One of the demonstrators tapped on my window; I opened it, partially, to be polite, and she handed me a pamphlet. The Turkey Lifers intended to inject tainted blood into any Christmas turkey that made it onto Natural Lee's meat counter. The demonstrator said that persecuting these shy birds had become another unhealthy aggressive American tradition; she hoped to educate people and stop the "wholesale slaughter of turkeys," and asked me to consider stuffing a vegetable marrow this year instead.

I didn't leave the car deck right away, but sat listening to the safety announcements. The world had become more preoccupied than ever with safety, and a part of me yearned for the freedom I had had, in comparison, when I was a hostage on Tranquilandia. The only people who spoke about safety on that lawless island were the drug barons, who equated safety with something found on a gun and advocated making the world a safer place for crime.

"We regret, no pets will be allowed above the car deck except guide dogs for the visually impaired," the announcement continued. Rainy would only agree to leave her python in the car if the HE left his rat. I told them to work it out, and took the steep flight of stairs to the purser's office on the ship's main deck.

Rainy and Frenchy joined me shortly afterwards as I waited in line for the key to my cabin. The HE and Say Muh had gone to steal snacks in the ship's cafeteria, Frenchy said, and Rainy worried that they were up to no good. Frenchy said the HE wasn't about to blow anybody up, not if there wouldn't be enough casualties to justify wasting the explosives.

One day they gon kill us all down, said Rainy, who didn't like the idea of her grandchild being used as a grenade before she had even popped out. On Tranquilandia, I recalled, it was considered the most efficient form of birth control — to kill guerrilleras while they were still in the womb.

I remembered what I'd heard on *Radio Peace and Love,* too, as I'd disinfected the hearse, earlier in the day. It had not occurred to me at the time that far from being pregnant, Say Muh had had, beneath her *jilbab,* enough explosives strapped to her body to blow us all out of the ocean.

❦ ❦ ❦

When their offspring didn't return, even after an announcement that the ship's cafeteria was closing, Rainy and Frenchy and I left the cabin to look for them. The HE fought hard when Frenchy dragged him out from under a table where she found him going *glock-glock-glock*, preparing to detonate. In our cabin he locked himself in the bathroom, making machine-gun imitations until Frenchy became convinced he was going to flush himself down the toilet.

Say Muh had disappeared. Rainy thought she might have gone back to the car deck to keep her twin company, and said she'd look there next if I would check the outer deck — she didn't want to go outside and have a hair wreck. We left Frenchy, her lips at a crack in the bathroom door, listing off large calibre sniper rifles, and went in opposite directions: Rainy took the elevator to the car deck and I climbed more steps to the solarium where families who hadn't reserved cabins were staking out little nests. An old man, naked except for a pair of happy face boxer shorts, called out as I passed, "there'll be a high tide tonight." I nodded to him and carried on past two blonde twins cross-dressing their Barbies, a man in a T-shirt that said "Will Work for Beer" munching his way through a bald head of lettuce, and a gang of teenagers on their way to a Marilyn Manson concert in Vancouver. But nowhere did I see a ghost in white robes embroidered with, I Have Special Permission to Enter Heaven.

As I searched for Say Muh I thought of the sign outside the Clínica Desaguadero, the bronze statue of a slave, his naked legs and arms breaking free of his chains. *No tenemos que pedir permiso para ser libres.* We do not need to ask permission to be free. I remembered, too, the attempt I had made to free myself, permanently, by taking my own life, when I was sixteen and my parents had refused to let me travel to Vancouver to see the Beatles in concert. My father found me before the pills took effect. Because of him I had missed my chance to become a teen suicide.

Since that time my body had stubbornly pre-empted every attempt I'd made to shortcut my journey from birth to death. Some, like Frenchy, would argue that the most valuable thing you could do with your life was to end it. But suicide required that you not only wished to die, but that you wished to kill, and be killed, also. While I had often wished for two out of three, I'd never had homicidal inclinations, despite what Vernal maintained, that those who do not wish to kill anyone often wished they were able.

I searched the outside deck but found no trace of Say Muh, and was on my way back to our cabin when I heard a familiar yelp. Toop leapt out from under a seat where he had been lying in ambush. He wrapped his front legs around me and covered my face with dog drool. "He remembers you," Hooker said.

I stooped to pat the dog, who had slithered back under the chair, the familiar 'W' creasing his forehead. "I told him if he didn't lay low he'd get himself busted and sentenced to a night on the car deck," Hooker said. He reached down and rubbed his dog's ears. Our hands touched, and I drew mine back, as if I'd been shocked. Hooker had that effect on me. I couldn't hide my pleasure in seeing him again, even though that pleasure was now tainted by fear — about what he might have done to Al and the role I had played in helping him dispose of the body.

Grace lay stretched out across three chairs, clutching the headless body of Baby-Think-It-Over and the Moses basket she'd woven for her baby, stuffed to overflowing with baby clothes. She still wore, I saw, the pouch containing the ultrasound photo, around her neck. She opened her eyes for a moment, then rolled them up into her head the way Frenchy did when it got too bright in my room. For a moment I thought she was going into labour, but she looked so frail now I wondered if that would even be possible. Grace seemed almost transparent, as if at any moment she might dissolve, leaving a baby in her place.

"She hasn't been doing so good lately," Hooker said. "I'm taking her off-island to get her away for a while."

I said I was sorry, and asked if I could help in any way. Grace opened her eyes again at the sound of my voice, hoisted herself up from her bed of chairs, and clutching Baby-Think-It-Over, headed in the direction of the washroom.

"If they would let her keep her kid . . . *that* might help," Hooker said, reiterating what Agnes had told me, once Grace was out of earshot. Social Services still insisted she had to give him up, but they would have to drug her and cut him out of her if they wanted to take him away. "If they think she's going to let him go without some kind of a fight, they don't know Gracie."

I told Hooker I had a cabin, and if Grace would be more comfortable there, she could have the bottom bunk. He didn't speak again until she reappeared making a bed for Baby-Think-It-Over in the Moses basket amongst the baby clothes. "You look sick," he said.

"Then don't look at me," she snapped. Her red hair hung over her face in greasy ropes; her pupils, black, unfocussed, had sucked up all the beauty from her eyes, making them look as if she'd left behind whatever happiness she'd known, on Kliminawhit.

Hooker told her I'd offered her a bed. "It hurts when I move," she said. "You take the bed. I'll be okay, I'll sleep here with Toop." She spread herself out over the three seats, resting her head next to the Moses basket.

Hooker covered her with his jacket and touched her cheek with the back of his palm. He told Toop to stay; Toop put his head down between his paws, his eyes full of that "I promise you I'm not going to do anything I shouldn't do" look.

"There'll be a high tide tonight," the old man, still in his boxer shorts, proclaimed, as we made our way back through the rows of sleeping passengers.

"Thanks for the head's up, captain," Hooker said.

When I opened our cabin door I saw Frenchy dangling Rainy by her ankles over the edge of the upper bunk. She dropped her when I switched on the overhead light, and Rainy landed, laughing, on top of Say Muh, who transformed herself back into a fine red mist. Rainy said she had found Say Muh in the children's play area, helping decorate a tree with snake's mirrors, her name for tinsel.

Hooker made himself at home; he hung up his jacket then sat down on the bottom bunk and took off his shirt. He pulled off his cowboy boots and let them drop to the floor, and got under the covers, still wearing his socks and his jeans.

Yo! Pistola! Rainy said, picking herself off Say Muh. She scuttled back up onto the top bunk where she lay on her belly, watching him. *He be a watermelon I eat him, seeds and all. I wouldn't spit him out.*

Frenchy peered over the edge of the upper berth, too, as the HE emerged from the bathroom, going *gack gack gack* trying to blow out the bullet that had lodged itself above his nose. Rainy said his hairball-vomiting noises hurt her headache.

He miss his boo, Frenchy said, defensively.

Boo hoo, Rainy said.

I took off my coat and hung it over the top of Hooker's jacket. Rainy grabbed my hand and held on to it. Her cold hand, at such times, squeezed my heart; she pulled me up onto the top bunk and I tried to get comfortable between the two of them. I didn't sleep, but went into a dreamy kind of meditation that involved carrying my baby in a sling, just high enough that he could see out above the line of my shoulders where he swivelled his head, like an owlet. Rainy nudged me fully awake and I heard, over the loud speaker outside our cabin door, "Attention passengers. Would the owner of a dog please come to the cafeteria. Would the owner come to the cafeteria immediately."

"That would be Toop," Hooker sighed. "Looking for a handout, no doubt."

"I'll get him," I said. I climbed out of the bunk and threw my clothes back on.

"I owe you one," Hooker said. "Tell Toop I'm keeping the bed warm for him."

In the cafeteria I found Hooker's dog, who had made friends with the cleaner, scarfing a chicken salad sandwich. I apologized, saying he must have escaped from the car, I'd make sure he was locked up for the night, and the cleaner looked at Toop, sympathetically.

Toop stayed close until we were out of the cleaner's sight, and then ran all the way back to the solarium where he hid under Grace's chair. I didn't have the heart to make him stay in the hearse with a python and a rat, so I took him with me to the cabin. When I opened the door he leapt into bed with Hooker, put his head on the pillow, and squeezed his eyes shut.

I told Hooker what had happened, and he laughed. "Toop's a sneaky Indian," he said. "He knows how to get out of the kitchen if there's too much heat."

As soon as the HE smelled Toop, he lost control of his body and began smashing his face against the door. Frenchy said the smell brought back memories — *he woke up ready to kill dogs* — as she slipped to the floor and tried calming him by repeating the names of sniper rifles: *AI Arctic Warfare .50, Truvelo .50, Mechem NTW-20, Barrett.*

I struggled onto the top bunk and tried to sleep. Beneath me I could hear Toop grinding his teeth.

"Let me know if it gets lonely up there without me," I heard Hooker say, before I drifted into sleep.

Neither Rainy nor Frenchy nor I had slept well, and when I woke early the next morning to an announcement that the ship was about to dock, Hooker and Toop were gone. Say Muh knelt on the bottom bunk blowing down the front of her blouse, trying to warm up her heart. The HE sat in the middle of the floor, jabbing his finger in the stripes of light where it came through the vents in the door.

When we'd made our way down to the car deck I found Hooker — holding Toop with one arm and supporting Gracie with the other — leaning against our ride, waiting. Rainy said Grace, even with a baby getting ready to pop out of her, still looked too skinny, like a body-of-Christ wafer. *She be like the Holy Uterus,* Rainy said.

Hooker apologized for leaving without waking me, but he had started worrying about Grace in the middle of the night. He asked if the three of them could bum a lift into town.

I said yes, of course, wherever they had to go. I left it vague, remembering that Hooker didn't like being pinned down: *when you make plans you interfere with the way things ought to turn out on their own.* Hooker thought Grace would be best off lying down so I unlatched the back doors of the hearse and made a bed for her out of the pillows. Grace went limp in Hooker's arms when she saw the wicker coffin. Riding in a hearse with a coffin, she said, pressing Baby-Think-It-Over to her breast, was what dead people do.

"Nobody's going to die," Hooker said. When he glanced at me I could see the questions in his eyes: why was I travelling with an empty coffin, in the very place we had laid Al's body?

I said Grace could ride in the front with us, if she felt well enough to sit up. "I'm sick," she said, but accepted my offer. Toop jumped in and curled up in the Moses basket I placed at Grace's feet.

Rainy forced Say Muh into the back, though she refused to share the coffin with the HE, who couldn't find his rat. I could feel every terrorist cell of his skin revolting against his loss, as if he wished his skin could wriggle free of itself, the way a snake's could, and escape from being dead. He threw himself on the ground, behind the rear wheels of the hearse, and began smashing his face off on the fender. Frenchy searched the hearse and came up with two whiskers and a small section of tail. She figured that Say Muh's twin, in her python-manifestation, had eaten the rat. When I looked I saw the python had a rodent-shaped bulge in its belly. The snake flicked out its forked tongue, as if taking the emotional temperature of the air, then slithered its way up between Rainy's legs.

I slipped in behind the wheel, waiting for Frenchy to get control of her boy. She kissed his bloodied face and whispered the word he loved most, the one she used when all others failed — *Kalashnikov* — like a mantra, or magical charm, in the hole where one of his ears had been. Gradually the HE stopped his smashing, his vacant eyes coming into focus as he let Frenchy lift him into the back.

"We ready to roll?" Hooker said. I got out and closed the back doors, but when the HE smelled Toop he began spitting and rolling his eyes and banging his broken head again. Rainy helped Frenchy wrestle him into the coffin; Frenchy closed the lid and sat down on it saying he could stay in there until he learned how to behave.

I eased ahead down the steeply sloping ramp. Rainy worried that I was going to put us all in the ocean, as I watched in the rear-view mirror the python crawl out from between her legs, undulate up her body and coil itself around her neck. Rainy unzipped her bongolock and the snake disappeared back into its nest of hair. A moment later Say Muh's no-name twin manifested herself back into her *kamikaze* form, and sat leaning against the coffin, stroking the bulge in her stomach.

We crept past the ferry terminal parking lot. It was still dark and raining, and the visibility was poor. Gulls flew in and out of the fog, their wings illuminated by the fluorescent dock lights.

Rainy, who had let down her hair and was nibbling at the ends, tried to squeeze in between Hooker and Grace on the front seat. *Front seat get to go everywhere first,* she complained, when I signalled for her to stay back. Toop opened one eye, growled and covered his flop ears with his paws.

"*Now* what's bugging him?" Hooker said. "We got *lumaloos* riding with us again, or what?"

I watched the ferry-terminal world recede through the side mirror, and had to pump the brakes hard and swerve to the left to avoid rear-ending a white stretch limousine that had come to an abrupt stop in front of us. A sign in the rear window read, "Ride in style — at no extra cost."

"I was supposed to get a brake job," I said. Hooker shook his head and said, "thanks for the warning."

I glanced over at Grace, who had green strings of mucous dripping from her nose. Her body was trembling and she was drenched in sweat.

"Been there, done that," Hooker said. "When you quit, cold turkey, you get life with its skin torn away."

I had never been addicted to heroin, but I knew what quitting everything but heroin was like, "everything but" being the cocktail of drugs I'd become a slave to on Tranquilandia. Even now I could start to shake and feel nauseated, thinking about that time. I crept up on the limo, and had to swerve onto the shoulder to avoid hitting it when it stopped, again, unexpectedly.

What they mean, ride in style for no extra cost? asked Frenchy, who'd been thrown forward into the front seat by my inattention to the road. *You pay for a limo you* want *people to think you rich and important.*

Grace moaned and began scratching at herself, digging her chewed fingernails deep into her skin. She couldn't stop shivering, even though I had the heat turned on high.

"Maybe we ought to do Grace a favour and drop her at Mercy first?" Hooker was saying. "Then I'll stop over at my cousin's, I guess." He had an address on the eastside of Vancouver, but figured he should call to invite himself first.

"A *favour*?" Grace cried. She felt too sick to go to any hospital, she said, wiping her nose on her sleeve. She said Mercy was for hardcore addicts who went there to die, not to dry out and have babies. She remembered a hotel, the Outer Planet, on the downtown eastside. "Not five diamonds or anything, but nice." Hooker reminded her that the last time they'd stayed there a man had been stabbed in the foyer, the couple in the next room had died of an overdose and they hadn't slept all night because someone kept banging on their door demanding that "Fuckface open up."

"I was just saying," Grace said. Her voice could have sucked the breath out of sorrow.

Morning had broken through the fog, a fog so dense I could see the suggestion of trees, but not their branches, as I pulled off the highway and drew up at a Petro-Can station. Hooker said, "back in a minute," and vanished into the gloom.

Grace, who hadn't stopped scratching, gradually nodded off. Frenchy figured Gracie was about to give birth in the dead-wagon; moaning and shivering were early warning signals. I said the baby wasn't due until Christmas, two weeks away. *That be Son Jesus' birthday*, said Rainy, blowing down the back of Gracie's neck. *Holy Uterus' boy be Come Back Jesus, best believe.*

Grace woke up, complaining about a draft. Hooker returned saying the telephone booth had been stolen. It took two more attempts — the Shell service station had got rid of its pay phone because too many drug deals were being made, and the Esso's had been vandalized so many times they had given up trying to fix it. When Hooker finally found a phone that worked, at a Mohawk station, his cousin's number was no longer in service. He remembered her telling him she was moving to the Interior to grow dope with her boyfriend last April, but he'd thought she was just trying to impress him.

They crib with us, Rainy whispered. *What else they gon do, bail?* She was right: what could I do but offer to take them home.

"You could stay at our place — there's plenty of room," I heard myself say. I said we would take turns watching Grace until she got through withdrawal. That way she wouldn't have to be hospitalized until she went into labour.

Hooker was quiet for a long time. "That's not a bad idea," he said, when he finally spoke — his way, I knew, of being grateful.

❦ ❦ ❦

Welcome to Astoria
"Your Gateway to Another Life"

Just past the sign we came up on a low, grey cement melancholy of a building shrouded in fog and surrounded by a chain-link fence. The words on the reader board under Astoria Collegiate had been edited, and now read, "End of Term Titeracy Fest Today 1:30 in the jism". Frenchy said all she'd ever wanted was for her boy to have the same opportunities as other boys his age.

What that be, chance to shoot off his gatt in a school cafeteria? Rainy said. She had pulled out a handful of hair and swallowed it without chewing it first. *You plan on shooting up any muhfo school, include me out,* she added, cutting Frenchy a look.

Frenchy let the HE out of his coffin so he could see the high-schoolers, standing in small groups waiting to go back inside. A few turned to stare as we passed. Hooker waved to a boy who stood apart from the rest — thin, with a shaved head and eyes that, even from a distance, looked empty in his head — but he didn't wave back. No one waves to a hearse, I knew. It might make the people inside feel even sadder.

Rainy had switched on *Radio Peace and Love.* "You are only fifteen-years-old. What was the main reason for you deciding to become a suicide bomber?" the reporter asked. A young girl replied, in Arabic, as a toneless translator drowned her out: "I did it because I didn't want to go to school. My parents forced me to go to school and I didn't feel like going. I wanted to be relieved of school."

You playing with power there, home girl, Rainy said to the *shahida,* the martyr-in-waiting. The Twin Terrorists leaned forward, one on either side of me, their ears tuned to the voice on the radio. I listened to the fifteen-year-old say that it is not possible for someone who is about to blow themselves up to look average or normal. "The height of bliss comes only with the end of the countdown," she said. "Seven, six, five, four, etc. and then you press the button to blow yourself up and then the boom and then you sense yourself floating to another life."

"I wonder how she knows," Hooker said, under his breath.

The HE had moved to the back of the hearse, as far away from Toop as he could get. "A human being himself is a weapon. No need to carry him. He will walk and explode," the young woman continued. I punched the radio off when she began speaking of personal sacrifice.

Looking good be a sacricide, best believe, Rainy said under her breath. *I get new shoes, my feet be killin me, that be shoe-icide.*

We were in traffic now. A crippled girl with legs as thin as the toilet plunger she carried in her hands, stepped onto the road, looking neither to the left nor right. I pumped the brakes and leant on the horn. Rainy covered her eyes, as if by not being able to see what would happen next, she could prevent it from happening. The girl didn't look up, but kept pulling herself along like a broken cricket. *She be street pizza, she do that enough times,* Rainy said.

Frenchy wanted to know why so many trees were decorated with lights, and why the lights didn't go all the way to the ground.

Jesus be the reason, said Rainy. *Chrimas be the season. When people — don't matter what they religion be — get together and worship Son Jesus. He rise up from the grave and cook hisself a turkey dinner.*

You think Jesus rise up on Christmas day, you think again," Frenchy said.

Rainy looked at her sideways. *Be more than one way to tilt a jello salad,* she said. She also informed Frenchy that the lower branches of the trees weren't decorated because people traditionally stole the lights that were within reach, at least when she was growing up in the hood. *God got a purpose for everythin he do, we don't always know what that be.*

I tried to focus on the world outside, sensed myself floating back to another life. But there was little evidence of the village of Astoria where Vernal and I had shopped when we lived in the nearby walled community. A McDonald's occupied the lot where the Scottish butcher had sold haggis and white sausages as thick as his fingers, and there was a coffee house on every other corner. The independent bookstore had been absorbed by Chapters; the Italian-run bakery where Vernal and I had bought weighty loaves of rye bread every Saturday morning had devolved into a pet deli called The Pawstry Shop.

We drove through a lighted candy cane archway up the main street of town, and stopped at an intersection where, on an artificial snow-bound traffic island, a nativity scene (what Rainy called a "negativity" scene) had been erected. A homeless man sat with his back against the manger, shouting at passing cars. Fake snow stuck to his eyebrows and his hair.

Painfully cheerful Christmas music leaked through the shop doors and windows onto the street and Frenchy, recognizing some of the carols, said they reminded her of the Condemned Row where every Christmas Eve a bunch of Salvation Army do-gooders had come to bring each of us a sack of leftover Halloween candy, and a copy of the New Testament. We also got a calendar, in a brown envelope stamped "Property of Heaven Valley Correctional Facility," so we could start afresh in the New Year, X-ing off our days.

Christmas hadn't been a reason for celebrating much of anything back at the Facility. We didn't have a real tree, just some contorted tree-shaped sculpture made from razor wire and meant to symbolize freedom or imprisonment — depending on which side of the fence you were on.

On the far side of town, in what had once been wilderness, we drove past a moonscape of used car lots, mini-storage units, a U-Haul rental company, and the Crossover Methodist Church. Next to the church, where there had once been a field of waist-high grass where Vernal and I had played hide-and-go-seek with Brutus, a new strip mall had gone up. The neon list of businesses included a food court, Heavenly Relics, a Colour Your World paint store, an Athlete's Feet, and a Drugs R Us. Hooker suggested we stop and pick up a bottle of Tylenol for Gracie, though I knew it would take more than an over-the-counter painkiller to kill the kind of pain Gracie felt today.

I entered the lot at the "Exit" sign and drove, against the arrows, in circles, looking for a place to park. Grace wiped her nose on her sleeve and said she only wanted to go back to the island, that she didn't want her baby to die so far away from home. "Nobody's going to die," said Hooker, for the second time since we had arrived on the mainland. This time, though, his voice lacked the same degree of certainty.

I slid into a space next to a sign that read, "Trust in God but Lock your Car", beside a stand of artificial Christmas trees marketed as "Stays Green All Year, Unlike Lesser Trees". Frenchy read the sign aloud and Rainy wanted to know what they meant by "lesser trees". *They be livin once, then chopped down,* Frenchy said.

Rainy looked away, her brown eyes loading up with tears. *Same thing as us,* she said. *We be actual once.*

Frenchy told her to stop being a sucky baby, her blubbering was steaming up the windows and she didn't want to miss anything, though I could see nothing to miss but grey fog and pavement beyond the steamy windows.

Hooker said he'd stay with Grace but asked if I would bring them a pizza. Toop's ears stood up. "Oh, and a chicken salad sandwich for His Royal Highness. Crusts off, remember?"

The HE, who thought he was being left behind, began making the *rat-tat-tat* sound of machine gun fire followed by the *thuck* of bullets hitting a body. Frenchy said he could come, too, and then Rainy said her twins had never been in a shopping mall, either.

We crossed the parking lot, through stacks of everlasting trees and baskets of plastic holly leaves, pinecones, and plump artificial berries. Rainy stopped to check out a fish-shaped plaque on a Toyota's fender — one with DARWIN on its belly and two feet sticking out below. She wanted to know what the fish symbolized. I told her it was possible the car's owner believed in evolution.

Mean he born against Christians, Frenchy said, and Rainy smacked the Evolve plaque with the flat of her hand. She got down on the asphalt and began chipping away at the plaque with her long fingernails that broke into more pieces than the DARWIN fish plaque. I said evolution was notoriously difficult to stop, knowing, at the same time, that wouldn't deter Rainy. She stopped to check each fender in the parking lot.

Everything inside the mall reeked of a bleary artificiality, shops the colours of pigeon feathers selling everything from garden gnomes to robot vacuum cleaners. I felt light-headed, as if my brain were being deprived of oxygen. The air smelled as if it had been continuously recycled through a popcorn machine.

We passed a wall of TVs, all showing the same image from the Middle East, an aid worker telling a reporter how much it hurt having to tuck children into bed every night in their small bloodied pyjamas. "For orphans, Christmas can be an even harder time of year," said the head of a charitable organization, soliciting donations. Rainy said you couldn't help feeling sorry for kids who got partly blown up, who didn't know they were being peeped out by millions of people on TV.

The camera panned over the village where the Red Cross had built a makeshift orphanage. Most buildings on the look-alike screens had been reduced to piles of rubble. *They got Sanity Claus over there?* Rainy asked. *Don't look like nobody got a roof left for him to chill on.*

Frenchy asked Rainy if she knew why "Sanity Claus" had no kids of his own, and Rainy looked at her suspiciously. *Because he only come once a year, and that be down a chimney,* Frenchy said.

Rainy thought about this. *They got no roofs over there, they don't got chimneys, neither.*

I left them on the verge of another argument and escaped to the food court where I ordered the Two-For-One pizza special with everything on it. I couldn't find a chicken salad sandwich at any of the fast food outlets, so bought a ham and cheese instead, hoping it would do. By the time I got back, my friends had gone their separate ways.

I found Rainy and the twins staring at a clothing store window display, photographs of Paris supermodels got up as Holocaust victims. The whole world, in the weeks leading up to Christ's birthday, seemed to have been infected with a virus of bad taste.

Frenchy and the HE sat on a bench outside Athlete's Feet that sold Boss Angeloss brand running shoes, like the ones that washed up on Kliminawhit, only in pairs. A pack of teenaged girls, each wearing a fibre-optic holiday hat, blinking Ho Ho Ho in sequence with falling snowflakes sparking across the brim, took over the bench, forcing Frenchy and the HE to move. Frenchy's boy took the festive atmosphere as a kind of personal affront, a reminder that his life had been cut short.

Drugs R Us was our last stop, where I bought Tylenol for Grace and Frenchy stole vampire's teabags and "clearless" nail polish for Rainy. On our way out of the mall we passed a shop selling floral bouquets and motivational cards. Rainy asked me what the sign said, and I told her, "Cut flowers."

Flowers hurt when you cut them? Rainy wanted to know, the water rising in her eyes like a river's in flood time even before I answered. To see certain things clearly, I thought, you had to be Rainy, with tears rolling down into your ears. Was it possible you had to be hurt to see anything at all?

We were almost at the hearse when Toop came slinking out from between two rows of Christmas trees, a single Boss Angeloss runner in his teeth.

Hooker had the door open on the passenger's side and Toop dropped the shoe in his lap. "Ten-and-a-half, left. Mission accomplished!" Hooker wiped Toop's drool off the runner, and then gave him a kiss, too.

"You shouldn't encourage him," I said.

Hooker said *you're right.* He kissed Toop again and then wiped his lips on the sleeve of his jacket.

We sat without speaking after that, in the mall parking lot, sharing the Two-For-One pizza. The HE pointed an imaginary assault rifle at every shopping spectre he heard slide past, going *glock-glock-glock* as he mowed bodies down. From the way his eyes shaved the warm and fuzzy off whatever crossed his sights, you could tell the HE had gone way past the hobby stage of shooting birds out of trees or taking potshots at crowds from the tops of tall buildings on university campuses.

I set the second pizza in the back between the rollers and Rainy, who had pulled out most of the hair on the right side of her head and had strands of it stuck in her front teeth, opened the box and began flicking pieces of red and green pepper onto the curtains — trying to make our ride look more Chrimassy, she said. Toop poked his nose into the ham and cheese sandwich I unwrapped for him, licked it once, then snapped his head back, as if he had been shocked.

"Sorry," I said. "It's all they had." Toop squeezed his body into the space at Hooker's feet, his head between his paws, looking bleakly misunderstood.

I drove to the gated community: a sign read, "Adult Living Restricted Entry: Authorized Persons Only", with "Visitors Must Report to Front Gate Before Proceeding" in smaller print underneath.

"Home sweet home," Hooker said.

"One of the reasons I left."

A video surveillance camera trained its unblinking eye on us as a sleepy-faced security guard approached, frowning as if trying to decide what our business might be. He bent down to inspect us through the window I had lowered. "Pick-up or delivery?" he asked.

Who deliver pizza in a dead-wagon? Rainy said.

I hesitated and before I could say anything Hooker leaned across me to speak. "Jus' visitin'," he said.

The guard's pen stopped halfway to the sheet of yellow paper attached to his clipboard, as if visitors were an anomaly within the walled city of his orderly world.

"You got a name? Person you're going to call on?"

I gave him the address and his face relaxed, simplified itself. "I know the place," he said, sounding relieved — he wouldn't have to file an incident report. "Belongs to that lawyer fellow whose clients always get off?" His eyes flicked over to Hooker and me as if to say gates and fencing worked best on a stable property with non-criminal, mature residents, which didn't include people like lawyers who defended social misfits who couldn't keep their noses clean. I felt the urge to defend Vernal's practice, tell the guard "you are only guilty if they can prove it," but stopped myself, and smiled, insincerely, gesturing with my hands — palms up and open.

The guard told me I could apply for a coded Visitor ID card so I wouldn't have a problem coming and going. I said I didn't foresee any problems and he said "suit yourself, ma'am." He handed me a booklet that I didn't look at but passed to Hooker, the *Visitor's Guide to the Adult Community at Astoria: Your Search for Niceness Ends Here!* that included a street map, the route to our former residence marked in red. The map let us know, in bold lettering, we were not to deviate.

"A lot of elderly people live here," the guard said, looking down at the hearse, as if he found it distasteful. "You are required to call Safe Arrivals when you reach your designated address."

I put up the window, and the electronic gates slid open to let us pass. We drove through an opening in a wall topped with broken glass set in concrete, much like the one surrounding the hacienda on Tranquilandia. Jagged glass that could shred a man's hands into lace.

The suburb had an eerie stillness to it, like the air before a dead wind rises. At one time it had been filled with the shouts of children playing street hockey at the end of the cul-de-sacs, and, in summer, their older siblings, lawn tennis on private courts. I missed the squeals of infants as their nannies fussed over them at the shallow ends of swimming pools. I missed the sounds of children growing up in a world where the worst pain they'd experience would be the sting of a parent's rebuke. Now there were no children, anywhere, to miss.

No poor people chill in this hood? Rainy said, as I cranked the wheel and turned right onto a wide, tree-lined street with no above-ground wiring.

Price of housin keep them out, Frenchy said. If *she* had been born in a killer-clean hood like this, she said, — *no drive-bys, no crack house on every corner* — she might have had a chance growing up. She might not have ended up getting executed on Death Row for killing her only kid.

Rich people don't need to kill their kids, Rainy said. *They hire up babysitters, they want to go out drinkin.*

God always been down on the poor, Frenchy said. She figured God must have invented poverty in order to entice poor people into doing mind-numbing jobs no one would think of doing unless they were flat broke first. Money was

God's most cruel invention — the only way He could get you out of bed and off to your minimum wage job. For once Rainy didn't contradict.

The competitive Christmas spirit thrived in this well-off suburb, and each outdoor tree outside every child-forsaken home was festooned with lights that went all the way to the ground. We drove past lawns studded with reindeer, penguins, carollers, candy canes and snowmen — many of them inside inflatable globes a-flurry with snowflakes. There was a lone bear holding a dreidel beside a giant menorah flickering neon purple, green and orange — and a lawn that held a cluttered mysticism of its own: Santa with his sleigh and reindeer parked next to an inflatable manger surrounded by camels, donkeys, and a dozen pink flamingos.

Sanity Claus be a fat-ass white muhfo, Rainy said.

Same as God be, Frenchy said. *Fat and white.*

§ § §

"This is it," I announced, "we're home." Aside from the "For Sale" sign mounted on the decorative stone wall, the word "Sold" imprinted on it, like a brag, the Walled Off and grounds looked the same as when I had left it behind, thirteen years ago. Now all the feelings I'd had of not belonging came lamentably back.

Rainy and Frenchy stared in awe at the house where Vernal and I had tried to live. The twins raised their arms in a gesture of praise and the HE rubbed his blind eyes with his hands.

I parked at the foot of the front steps and opened my door. Toop jumped out ahead of me, as a ball of fur the size of a tea cozy, wearing wrap-around sunglasses, darted from under the evergreen magnolia Vernal had planted to mark the celebration of our first anniversary, a tree that had never bloomed. The fur ball lunged at our tires, and when they failed to fight back, turned his attention to Toop, sniffing the place where his leg had once been.

"He's got an amputee fetish, what can I say?" a familiar voice came, as I started up the steps. When I looked I hardly recognized him, he'd aged that much. He wore his brown hair, now streaked with greyish-white, twisted at the back of his head into a small cluster of unruly curls. As I got closer I could see he had lost a few more teeth since we'd last met. But it was his nostrils — big enough to be vacuum cleaner attachments — that gave him away. In the early days of my marriage, I-5 had visited our home on a regular basis, packing a pocketful of cocaine and a pistol under his *ruana*. We hadn't been close.

"Place ain't on the market, not now. Sold, in case you can't read." I-5 wore sunglasses to match his dog's, a white T-shirt with "International Terrorist" and a picture of George Bush on the front and a belt with a silver buckle inlaid with nubs of turquoise. A pager and a cell phone were clipped to the belt; I gathered he was still in the business. I stepped around him to go inside, but he moved to block the way. "This ain't the Vatican. We ain't open to the public," he said.

"I-5, it's me," I said, testily. "I used to live here. Remember?" I tapped my forehead to help him remember the place where memories, and names, are stored. His real name, the one that appeared on his numerous arrest warrants, was Primero Segundo III, but no one — no one who retained a full complement of limbs — ever called him that.

The sound of his *nom de guerre* had the desired effect: his face grew more open and he began to take an interest in what I had to say. He removed his glasses, as if looking at me with naked eyes would help him recollect.

"Hey!" he said suddenly, snorting through his throat, the way I remembered him doing — one of the many irritating side effects of being who he was. "Chicken Quito Ecuador! Long time no see!"

Whenever I-5 had come to the house I'd stayed in the kitchen preparing Chicken Quito Ecuador from the *Time Life Cookbook*, a dish Vernal requested but never ate, after inhaling a few lines of I-5's anti-appetizer. As he left the house I-5 always turned to me and said, "Next time I come for dinner I'm going to leave room for more of your Chicken Quito Equador."

I-5 looked through me, not at me, the way he always did.

"What are you doing here?" I said.

"Looking after the place. Didn't anyone warn you?"

"Vernal didn't say who, just that he'd found someone."

I-5 said the *jefe* had offered him a place to stay because he was, at the moment, under house arrest, "Except when I go out to do that community service."

I told I-5 I would only be staying at the Walled Off until I got the rest of our possessions packed and my mother's affairs straightened out. As I spoke, I saw him draw himself up and puff out his chest a little, looking away from me to the right, over my shoulder. I followed his gaze down the steps, saw Rainy and Frenchy squeezing out with the twins and the HE, who stooped to fill his pockets with gravel from the driveway. Seconds later they were all hovering beside me.

Their presence was not what had precipitated the change in I-5's demeanour. His eyes had come to rest on Hooker, bending over, reaching to catch hold of Toop, who had jumped onto the hood and was licking his stump, as if he had suddenly become awkwardly aware of it.

"They lick themselves it's a sign they're giving in," I-5 said, as Hooker went around to the back and began unloading the coffin.

"Toop's not giving in," I said, protectively, "he's just being polite. He doesn't like to kill anything that isn't his own size."

"That ain't *anything*, that be the Bomb," I-5 said, as the deranged tea cozy attached himself to Hooker's leg, and began pumping. "I don't let him out much. He's more of an inside dog."

Hooker swore, shook his leg once, and the Bomb, along with his sunglasses, flew off and landed upside down on the gravel. Toop sighed at the enormity of it all and settled his chin on his paws.

I-5 told me to go ahead inside, and make myself at home. "*Su casa es mi casa, comprehendo?* I'll let the front gate know you're here." He touched the cell phone on his belt. "I can help your boyfriend with your luggage while I'm at it."

To his credit Vernal's criminal-element caretaker didn't ask why I travelled with a coffin. Maybe he thought it an accessory that came with the vehicle. I didn't bother informing him that Hooker wasn't my boyfriend, or that Hooker's sister was lying on the front seat, pregnant and trying to kick a full-blown heroin habit. He'd find out himself, soon enough.

I-5 reached the bottom of the steps and began shouting obscenities at his little dog, who danced in circles around his feet. I-5 tried to swat him and the Bomb bolted, yelping, into the garden, his stubby hind legs bumping into his front legs as he ran. Toop slithered off the hood and went limping after him.

Rainy and Frenchy stood on either side of me, watching I-5 help Hooker ease Grace from the hearse. *I make him for a blow-boy*, Rainy said, *way he pimp out that gay ass dog.*

He look burned out like a housin project in the hood, Frenchy said. *In dog years, that boy be dead his own self.*

I stepped into the entrance hall where the walls were still covered with photographs from the nineteenth century, drenched in sepia light, portraits of children who had been born but never wakened. Vernal had started bringing them home from the flea market and second-hand stores after our dog died, to become the family we would never have. He called them his heirless heirlooms — dead children whose families had forsaken them, left them to descend through the hands of generations of strangers — he'd hang them wherever he could find a bare space in our house. "I like to think I am giving them another life, just by hanging them here," he would say, to anyone who asked about their histories.

Home be where you hang yo self, best believe, Rainy said, as we edged our way further into the house filled with the rich madness of my mother's life, and pushed through to the living room, trying not to knock over the multitude of antique floor lamps with irreplaceable parts missing and stands full of broken umbrellas nestled together like crippled bats. At her age one would be entitled to maintain a cluttered house, crowded with almost a century of assorted and sundry belongings, but my mother had never been content to own *one* of anything, or anything that was in some way not in need of repair. She only seemed to find beauty in broken things.

Rainy and Frenchy came after me with their kids, but Rainy didn't get any further than the big-screen TV inset in the massive stone fireplace. I-5 had the TV tuned to a station that broadcast a log fire burning.

I hadn't grown up with TV — my father had always said television had been invented to convince people the world was not a mysterious place, and wouldn't allow one in the house.

When Brutus died Vernal bought the TV and it had become his primary avoidance technique. He would sit, staring at the log fire burning for hours on end, as if there was nothing else left to do, and I would have to tell him, with rough mercy, to turn off the television, read a book, get some work to do.

Hooker came in carrying Grace in his arms. I took him to the sunroom — where I had napped away many an afternoon, waiting for Vernal to come home from work and order in dinner — and cleared a pile of magazines off the loveseat, covering her with a blanket.

I-5 brought Baby-Think-It-Over in the Moses basket and set it on the floor, beside Gracie's head. I moved the cat litter box "so the Bomb doesn't make a mistake in the house," I-5 said, out of the sunroom into the hallway where Grace wouldn't have to look at it. I-5 led us through the dining room filled with empty packing boxes, into the kitchen. He said Vernal had instructed him to pack up my mother's things, but never called back to say where he wanted the boxes sent. He said he had his own "oddments" stored down in the basement but he had no clue where he'd be moving to himself when "the slants who'd bought the heap" took possession on the first of February.

I went to the kitchen window that overlooked the neglected garden, the scene of my mother's fatality. At one time I would have had a view of the heart-shaped swimming pool, but Vernal had filled in the pool after Brutus drowned.

I watched I-5 as he cleared most of a week's worth of coffee cups and dinner plates off the table and added them to a pile in the sink where lumps of congealed egg white, like beluga flesh, floated in the dirty water. The counters, too, were choked with cutlery, saucepans and empty sardine tins. Hooker said he'd bring in our luggage and I-5 repeated his earlier offer of help. I asked Hooker to put the coffin upstairs in a corner of Vernal's office where it wouldn't be in the way.

Frenchy had gone to explore the house with the HE; Rainy and the twins watched the log fire burn on TV, inching closer, trying to squeeze some warmth out of it. I heard Toop sighing through his teeth outside, and the Bomb flinging himself against the backdoor screen. I let them in. The Bomb, without his sunglasses, had a squinty expression on his face, and when I looked at him more closely I saw he was cross-eyed.

I opened the remains of the Two-For-One Pizza, and sat down at the kitchen table. The December issue of Martha Stewart's *Living* lay open next to a partially eaten can of sardines. I flipped through *Living*, wishing that "Holiday Stains and How to Treat Them," was the biggest problem I had to contend with, and heard Hooker and I-5 re-enter the house, carrying the Chrysalis upstairs, laughing as they bumped into things. Hooker said, "your end needs to go up further," and I-5 said something back, and they both laughed again, but they'd reached the upstairs landing, and I felt left out, I couldn't imagine what they had to laugh so hard about.

After a while Hooker came back downstairs. I heard him stop and check on Grace, before joining me in the kitchen.

"Well?" I said.

"She doesn't look good," he said quietly. "But she's still breathing." He picked the pineapple off the pizza, making a tipi out of it on his plate. I was about to suggest we call the hospital, have Grace admitted to Mercy *without* her consent, when I-5 interrupted us. He stood at the sink, with the Bomb under his arm, eating sardines, two at a time. "You swallow them in pairs, they don't get so lonely going down," he said, glancing at Hooker.

He offered me a couple; I shook my head. Rice topped with a mixture of pasta and chopped sardines, or a soup of sardines thickened with pasta and potatoes, had been my daily diet while I was a hostage. I said I had never understood why people thought it was acceptable to eat every part of the sardine — bones, guts and excrement — just because it was small. "Sardines are all right, I guess," Hooker said, as if he didn't agree with me. "Some of the time, anyways," he added, when he saw the look of betrayal on my face.

I-5 asked if I had been talking to the *jefe* lately. I told him about Vernal's fall.

"That guy's gonna get himself an injury to himself one day," I-5 said, pensively. "Why don't he just buy a bottle and do his drinking at home where he can pass out on the floor without hurting himself."

I said I wished Vernal had thought of that years ago when we were newlyweds and our life together still had a chance, and asked I-5 if I could use the phone to call St. Jude's. When I enquired about Vernal, the receptionist said no one had been admitted under that name.

I had spoken to him less than a week ago. "He must have been discharged already," I said. "Or else he checked out early."

"He checked out he would have called home," I-5 said. "He'd want a drink — they don't look after you so good in those places."

Hooker laughed — a laugh I felt excluded from again, and I began to have strong feelings of resentment towards I-5 — how quickly I felt him intruding upon my life. I got up and left the kitchen as I-5 began regalling Hooker with stories of his depraved childhood, how he attended the sort of elementary school where you packed a box knife in your lunch box, but when you graduated to high school you needed a good Italian switchblade because it was over three inches to the heart, and shorter knives wouldn't go the distance.

Rainy and her twins had abandoned the fire — I found them upstairs with Frenchy, in Vernal's office. Frenchy had logged onto the Internet where she'd at last found a Twelve Step program that made sense to her, called *AfterLife Anonymous* (ALA). I listened to the First Step: "We came to believe we had attained a level of self-sufficiency not available to the living and that our lives, as we had known them, were finally over." Rainy asked Frenchy to explain what this meant in plain English.

It mean you be MIA, Frenchy said. *Once you accept that, you start to move on.* Frenchy said most people would feel a lot happier about being dead if they knew they'd lose weight and stop getting older; dead and naked you looked a lot thinner, and sometimes even younger. In death you grew older, you just didn't age.

The HE sat huddled in a corner picking shrapnel from his skin, making coughing up hairball noises, going *glock glock glock.* The Twin Terrorists had driven him from his end of the coffin where they lay planning their post-mortem martyr banquet, especially the kind of cake they'd like served at their funerals. Say Muh wanted it to be chocolate with coconut flakes, her favourite. Her sister thought angel food cake would be more fitting.

I went back downstairs where I-5 was rolling a joint, explaining to Hooker how he had killed a boy by accident with the knife, but he hadn't murdered anyone. "Killing is something the world makes you do — when there's no other way. Murder's something different. I've killed a few men, but I never committed murder."

I stopped listening and went into the sunroom, expecting to find Grace where Hooker had left her, lying on her back next to the lifeless doll. I'd seen Rainy go through the same thing enough times when she tried to kick. It was never pretty.

Grace lay face down on the loveseat and didn't move when I shook her. Her limbs were flaccid, and I knew something wasn't right. When I turned her over I saw her blue lips, the needle sticking in her neck, and blood all over the blanket and the loveseat's upholstery.

I shouted her name, turned her over and hugged her to me, held her away from me and slapped her cheek, tried to make her sit up, but she felt like a dead weight however I positioned her. I grabbed a cushion and put it under her head, shouting for Hooker who came flying out of the kitchen, yelling at I-5 to call 911. Hooker and I lifted Grace off the couch and dragged her across the floor to the downstairs bathroom, knocking over everything in our path. I-5 said an ambulance was on its way, and helped Hooker lift Grace into the shower. Hooker told me to turn on the cold water while he tried to hold her up. Grace fell against a wall, her legs and arms flopping, no flicker of pain, or hope, no life on her face. It was as if her eyes had led the way out of her body and the rest of her had followed.

Hooker got her to her feet, gripped her from behind, and tried to make her stand, but nothing he could do would move her back to life. Each moment was crucial, I knew, but Grace had to make up her own mind whether or not to come back.

I heard I-5 trying to speak calmly, though his voice and Hooker's both began reverberating through me. "Hold her up! Walk her. Keep her moving. Don't let her fall." He looked over at me. "You know what to do?" He pulled the syringe from Grace's neck and thrust it at me.

I remembered Frenchy telling me what to do "the next time" Rainy overdosed, but I couldn't remember how much salt to water you used, whether you boiled the water first, or heated it to make sure the salt dissolved. I raced to the kitchen, found the box of salt next to the baking soda, and spilled half of it on the counter trying to pour it into the syringe. My hands were shaking; I feared I was already too late.

I somehow managed to fill the syringe, then ran back with it to the bathroom. Hooker was still holding Grace upright and I-5 had lifted her inert arm to try and find a vein. I-5 grabbed the point and started poking, but nothing happened. "No veins left," he said. Hooker said, "try her neck again," but I-5 gave up and pushed the point into a muscle. Then he got behind her again, took her under her arms and started shaking her, violently, as if he could shake death out of her. Hooker kept trying to feel for her pulse. I listened for a breath. Nothing.

I heard the siren, and wondered what the guard would think: first a hearse, now an ambulance, both going to the same address. Usually it went the other way around. Hooker said he figured the ambulance attendants wouldn't be able to get a stretcher through all my mother's clutter, so the three of us heaved Grace's body into the entrance hall.

Hooker said he would ride with Grace and asked me to look after Toop, who tried to jump into the ambulance with him. I held on to him long enough for the paramedics to get the door shut, but then the Bomb began to wail, harmonizing with the siren, as the ambulance sped away. Frenchy said he sounded like a peacock in heat.

Rainy and Frenchy took the guest room across the hall from Vernal's office. Neither of them liked the idea that I would be so far away from them, sleeping downstairs in the room Vernal had renovated for my mother, and where she must have spent a lot of lonely hours during the last few years of her life. I told them I needed the space, it was my way of saying goodbye to my mother who, for all her idiosyncrasies, had been a good mother to me.

She never leave you in a dumpster, walk away? Rainy said.

My mother used to say she was glad she raised me before child abuse was invented, but I'll say this much for her — she would have given me up for adoption before leaving me in the trash. "My mother wouldn't have known what a dumpster was, let alone where to find one," I said.

Rainy's definition of a good mother was one who left her baby in a dumpster but then had a change of heart. She took great pride in the fact that her own mother had left her for dead, then come back for her before she was compacted with the day's garbage.

My mother's room had not been touched, as if I-5 had known at some level she wouldn't have approved of him going through her underwear drawer or her medicine cabinet. The room looked as if she had just finished making her bed and had walked out the door into the garden she called her labour of love where she would spend most of the day trying to impose order on the "riot" other people called nature.

My mother's tortoise-shell hairbrush, comb and mirror set, sat side-by-side on her dressing table. The brush still had strands of her hair in it, thin and white, and I pictured her sitting in front her mirror brushing her waist-length hair, counting out a hundred strokes, up until the end. There was a vase full of tea roses that had shrivelled and turned black. They were beautiful, in their own way, but my mother would have dismissed them as 'deadery', and tossed them out.

Also on her dresser, in their glass cabinet, were the look-alike china dolls that as a child I'd been forbidden to touch. My mother had kept them locked up where even the dust could not violate them. She told me, years later, that the key had been lost, but today when I tugged on the tiny gold padlock it came apart in my hands. I opened the glass doors, and let the dolls breathe fresh air for the first time in so many years.

I lay on my mother's bed, unable to sleep. In the distance I could hear sirens, a night train's mournful wail, and closer, in the hallway outside my room, Toop, missing Hooker, getting up, pacing back and forth, then lying down with a great exhalation of breath. I heard my heart, too, beating away in the darkness of my body. *Only temporary*, it seemed to say. *Only temporary*.

I rose before daylight. Frenchy had already logged on to her ALA Meeting, and had skipped a few steps (when you were dead, she said, the order of things like the steps you took didn't matter) — to the Fourth: "Forced ourselves to remember and relive every nauseating detail of our former lives (especially the way we treated our children)." The HE stared at her with his blind eyes that could appear playful when he didn't have detonating on his mind.

Rainy, with her twins propped up on either side of her like deadly bookends, sat on the living room floor, eating candy canes for breakfast in front of the TV where an all-male panel discussed the modern woman's role in suicide bombings, in particular the recent terrorist attack by the all-female Army of Roses. There were long queues of young *shahida*'s-in-waiting more than willing to join the road to heaven, the panel's moderator said. One panelist argued that we shouldn't expect women, known to be bearers of life, to be efficient killing machines. Another said the very people we were least likely to suspect, the givers of life, might be those who were dying to kill. It was his opinion that a woman should be required to produce one son and one daughter before she be allowed to blow herself up. After she had fulfilled her demographic role, only then should she be permitted to participate in armed struggle.

Holy Uterus be one more stinkin old needle sticker, Rainy said, lifting Baby-Think-It-Over from the Moses basket. *This be where she hide her stash.* She reached into the doll's gutted body and pulled out the syringe, a spoon, and the fistful of empty flaps she'd discovered. She had also found the leather pouch where Grace kept her care-key and the ultrasound photo of her baby, under the loveseat in the sunroom. If you looked at it long enough, she said, you could see Son Jesus in the arms of the "Version" Mary in the black and white photo.

I glanced at the grainy photo of Gracie's baby swimming in his sea of dark. Rainy was hardwired for Jesus — she saw him everywhere she looked, and especially in everything she ate. Since I'd known her there'd been a Holy Tortilla, Christ crucified on a pretzel, and Jesus rising from his tomb out of a jar of Prego spaghetti sauce. Rainy had started toying with the needles that held her head on her neck. I hoped to God she wasn't thinking about sticking one of Gracie's needles in her arm, going back to her old ways, trying to blot out her life. I threw the doll to Toop. "Go and bury it in the garden," I told him.

Hooker had called during the night and left a message on the machine. I listened as he said Grace was going to be okay, and ran my finger around a heart-shaped bloodstain on the loveseat as he said he would stay in town where he could be close to her. His message was punctuated with long silences, as if he expected the machine to speak back. He didn't leave a number; he didn't even ask about Toop. He said he would try to call again in the morning.

I went to the kitchen, wondering out loud how I was going to wash Grace's blood off the loveseat; Martha Stewart's holiday guide to stain removal hadn't included bloodstains. I-5 volunteered a home remedy he had learned "from what he used to do for a living," a paste made of meat tenderizer mixed with water and then rubbed into the fabric.

I-5 had spent a lot of years in federal never-never land as a result of what he had done for a living. Besides retailing drugs he had been the sort of landscape artist who gives wooded areas a bad name. He lured people who didn't pay him into the bushes and killed them. (It was from this career path that stemmed I-5's need for Vernal's services as a lawyer.) Vernal had got him off his most recent murder charge on a technicality. The Crown had claimed, in their written argument to the judge, that I-5 had "repeatedly" killed the deceased. Vernal argued that it should have been "reportedly."

I watched I-5's hands as he sponged off the meat tenderizer-paste, thought about the blood that had stained them, the blood on the hands of a man who kills but does not commit murder. When he'd finished, and left the sunroom, I sat down to use the phone. The first call I made was to Mercy.

An operator informed me visiting hours were from one to three, adding that patient Moon was in B-Unit — as if I would understand the implications — and there were no phones in any of the rooms for reasons that had to do with security.

I called St. Jude's, and asked for Vernal again. The receptionist was more helpful than the last one and told me Vernal's doctor had discharged him three days ago, and moved him to a recovery centre.

By noon, when I still hadn't heard from Hooker, I decided to drive to Mercy to visit Grace myself. Rainy and Frenchy wanted to come for the ride, but the twins had found *The Simpsons* on TV and insisted on staying behind. The HE remained upstairs, guarding the coffin that he had repossessed, picking at the shrapnel trapped beneath his skin.

I'd spent less than twenty-four hours at the Walled Off but already I had started feeling the way I'd felt in prison when I didn't own the keys; I was glad when a guard waved us through the front gate and we were free. I took a back road into Vancouver, to avoid the busy highway, a route that led past the Perpetual Life Pet Cemetery where there had always been more flowers on any given day than in its human counterpart further along the road. It was easier, I supposed, to love something when there was a good chance it wouldn't outlive you.

I switched on the radio where there was nothing but Christmas music, and turned it off again. We stopped at a red light as we headed into the downtown core and I watched a garbage bag being buffeted about, caught in a whirlpool of air, a lost soul trapped in the centre of the intersection. Rainy wanted to jump out and rescue the bag, but then the light turned green and we left it, fluttering and ragged, a wind-grieved ghost in the middle of the road.

Our Lady of Mercy had been built as a mental hospital at the turn of the century, and after that had served as a remand centre, a dismal place where prisoners were held awaiting trial. In recent years it had become a hospital again, with an infamous psychiatric unit and a ward for the criminally insane. It was, too, as Grace had said, the hospital for hardcore addicts.

The parking lot in front of the hospital, reserved for doctors and emergency vehicles, had been built around a fountain in the middle of which a nude boy cavorted with dolphins. The public lot in the back was full, but I found a vacant spot in an area marked Shipping and Receiving, parked and stuck the "On Appointment" sign in the front window. We walked back around to the entrance where two gold-painted lions lay in repose on either side of the steps leading up to the main doors. Rainy asked why the fountain boy's swipe wasn't hard. *Boy's swipe only be publicly hard in kiddie porn on the Internet*, Frenchy told her.

Once inside we passed a gift shop selling an array of forlorn looking objects the mental patients made in their occupational therapy sessions. I bought flowers, blue and green carnations because it was all they had, and went into the waiting room where I took a number and sat in one of the chairs bolted together in multiples of threes. People — it was hard to tell which were patients and which were visitors — stood in little groups around the room. A man in a wheelchair backed into my legs and told me to watch where I was going. *Dudes in wheelchairs they be used to pushin people round*, Rainy said.

A notice on the wall advised that anyone with information leading to the arrest of individuals bringing drugs or other contraband into the hospital should report it at once, "anonymity assured." The hospital, though, seemed to be trafficking in drugs of its own. A poster showed a mother and child skipping together across a flawless stretch of sand. Beneath the grainy photo, a note scrawled in crayon, "Thanks, Paxil. I got my mommy back." Another depicted a woman just out of bed but impeccably groomed, wearing a white terry cloth robe. A marmalade cat, a youthful version of Aged Orange, perched on a shelf above her bathroom sink. The woman breezily tickled the cat's chin with her toothbrush. "A new day. A brighter outlook. Make it happen. The Zoloft morning."

A newspaper lay on the floor under the seat across from me. I drew it towards me with my foot and scooped it up as the receptionist called my number.

I told her I was here to see a friend, Grace Moon, in B-Unit. The woman looked away, somewhere over my left shoulder. "B-Unit's a locked ward, under 24-hour surveillance; only immediate family members can visit a patient there." When I didn't make a move to leave, she looked at me as if I were yet another irksome member of the public trying to make her life difficult. "I can't wait until this day is over," she said, under her breath.

I asked if I could leave a message for Grace, and she shrugged. "Suit yourself. There's no guarantees. Even if it gets to her, and I can't say it will, doesn't mean she is under any obligation to read it." I said I'd take a chance, wrote "Grace, call home," and printed the phone number underneath.

Bitch and a tampon do the same muhfo job, Rainy said, as we left. *Both be stuck up cunts.*

The story appeared above the fold on the front page of the paper I brought home from the hospital: the charred remains of a man's body had been found on Kliminawhit, in a wooded area near the Port of Mystic. Anyone with information should call the RCMP Homicide Division.

I wondered if Hooker had seen the article, thought of what he'd said the night I'd left him at the dump: *don't worry, I always clean up after myself.* I tried not to think the worst as I busied myself for the rest of the afternoon emptying my mother's cupboards of everything from her ninety-six-piece Wedgewood Dinner Service ("some chipped") to a box of toast caddies that needed replating. My mother had loathed the idea of people running their hands over her beautiful things once she had shuffled off, and here I was, doing what she had had reason to dread; my task was to reduce my mother's life to a series of inventories — what to keep, what to be sent to the auction, what would be donated to charity and redistributed to the needy.

I put aside a box labelled Hurt Books (my mother had not been the sort of person to pass up a book, or anything else in this life, because it had been damaged), and another of the empty picture frames she had bought at rummage sales, hoping to fill them with photographs of the grandchildren she never had. If I had learned anything from my mother it was how to appreciate everything that mattered to me, before it was gone. So much of what helped us through our lives, the things we really cared about, were things we took for granted, until they broke or stopped working: only then did we started paying attention to them. I remembered dropping a Venetian glass vase Vernal had given me, then weeping over the pieces. I had never realized how beautiful it was until it was on its way to the ground.

I knew I had a lot to learn from the earless teacup, the silver teaspoon I had bent, as a child, trying to scoop rock-hard ice cream into a bowl, the wayward thread on a lacy tablecloth's hem. Now I had to glue a handle on the teacup, unbend the spoon, tie off the thread on the hem. I would have to give these broken things a new life, and in doing so, find a simple gladness in my own, and learn to feel grateful.

But would I ever find the time to reshape the wire coat hangers my mother had saved, the ones Vernal had straightened to break into his car when he'd locked himself out? Would I fix the spring on the broken mousetrap, sharpen the blunt nail clippers, restring the badminton racquets, patch the garden hose? My mother had always said even a broken thing of beauty could be a joy forever, but when it came to her cedar chest full of burned out Christmas lights — forever, I decided, would be stretching it; I set them aside for the dumpster. Thinking of the dumpster reminded me again of how I'd dropped Hooker with Al's body at the Mystic dump, how I knew I was somehow more involved than I had ever intended to be. I was, as Vernal would say, "implicated."

I saved a few of my mother's unbroken things with Christmas gifts in mind — an umbrella that still opened and closed, for Rainy, my mother's tortoise shell hair brush, comb and mirror set for Frenchy, and the look-alike china dolls for the twins.

By the end of the afternoon the dining room table was piled high with all the treasures I couldn't throw away, but didn't have room for in my life, like the carpets she'd stored under her bed so they wouldn't fade in the sunlight and the box of pine-scented Christmas candles I remembered from my childhood. My mother had arranged them in the same centrepiece every year, but never lit them — that would have been wasteful. She had stored the candles in the linen closet next to the hot water heater, on top of the expensive linen sheets Vernal and I had bought her, and she had considered too good to use. The candles had melted on the sheets, leaving permanent red and green stains.

I had just opened a shoebox containing my mother's collection of thirty years' worth of Christmas turkey wishbones, when I heard the phone ring. I heard I-5 say, "Will do, I'll pass it on. Sure thing. You got it. We got everything covered. Yeah, yeah, okay boss. I'll give her the 411."

I went into the kitchen as he was hanging up. "The *jefe*," he said, as he picked up where he'd left off, clipping the Bomb's toenails on an unravelling Persian carpet my mother had never allowed us to walk on. I-5 said that ever since Toop had come into their lives his pooch liked to be groomed more frequently.

"And?"

"I already gave him a Xanax a couple of hours ago. He's been getting these hair balls around his, you know, his, you got to wonder what those two are getting up to when we're not looking. He hates it when I start cutting . . . "

"What did Vernal say?" I interrupted. Something in my tone made I-5 look at me in a new way. He put down his toenail clippers and held up his hands in a gesture of surrender.

"Whoooa, killer. Don't get your shirt in a knot. The *jefe's* checked into some place . . . they don't allow contact with family members. Not for the first three weeks, they do some kind of assessment on him."

"What sort of *place*?"

I-5 shrugged. "One of those treatment centre type of deals. You want my opinion, the *jefe* needs a stiff drink, not rehabilitating." He began clipping his own nails even though anyone could see they weren't in need of clipping.

"A drink is the last thing he needs."

He shrugged again. "I got this friend of mine, gave up everything. Pills, booze, crack, junk, even quit smoking. Now he goes to church, his wife's divorced him, and his kids have to leave the property when they want to get high. When you're sober and clean, it's the rest of the world that's fucked."

I realized, as he spoke, that Vernal wasn't doing I-5 a favour by having him live at the Walled Off, it was the other way around. As long as Vernal kept I-5 close, he would always have an excuse to drink and do drugs, especially since he wasn't planning on living forever, as he had reminded me numerous times.

I went upstairs to begin packing up Vernal's office. Frenchy was online explaining to her ALA group that because Step Four had encouraged her to dredge up and relive every nauseating detail of her former life (especially the way she had treated her son) she had decided to skip right ahead to Step Five: "Shared these details with the dead (as we understand them to be) who have begun to manifest themselves in unexpected ways."

The Twin Terrors had driven the HE from the coffin again, and had removed their veils for the first time since manifesting themselves as martyrs-in-waiting; their faces looked at peace. The HE squatted on the opposite side of the room with the pocketful of rocks he had collected from the driveway, trying to drive the twins out of the coffin by throwing the rocks at their exposed heads. Even though he was blind, he was right on target. But the twins never lost their composure, not even when the gravel imbedded itself in their foreheads, or left pockmarks of blood on their cheeks.

Frenchy quit her meeting before it was over to take the HE for a time-out in the hall closet. When they'd gone I began emptying the drawers in Vernal's desk. Vernal had saved every letter he had ever received from me in prison, and tied them together with a length of butcher string. In prison we had relied on letters — both writing and receiving them — to combat the ills of daily existence. The longing I felt for certain letters — those from my family in particular — allowed me to remember what it was like to be real.

I had packed everything but the computer and started down the stairs when I came across Rainy sitting on the landing with a light bulb, like a giant white tear, between her knees. She had been on her way to replace the bulb that had burned out overhead, when she'd heard me coming.

Look like someone et up yo cake, she said, turning the conversation away from herself. I told her it wasn't easy, packing up your dead mother's life, and that Vernal had checked into a residential treatment centre and I wasn't allowed to speak to him.

You make your grave, you lay in it, aight? Rainy said. Rainy didn't have a lot of sympathy for other people's weaknesses, especially those who were wealthy enough they didn't have to steal to get high. *You rich and white you got a dependency problem,* she said. *You go on TV tell everybody you sorry, then check into a place for rich fuckups. You be poor and black with a crack pipe and a gatt you get shook down by the cops, get a beatin laid on you and yo sorry ass be hauled off to jail.*

On Tuesday morning, I-5 woke me from a dreamless sleep. I went downstairs, picking at a shred of skin coming loose along the side of my thumbnail. It peeled away easily, but left a burning sore.

I put the phone to my ear, hoping it would be Hooker, but heard a small voice say, "It's me. Gracie?" the last syllable of her name rising like a question.

"I'm on a different ward, now," she said. "I'm allowed visits. They even let me out of my room to make this phone call."

Rainy didn't want to come to the hospital again, not *twice in one row*. Frenchy said she would take her to do some Christmas shoplifting, and I dropped them at the mall. A true gift, in Frenchy's eyes, was something you personally stole. *You* know *it come from the heart, person take time to steal it for you.*

At the hospital I was informed that even though Grace had been transferred to a lower security unit, I would still have to leave everything I'd brought with me in a locker. I couldn't take items such as money, food, a comb, even a book or magazine, to the detox ward.

I locked up my car key, then followed the overhead signs; the double doors were electronically sealed and when I pushed the buzzer a male nurse peered at me through a wire-thread grid imprisoned in glass. The door opened inward, and the nurse, his face worn, featureless as his uniform, said he would escort me as far as Room C12.

The hall was dark, poorly lit. The only light I could see came from the ruddy glow of an "Exit" sign at the opposite end of the building. When I asked the nurse why the lights were off, he said, in the most matter-of-fact way, that light bulbs got stolen as fast as they could be replaced, their filament wire being just the right size for reaming the #25 needles junkies liked best. "Patients call this ward Drugless, what a joke." When we passed the nurse's station I watched an orderly slip a condom over the mouthpiece of a telephone before putting it to his lips.

The nurse unlocked Gracie's room that had a green sticker on the door — a child in the fetal position, inside an eye shedding a tear. The nurse told me visiting hours were over at three, and locked the door behind me. Even though the room was brighter than the hallway — a barred window took up most of the outside wall — the darkness just got darker. I stood, feeling as if I were a prisoner again myself.

A TV screen hung suspended from the ceiling in the middle of the room where you couldn't reach it to adjust the volume or change the channel, just like the ones we had in our cells at the Facility, only this was tuned to the Weather network. TV, on the Row, had been used as a kind of electric Thorazine: an inmate who practised a slumping vegetable life in front of her TV was a tranquil inmate, cheap to accommodate. "Ladies who don't enjoy watching TV are the ones who get into the most trouble," our care and treatment counsellor had said, when I went to ask her permission to have my television permanently disconnected.

There were four beds in Grace's room, three of them occupied. A girl with half a face looked up at me and moaned, "you pay me first then you take my fuckin' picture." A woman with a birthmark shaped like an inflated kidney bean on her neck lay in the bed next to Grace by the one section of the window that opened; a breeze rippled the shadows of the bars that fell across her body, making her appear fragmented. Grace turned her head when she heard me enter. Her entire being looked sad, even her fingernails and her skin. She had that look people get when they are about to tell you something that will change your life.

Grace, and both the other women, had green stickers on their charts, the same as I'd seen on the door. She made room for me on the bed, told me to sit, and patted her belly as if she were encouraging the life inside her not to give up. I put my hand on top of hers, toyed with the plastic bracelet listing her allergies — penicillin and honey dew melon — on her wrist.

"You're the only one who came," Grace said, after we'd sat in silence. "Hooker said he'd come back, but he didn't. When you look like you're going to die the whole world starts caring about what's going to happen to you. And then, when they save you, they get mad if you say you didn't want to be saved."

"Hooker cares, Gracie."

"Not even."

"I've talked to him. He cares, he just doesn't know how to show it."

Grace said he wouldn't have left her a prisoner on a locked ward if really cared. She said she didn't belong here. They fed her jello salad. The TV never changed, unless you could afford to pay for it. They had installed cubes of ultraviolet light in the bathroom so you couldn't find a vein to shoot up in.

She looked away as she spoke. "They don't trust us. They hate us. They make jokes behind our backs. They think we deserve to get AIDS. They hope we'll die."

I said it wasn't true, everyone wanted her to feel better. Grace said she didn't *want* to feel better. She didn't want to live. She'd rather die a bleeding scabby death in a dumpster alleyway, than live this way. Her eyes came to rest at the bars on her window.

"Hooker cares," I insisted. "You're all he's got."

"Hooker only cares about himself," Grace said. "Strike a match on his soul, he wouldn't even flinch."

I sat, not knowing what to say, wanting to ask more about Hooker, wondering how much, if anything, Gracie knew. I told her about Vernal's call. Grace perked up at the mention of Vernal's name, when I said he had checked into a dry-out centre on the north shore.

Grace said she knew how he felt. She'd been in and out of detox most of her life. "The last time I checked in I thought this is crazy, I don't need this.

"The guy I was with, he wanted to stay high. When they wouldn't give him his keys he left on foot, towing his suitcase behind him down the road. I looked around the place and I started getting this wrong idea that I didn't need anybody's help, I could get clean again all by myself. I had will power. I called home. 'Naha,' I said, 'come and get me. No one here has any teeth.'

"'Have you looked in a mirror lately?' my *naha* says. I looked in the mirror. I didn't have any teeth, either!"

Grace gazed somewhere beyond me. "One guy in that place, he lit himself on fire. I'm the one who found him — I tried to put him out. Normal people, when they burn, they burn with a blue flame. When a heroin addict burns . . . well . . . the flames are green."

I'd been locked in the room with her for less than five minutes when another nurse came in, ostensibly to check Grace's blood pressure and take her temperature, but in fact, Grace told me after she left, to see if I had brought drugs with me that Grace hadn't had time to hide. The nurse looked in the drawer in the table beside Grace's bed, flipped through a stack of old magazines — including the *Newsmakers* with my face on the cover — and a Bible, checked under her tongue, and between her legs, then narrowed her eyes at me. Who else but another drug user, her eyes said, would be visiting an addict on Drugless?

"Any problem with your medication?" the nurse asked Grace, still looking at me as if I were a bad influence.

"I already told you," said Grace, "there's a problem. I keep telling everyone, I don't want to take it."

The nurse ignored her, as if she knew what was best, and handed Grace a small white paper cup with a hexagonal orange pill in the bottom, and a round white one. She waited until Grace went through the motions of putting them in her mouth and swallowing.

As soon as the nurse was gone, Grace spat the pills out and gave them to the woman with the birthmark on her neck. "She'll swallow anything," Grace said, "even if she has to chew it first."

She lowered her voice. "You bring anything, a pick-me up? Coke? Percocets? They don't let you have painkillers in here. It might make you feel less worse."

I got off the bed and went and stood by the window, looking down into the courtyard where two men in sky-blue pyjamas were planting plastic flowers in the dirt, blossoms first.

"Hooker killed Al, didn't he," Gracie said, suddenly, but as if it had been on her mind all along. "It doesn't matter now," she said, before I could reply, "He didn't pay his way. He didn't even pay for his toilet paper. I'm glad he's dead now. I wouldn't have been able to say that a month ago."

Grace asked me for the pencil that was in the drawer beside her bed, and to pass her the Bible. She tore a page out of the New Testament and wrote on it, then folded it into a tiny square and told me, using hand signals, to put it somewhere safe and read it later. Then she asked if I could bring her the bedpan because it hurt too much to get out of bed. She pulled the sheet off and pushed away the pillows she'd placed on her belly. Gracie looked like Baby-Think-It-Over, her body emptied out.

"Oh my God, Grace," I whispered. "What happened?"

"I lost him," she said. She raised her eyes to the sticker on her chart. "That's what you get when you lose a baby here." She made a face. "It means you're on suicide watch."

I stood there holding the bedpan, not knowing what to do. At first I thought she meant her baby had died at birth, but then Grace said they came for him in the middle of the night, gave her an injection, and when she woke up she saw her baby's soul squeeze out between the bars on the window, and fly up into the air.

"Heroin makes you the loneliest person on earth," she said.

She thought she knew everything there was to know about loneliness until they took away the one thing that might have mattered to her, the small piece of heaven that had popped out of her like a shiny lifesaver.

Grace asked me to find Hooker. He had promised her, if they took her baby away, he would get him back.

The light was beginning to fail as I drove into the downtown eastside. Every plywood wall that had been erected around a condemned building; every brick wall overlooking a vacant lot; each lamppost, hydro pole and garbage can was a frenzy of Missing posters — the older ones choked out as the more recent fought for their own fifteen minutes of breathing space — pictures of missing women who had, long ago, become lost in the helpless privacies of their beings. As I waited at a stoplight I saw a poster of a "Missing" boy: he looked as if someone had told him "smile if you know what's good for you," when all he wanted to do was cry. "Lick Me Diddle Me," had been scribbled across his face.

I passed a pawnshop, with a baby's car seat and high chair in the window. There was nowhere I could go any more, nowhere that wasn't emptied of meaning, of love.

I hadn't read the note Grace had scrawled on the scrap of paper, addressed to Hooker at the Outer Planet Hotel, until I'd been alone: "Help me, pleas." I parked in a Commercial Loading Zone a block away from the hotel and when I got out I realized the socially disadvantaged types who might have been thinking of mugging me were instead eyeing me with a mixture of curiosity and fear. I placed the "On Appointment" sign in the window and walked, purposefully, as if going about some deadly business, past the panhandler whose tongue lolled from his mouth in a wad of flesh, past the woman sleeping half-naked in the back of a pickup full of empty beer cans, past a row of dark, unloved apartment blocks. I kept my face closed and, as I walked, people moved away from me, even crossed to the other side of the street, as if I had one of those diseases you can catch from standing too close to another person. There was no sign of the impending Christmas debacle in this part of town, no flashy displays of lights, no halls decked with anything but misery, though there were "negativity scenes", the bona fide kind, in every doorway. In many ways I felt more at home here, more vibrantly alive (my mother would have called it having a taste for the gutter) than I did at the Walled Off or even at the farm. I worried that, having lived in prison for so many years, I would never be satisfied, now, to live a life rich with possibility and choice.

I read the fading words, "Rooms for Rent in the Outer Planet: Hourly and Weekly Rates", in a ground floor window and went inside. Someone had screwed a red light bulb into a socket in the ceiling above the counter, a concession to the season, I guessed, or a clue — for those who couldn't read the sign — as to what kind of negotiations went on behind closed doors. *Not five diamonds, but nice.* I looked around, but couldn't see anybody, and was about to ring the bell when I smelled smoke coming from the other side of the counter. I looked down and saw a man in a wheelchair, a cigarette between his lips, sucking smoke in through his teeth.

"I'd like to speak to the manager," I said, before realizing the nametag he wore said Manager. He reached up and stubbed out his cigarette in an ashtray full of what looked like pubic hair, and the lobby filled with another, more disturbing odour.

"Some towns adopt a highway. Mine adopted a minefield," he said, assessing me with the expression a marksman might have, concentrating on his target in a firing range. "That's supposed to be a joke," he said. "My sick idea of a joke, anyway." He toyed with the fringe of the blanket covering his lap. From the way the blanket hung, I could tell he had lost both legs. I looked away, behind him to where I could see rows of room keys hanging on hooks.

"What can I do you for?"

I said I was looking for a friend, Hooker Moon.

"Everybody's looking for somebody," he said, smiling enough to show off his yellow stumps of teeth. He looked like the sort of man who smiled as a tactic, not because he felt there was anything worth smiling about. I opened Vernal's wallet, found a fifty-dollar bill, and smoothed it out on the counter.

The manager reached for the bill, inspecting it to see if it was a fake, then set it down on the ashtray. "Native guy? Long hair? Good-looking? Yeah, he was here. Stayed one night and then left. Never saw him again." He looked at his watch as if he expected it to back him up. "Police came looking for him, wanted to ask him a few questions. I think it was yesterday. He done something I should know about?"

I said I had a message for Hooker from his sister.

"Yeah, well, he seemed like a regular guy to me," the manager said.

I took a card with the hotel's phone number on it from a chipped dish on the counter, and left. When I got back to the hearse I didn't feel like going home right away, so I drove out to the university and parked on a cliff-top with a view of the ocean, thinking of Kliminawhit, how Hooker had been right, that life had been so much simpler there.

§ § §

Rainy and her twins lay sprawled in front of the television watching *The Simpsons.* "Aren't we forgetting the true meaning of Christmas?" Bart said, as I locked the front door. "You know, the birth of Santa Claus?"

Rainy's eyes were half-closed in her head that seemed to have come unattached from her shoulders. When she heard me come in she said she was going upstairs to say her prayers and I said I'd go with her, but when I went to switch on the light on the staircase, nothing happened. I looked up, saw the bulb had been removed, and remembered I'd found Rainy getting ready to change it, earlier in the day. I thought of the hospital and the nurse saying how many light bulbs got stolen. Frenchy was online chatting with the founding member of her ALA group.

What he do, anyway, get hisself killed on down? Rainy snapped at her, as if she resented Frenchy having anyone else in her life.

Frenchy shrugged. *Most likely gatt some white boy. Nigga blow away another nigga, they look at it like he doing the world a favour.*

Rainy knelt down by the window and began reciting her version of The Lord's Prayer.

. . . .And cut me some slack, Blood
So's I be doin' it to dem dat diss me
Don't be pushing me into no jive
And keep dem muhfos away

Cause you always be da man, G,
Straight up, Ahhhhh, man, Ahhhhh, man . . .

Frenchy waited until she said her final *Ahhhhh, man* before saying she should listen to Step Eleven instead of investing any more hope in prayers: "Understood (through our prayers never being answered) that there is no God, that we are born alone and that we die alone and in between being born and dying there is nothing but isolation."

You smokin like an old pistola, Rainy said. *Holy Spit-it be everywhere, big time, best believe.*

I went to bed and fell asleep right away, but then woke an hour later from a nightmare. I stumbled from my mother's bed, found my way upstairs and cracked open the door to the room where Rainy and Frenchy slept. The twins lay at rest in their coffin and the HE squatted by the window, not sleeping, but with his eyes closed against the need to meet mine. Rainy lay spread out across the bed, grinding her teeth the way Toop did, Frenchy beside her with tampons protruding from her ears.

I heard weeping, and when I went back into the hallway I realized the sound was coming from inside myself. I buried my face in my hands, and the crying only came harder. Nothing I could think of would stop it, and after a while I didn't even try.

I-5 came upstairs when he heard me. He was high: I could tell from the way his eyes slitted around the hall to see what had upset me. I told him, through my tears, that I must have had a nightmare that I'd been smoking freebase cocaine again, because I had smelled it so strongly it had wrenched me from my sleep. "You live long enough you become like the rest of us. Unrehabilitable," I-5 said.

He put his hands up over his head in what was getting to be a familiar gesture of surrender, then lowered his arms and gave me a look only another addict would recognize. "Sometimes life just seems to be going on for such a long time. Polish off some of your hurt?"

That's all it took. I got to my feet and followed him down the stairs.

In the kitchen I-5 poured me a *tinto* — sweet black coffee — in a tiny cup, and then produced a bottle of licorice-flavoured *aguardiente,* from a cabinet. I hadn't tasted either since Tranquilandia where each day began with *el blanco y negro,* two big rails of cocaine and a tiny cup of *tinto.* I would cut out my white lines and drink my coffee, and let the rest of my life, the world, float away. I wanted only to feel the hum in my veins, the freeze creeping into my gums, the *nosola* burn, the bitter tang of cocaine mucus down the back of my throat.

I sipped the thick black coffee. I-5 took a flap from his wallet, and laid out four white lines as long and straight as the Interstate highway, the one he'd been nicknamed after, that ran the length of Florida. I knew at once I was in trouble by the way my mouth watered and my palms began to sweat.

I-5 called it "hitching up the reindeer." Outside I could hear the wind getting up as if it had decided to come inside, where the party was, and join us. On the wind's heels a light snow drifted in through an open window and melted around my head in a cloud of breath.

You never understand the nature of the drug, you only understand the sorrow. Somewhere deep in my old brain there must have been a memory stored from the first time I ever did a line and cocaine had become my fate, my sweet annihilating angel.

I didn't get to bed that night because after we had cooked up and smoked what was left in the flap, I-5 went to his stash in the basement and came back with more.

Vernal had always said I had a sensible streak, but there is nothing sensible about cocaine. I only used what I needed which was, of course, an immeasurable amount. That is to say, if there was any in the room I couldn't let it go unused, but the minute I'd done a line I wanted to be straight again, and then I'd do another line, and another, until it was all gone and I found some sort of peace in coming down. Meanwhile every line I snorted, every base toke I took, helped obliterate my life.

When I opened my eyes late the next day, got out of bed and stumbled up to Vernal's office, full of remorse, I found Frenchy where I could count on finding her, at the computer. Rainy sat on the floor with Say Muh's head in her lap, going through her hair with the fine-toothed flea comb I-5 used on the Bomb, looking for lice. Ever since the twins had removed their veils they'd been scratching at themselves, she said. I told her it might help if she tried washing their hair once in a while.

Frenchy said *shhhhhh* because she couldn't concentrate with us distracting her, conversationally. Frenchy had reached the Twelfth Step: "Having reached a state of spiritual exhaustion as the result of all the other steps we've taken, we were ready to carry our message to others who were newly dead and looking for a way to live well in the afterlife."

So many steps, only two feet, Rainy said, sulkily. *What you gon do now, you finish settin your wreckful life right?*

Frenchy looked up at her, and shook her head. *Shoot bullets through me, why don't you?*

Rainy shrieked — she knew this always got Frenchy's attention — hitting a pitch that caused the computer screen to crack, from one side to the other. Rainy took hold of the twins by their hair and went back downstairs.

She be high as a nigga pie, Frenchy said, confirming my worst fears.

I went down to join Rainy who was watching the noon news. I had missed the beginning of the story but caught, " . . . believed the child's mother, who may have had outside help, kidnapped the premature baby who was being kept in a Natal Intensive Care Unit and left the hospital early this morning. A hospital spokesperson said, 'We have checked the area thoroughly and there is nothing to indicate that the child is actually lost, other than the fact that he is missing.'" The reporter said the baby had been under the protection of Human Resources and was in the process of being adopted, that the infant's birth mother was an intravenous drug user who was being held under observation at Mercy, and that the missing baby was now the centre of a city-wide hunt.

Rainy sniffed, pressing her nose flat with her forefinger the way she used to do in the Facility to show she was not pleased with the world. *You jack what belong to you, they still call it stealin?*

I said most people would see it that way. Grace was one of those about whom others say, "she should never have been a mother."

I heard the phone ring, got up and went into the kitchen, just as I-5 was hanging up. "We got a situation," he said. "Let's go. Right now. Fast."

§ § §

The twins wanted to watch TV, so Rainy said they could stay behind again. The HE had changed into a clean, white robe, covered his head with his black and white checkered scarf, and put on the green bandana with the Arabic lettering. His eyes, for once, looked beatific, as though his soul resided, already, in another place.

As we piled into the hearse, Toop came around the corner of the house, the dirt-encrusted body of the headless Baby-Think-It-Over in his mouth. Rainy wrenched it from him, and clutched it to her own damaged body.

I-5 kept giving me directions, even though I knew where to go. Frenchy tried to restrain the HE as he flew from one side of the hearse to the other, gulping down the fast-paced downtown air, as if he had been starved for chaos.

When we reached the centre of the city nearly every parking lot had been cordoned off by yellow crime-scene tape in the aftermath of the Marilyn Manson concert. I no longer recognized where I was. The neighbourhood had changed since the days the legal crowd had frequented the restaurants and I had joined Vernal at the Hung Jury Inn, with prosecutors and other defence lawyers, for long boozy lunches. Now the local businesses had more bars on their windows than your average Death Row facility.

I-5 pointed to a vacant spot in front of the Salvation Army. I parked, and he went to open the passenger door, but a woman on crutches, wearing fire-engine red boots up to her crotch blocked his way, and made a sign for him to roll down his window. Her skin was a urinous yellow, her nose brimming with doper's drip. She asked if he had a cigarette, or five dollars for bus fare, and he shook his head. "Not for you I don't, sweetheart."

"What about crutches, you need crutches?" she asked, ignoring him and turning her attention to me. "I can get a good pair, cheap. I give you a deal."

"Does she look like she needs crutches, she's driving, ain't she?" I-5 opened his door and the woman stepped backwards, mumbling "fuck you very much," then crumpled to the sidewalk as if her bones had been pulled out from inside her legs.

I put the "On Appointment" sign on display in the window, got out and locked the doors. I glanced at a plaque: Salvation Army was invented to save souls, to grow saints, and to serve suffering humanity. It was hard to imagine any kind of saint growing or thriving in a neighbourhood such as this one. *Look like everyone fall out of an ugly tree and get broke by branches on they way to the ground,* Rainy said.

The smell of cigarette smoke hung in the air. We had to run the half block to keep up with I-5, who disappeared inside a McDonald's whose golden arches had long ago fallen. A sign on the temporary plywood door read, "Sorry For Our Appearance. We are Undergoing a Face Lift".

A girl, presumably a server, leaned on the counter, twitching. A man with the top of his head wrapped in bleeding newspaper sat at a corner table collecting his spit in a wide-mouthed Mason jar. A woman stood over him, pulling his ear, saying, "Dave, I thought you loved me? Dave?"

At that moment the HE, who had come in after Frenchy, twisting at a piece of shrapnel under his skin, started going *glock-glock-glock* clutching at his throat. He made the same coughing-up-a-massive-hairball sound I was accustomed to hearing, accompanied now by an even more heroic clearing of lungs, a gurgling sound, like the death rattle issuing from the throat of a dying man. But this time, as he blew his nose over and over again into his *kaffiyeh*, a projectile that had struck him between his eyes and lodged itself above his nose all those years ago, flew out and landed at Frenchy's feet. The HE slapped his head hard, only once, with his open hand, and then stopped, opened his eyes, and stared at his mother as if seeing her for the first time.

Frenchy fell to her knees on the floor before her son, telling him she had never given up hope that he would find his way back to her. Even though the HE had regained his sight, he couldn't hear her. He just went on smiling down at Frenchy with that half-embarrassed smile the dead get, as if they're sorry to be a burden on you, for the grief you're going to get.

You go ahead, girl, Frenchy said to Rainy. *I catch up widju later.*

I-5 headed straight through the building to the door leading into the alley behind the restaurant. Rainy hustled me outside in time to see I-5 reach into a dumpster and pull out a green garbage bag. He opened it, looked inside, then told me to have a peep: I saw a baby, wrapped in crime-scene tape like a tiny mummy, with his head poking out, sucking a pacifier that had been fixed in place with duct tape so he couldn't cry and draw attention to himself.

The baby looked up at me. He had Angel's caramel eyes — eyes that at first just looked warm, but which, like little windows in furnace doors, only gave a glimpse of the heat inside.

I-5 made kissing noises as he lifted the baby out of the bag. I unzipped my jacket, tore open my shirt, and loosened the yellow tape from around his body. When his arms were free, he balled his hands into fists and began pummelling the air, like Angel used to do.

I removed the duct tape and took the pacifier from his mouth, then tucked him inside my shirt, and held him against my bare chest like a piece of my mother's bone china, one with a hairline crack that might break all the way if you looked at it too long, or too hard. I felt peaceful, suddenly, and whole again, having him there, as though a part of me that had gone missing had been temporarily restored.

"Youngster could have starved to death," I-5 said, giving the baby a proprietary look. He turned the bag upside down and a plastic baby-bottle, a jar of Coffee-Mate, and a note saying, "Feed me, pleas," fell out. I recognized the scrawl.

This be Son Jesus come back early for his birthday, Rainy cried, as she danced around me, swinging Baby-Think-It-Over high over her head, reciting snippets of nursery rhymes because she was too excited to remember any of them all the way through: *Rock-a-bye Jesus, Be hip-hoppin up da hill, Son he felt down, An busted he ass, the whole muhfo crib rock on.*

The baby fixed Rainy with an open-mouthed stare. When his eyes shifted their focus onto the headless doll, his face, for a moment, became pinched — he seemed to be trying to make up his mind whether he should be afraid or amused — his eyes darting from the doll's severed neck to the centre of its gutted body. His decision made, a frown pulled down the corners of his mouth, his bottom lip began to quiver, and he began to wail. There was no consoling him. He continued to scream until Rainy stuffed Baby-Think-It-Over in the garbage bag, and tossed it in the dumpster. It was as if he had sensed, in that headless, emptied out body, what could have been his fate.

Rainy asked if it was safe to touch him, and when I said "go ahead" she reached inside my jacket to rub his shiny head. She said he looked hungry, that we should stop and pick up a pizza on our way back to the house.

"Babies don't eat pizza," I said. "You have to have teeth."

Even the ghost of a dog got teeth. Babies don't eat pizza, what they do eat? Rainy stared at me as if the baby might be better off scavenging in a dumpster than having me as a mother. I thought of my own son, how I had watched him sicken, grow thin, his eyes as big as mouths, his heart all hunger. I didn't know anything about taking care of babies, then. I could hardly take care of myself, let alone a hapless child who needed me.

"Milk," I said. "Babies need milk."

♊ ♊ ♊

With the child snug against my chest, I walked back inside the restaurant, with Rainy and I-5 right behind. The place had emptied, and Frenchy stood frozen by the front entrance where the HE was going *glock-glock-glock*, his eyes as fixed on Frenchy as the eyes of a newly dead person. Even by his own standards the HE didn't appear normal.

As I watched, he began to peel off layers of his clothing. I realized then what Frenchy's boy was about to do.

Beneath his robes he wore a vest that covered his entire upper body, a vest lined with cylinders of explosive. He started counting backwards from ten, at the same time fingering the on-off switch on the belt.

The height of bliss comes with the end of countdown then boom! You sense yourself floating to another life.

Bounce! Now! Out of his way, Frenchy screamed, the words cutting through me like a blade of cold wind. I broke open the doors, dragging Rainy after me.

We hit the pavement and rolled into the street, just as I heard the dry *ker-boom* of the detonation. The echo of the blast continued to hang in the air for a moment before everything became so quiet it seemed as if the explosion had blown away all other sound with it. I turned and saw clouds of dust rising from the site where the fast food outlet had stood, and the remains of the fluorescent sign saying, "Billions and Billions Served".

🖐 🖐 🖐

Neither Rainy nor I spoke as we drove. Frenchy, I assumed, was dead all over again, and I-5 hadn't made it out, either. All I could think of was getting away. Whenever we came to a red light I reached over and slid my little finger into the baby's tiny grasping hand.

I could hear sirens. Rainy held the baby in one arm as fiercely as she had held Baby-Think-It-Over. He was still loosely wrapped in crime-scene tape, but he had kicked free his skinny little legs, and wriggled with life, as if he could swim through the air. I saw no fear in his eyes, just a question, but then I looked at him again and thought, wasn't he too new to be capable of forming a question? One lazy eyelid fluttered like the heartbeat of a baby bird and his tiny mouth stretched into a lopsided O, so much like Angel, my heart did a double flip.

Rainy's mind, I could tell, was on Frenchy. When I went to touch her hand, she put her free arm around my shoulders. *Way I see it, Frenchy catch up wid us later, just like she say. Best believe.*

I didn't answer, kept my eyes trained on the road.

I look at you, don't see no waterworks, Rainy said. *You see me cryin tears?*

I wanted to tell her, sometimes we cry with everything *except* tears, but I kept quiet.

Frenchy be dead again, we both be spoutin, Rainy continued, studying the baby's wrinkled face.

She said this as we came upon a billboard, plain, white, with 1 CROSS + 3 NAILS = 4 GIVEN in red. I remember Grace saying her baby was a gift, a hard gift to accept but one she'd forgiven the rapist for bestowing upon her. Staring up at that billboard then, I knew what her baby's name was going to be.

§ § §

There was no convincing Rainy that Coffee-Mate wasn't a reasonable substitute for mother's milk. "Babies drink milk," I told her over and over again, until we reached the mall where I stopped to buy formula and diapers. Formula, I tried to explain, was what you used when you couldn't produce your own milk.

When we got back to the house, and the twins saw Given, they abandoned *The Simpsons* and took turns holding him, as if they had finally discovered something more interactive than bombs *or* TV. When they hugged him, Given squeaked. The Bomb must have figured that Given was a life-size toy; he got so excited when he saw the baby he wagged his whole body and put his tail out of joint. Toop lowered his eyes and looked away, like a boy with a crush on his first grade teacher.

Rainy drew Given a bath, singing *Way Down in Bath-I-Am,* while I fixed a bottle and made a sling out of a towel. "I've got something else for you," I whispered, as he gulped down the warm milk. I reached into my jacket pocket for the shoe, saw Given curling his toes the same way Angel always did whenever I tried to slip his foot into one of his little boots.

The shoe fit beautifully, as if it had been hand-tooled for his foot alone. Rainy spun around and disappeared upstairs, returning with a parcel she had been keeping for me, she said, underneath the bed. She insisted I open it now, even undid the tape for me, being careful not to tear the motivational gift wrap depicting a deserted beach and a lyrical sunset.

The beach looked like the one Hooker had taken me to on Kliminawhit. I peeled back the paper and began lifting the lid of the box, cautiously, as if something might be waiting to jump out at me. Rainy couldn't contain herself. She grabbed the box from my hands, tore off the lid, and held up the shoe, identical to the one I had found that day in the sand. I wiggled Given's foot into it — the perfect match to the smallest running shoe ever made.

Rainy, I could tell, was pleased with her gift. She'd found it in an odd-size bin at the Athlete's Feet and Frenchy had had no problem pocketing it. She beamed as she went through the Moses basket for baby clothes, then helped me unwrap the remainder of the crime-scene tape from Given's body. I showed her how to test the bathwater, with her elbow, to make sure it was the right temperature before lowering him in.

I remembered the first time I'd given Angel a bath, how hard I'd fought to keep hold of his skinny arms and legs, slippery as cooked spaghetti. Then I'd taken him into bed with me — something I'd been afraid to do lest I rolled over on top of him in my sleep — and felt so — glad. Such a small thing, but you don't always know what will make you glad when you think back on it. Or what you will wish you had done differently.

Back then I thought my choices would always be in front of me. Now it felt like the important events of my life had already happened, and when I conjured up Angel I pictured a little ghost, weighing less than a puff of wind. Most of the catastrophes I had suffered in my life had never happened but losing my child was one catastrophe that *did,* and I had been willing to forfeit my life for him. I'd wanted to die so badly at one time because then I could have joined him in that black, unappeasable earth under the guaiac tree, the Tree of Life.

Toop barked once; it startled Given enough to make him open his eyes wide, and look at me to see if either of us were in any danger, as if he wanted the world to continue a while longer just so we could be together. The Bomb sat poised at the bathroom door, ready to leap into the water and rescue him, if I gave the word.

Given's tiny body seemed dwarfed by the ocean of the bathtub; I held on to him so tightly he must have felt my fear. I cupped his head in one hand, to keep it out of the water, and squeezed a sponge over him with the other, then plucked him from the bath, dried him off, and balanced him on the palm of my hand, where he quivered like a soap bubble. It felt so fine — to be able to hold all that mattered to you in the palm of one hand.

Vancouver's first suicide bombing was all over the six o'clock news. Rescue crews had recovered a green bandana with *Allah Akhbar* on it. This meant, "Our God is better than your God," the reporter explained with the breathlessness of a sports announcer caught in the spirit of competition. A police officer was interviewed saying, "There is no way to stop 'these people' once they make up their minds. What are we supposed to do? Threaten to shoot if he blows himself up? We're dead if we do, dead if we don't," as if suicide bombing had become a feature in our lives. The camera panned to workers at the Sally Ann covering their windows with bombing net, and a dumpster filled to the brim with broken glass.

A priest tried to make sense of the event from a religious extremist's point of view. "We can't stop it. A living person, to these people, they're nothing. As a dead person you can become a hero. It doesn't make any difference to him anymore whether he's shot dead while throwing stones or he blows himself up." A municipal worker said they were considering padlocking all the garbage cans in the downtown core so people couldn't leave their bombs in them. "All they have to do is push a button that will trigger the time mechanism so it will explode an hour later. They have time to get away."

A bystander who had been to Jerusalem on a bus tour was interviewed as an expert. "The worst thing is when someone blows himself up in a bus: it takes weeks for you to escape from the smell of burnt flesh. You never forget it." A soldier who'd been on a peacekeeping mission in Afghanistan said, "It's hard to believe the dawn of civilization began over there. They don't even have a McDonald's." A panhandler, with a Starbucks cup full of the spare change he'd earned said he thought the problem had to do with immigration, and that "whoever did this should be consequenced."

Rainy kept quiet as we watched, holding the twins close. She said she would clean out their coffin so Son Jesus would have a place to crib, but I told her I didn't want to see another baby in a coffin again, ever, and laid him in the Moses basket Gracie had woven for him. Rainy cried *yo!* and I looked up in time to see Gracie's picture flash across the screen.

A police officer said he hoped Grace would give herself up. "We want to help her, to get help for her as best we can." Anyone with information was asked to call the number that flashed across the bottom of the screen.

Rainy snorted. *Since when they want to help anyone? They rather bust her ass. Haul her sorry ass off to jail where cops eat Score bars in front of her when she be jonesin and sick. I never seen any situation so bad cops don't make it worse.*

Given squeaked and Toop stuck his nose in the basket, sniffing. He licked dribbled formula from Given's chin. Given didn't object; he wasn't a complaining baby.

The professional couple who'd planned on adopting the newborn declined all interviews. They'd been through enough, their lawyer said. After the lawyer, a social worker said they were concerned only for the welfare of the baby who was withdrawing from crack cocaine and cried all the time.

That be a lie, Rainy said, indignantly. *Son Jesus never cry, he only squeak.* She told me not to worry, once everyone realized the baby wasn't white, she said, they would stop caring about his plight. Not too many people were interested in trying to save a crack-addicted Indian baby.

I shifted Given in my arms. He had hold of a strand of my hair, the way Angel used to grab on to it, and was twisting it around in his fingers. When I gazed at Given I still felt Angel's spirit, connected to me by something deeper than blood.

When you are born, if you are one of the lucky ones, you begin your life at the mercy of two people who love you. Good luck, I knew from experience, was often just as baffling as the bad, but Given stared up at me again the way Angel used to do, as if to say never stop believing in the goodness of this world. From now on he would have me to love him, and, looking at him, I knew *I* was the lucky one.

Toop missed Hooker, I could tell. I would catch him sitting by the gate, his head cocked to one side, his eyes watchful. When it began to grow dark he would come to the back door, scratch at the screen, and I'd let him in. I'd tell him we were going home soon, and he would lie down, his face on his paws, and try his best to act as if there was nothing missing in his world.

The Bomb, given to spells of nervous fatigue, spent hours swooned on the loveseat in the sunroom. When this didn't get Toop's attention he would dart madly from room to room flinging himself into walls and against the furniture, barking at empty corners. After sniffing the floor in the kitchen where I-5 had stood, opening can after can of sardines, he spit up on the loveseat, chewed the telephone cord, snarled at the television, his food, or nothing at all.

At night Given slept in the Moses basket beside me and during the day I carried him, facing me, in the sling I had made — he liked the view from my shoulder. Having Given to care for and to love helped me as I waited for a call — from Hooker, Grace, or even Vernal — but by Monday I'd heard from no one. Missing the ones I loved had been, for years now, a kind of grieving for me, the grief being so much worse when the ones I missed weren't dead, but simply gone elsewhere.

When I finished clearing out the rooms upstairs, I went down to the basement. Given dozed on my chest; I sniffed the top of his head that gave off a warm, sleepy fragrance. My mother's freezer had been shoved to a far corner to make room for I-5's oddments that included boxes of dog food, canned sardines, back issues of Martha Stewart *Living*, cases of California wine, burlap sacks full of marijuana seeds, and a 12-gauge shotgun along with three boxes of shells.

I found the urn, after much searching: either Vernal or I-5 had packed it in an ice cream bucket that was nestled between a package of Pizza-Pops and a cracked Ziploc container of applesauce, and lifted my mother — who now weighed slightly less than a bowling ball — from the cold. I was about to close the lid when I remembered I-5 going down into the basement and coming back up with more cocaine. I had convinced myself I'd only had a "nice little relapse", that one night when

I-5's reindeer flew me somewhere I hadn't planned to go. I'd told myself, "no more, never again". But in my heart, even as I said these words, I knew it was too late. Many years ago I had stopped wanting cocaine. From that point on it had wanted me.

At the bottom of the freezer I-5 kept an addict's Emergency Preparedness Kit — a bottle of Irish whiskey, a pound (at least) of BC bud, a selection of good Cuban cigars, and three ounce-bags of cocaine. If the end of the world ever came, I-5 had not planned to live through it straight.

I took the baggies upstairs to stash under the receiving blankets at the bottom of Given's Moses basket. Rainy and her twins were watching a Christmas special on the Faith channel. A man, whose face was as shady as the Shroud of Turin, said Jesus and the Virgin Mary's divinity was so blatant, their souls so expansive that when they died their spirits were distilled into atoms, and they coated the world, the way teflon coats a frying pan. He said it was time to take another break, "don't go away we'll be to be right back with our viewer's personal stories of Jesus and Mary sightings."

I returned to the basement for my mother's remains, then sat at the kitchen table, placing her next to me on a chair, as if she were a guest who had dropped by for tea. When I heard Rainy and her twins heading for the kitchen, I got up and made formula for Given who had woken from his nap and seemed to sense my somber mood.

The twins had manifested themselves back into their red mist and Rainy was gnawing the ends of her hair. I imagined a knotted tumour of hair taking root and growing in her stomach.

She saw the ice cream tub and reached for a spoon.

"It's not what you think," I said.

GIVEN

§ § §

"Now I've seen everything," Tod, at the rental agency said as he helped me hook up the U-Haul. "Old saying goes, you can't take it with you; you never see a hearse towing a U-Haul . . . " He shook his head, a strand of thin hair falling in his face. "There's got to be a story."

"My mother died," I said. "She was a bit of a pack rat."

"Tell me about it. My mother passed away recently, too," Tod said, in that way people have of deflecting the tragedies of others onto their own. "Of course she didn't die without making the rest of us pay for it. Mothers never do."

"Right," I said. My mother had spent a lifetime refusing to die, by degrees, ever since I could remember — a process that had both wearied and exasperated me in equal measure.

"When mum died dad smashed every window out of the kitchen. It was the start of his healing journey," Tod said, swiping at another renegade strand of hair. He knew it, he said, the very second his mother went into spirit. He felt her soul lifting out her body like when you pry a pit out of an avocado pear.

I'd felt nothing so physical when my mother died. No gust of wind shook my cell or flung open my door as if the keeper had kicked it harder than usual.

I asked Tod how much extra I'd have to pay for dropping the U-Haul at the ferry dock on Kliminawhit. One of his eyebrows shot up. "Kliminawhit, eh? I took my mother there for the weekend, before she forgot who I was and why I was calling her Mother."

While he continued talking I saw the newspaper on the counter. "Investor's Son Victim of Mystery Island Slaying: Couple Sought for Questioning."

"She thought my name was Ted. 'Ted drove me around the Bend,' she liked to joke, but actually it was the other way around. I don't know how many times I told her, 'it's Tod, Mum, not Ted. It's Tod, not Ted'."

I listened with my nerves, not my ears, while I skimmed the article. A shoe, similar to the one the victim had been wearing, had been found, partially buried, after a search had been conducted of a property in the First Nation village of Old Mystic where the victim, Allan Lawrence Porscher, 35, had resided for some time. The victim's girlfriend and her brother were wanted for questioning though neither were considered suspects at this time.

ऄ ऄ ऄ

In the late afternoon, as the sky loomed black in the west, we packed the last of my mother's belongings, the things I couldn't bear to part with, in the U-Haul. I tried, but there was no way I could find room for her television. The moment they saw me pick up the TV to return it to the house, Rainy's twins manifested themselves back into martyrs-in-waiting. They stared at me with eyes almost alive but gazing off in some infinite direction no living eye could follow, made a whistling sound meant to imitate mortars, and pleaded with Rainy, in one voice that was all sweetness — a lid of light over a cauldron of darkness and need — to make room for the TV set even if it meant leaving the dogs behind. Rainy placated them by promising we'd decorate a tree instead, something they could stare at all day, without being interrupted by commercials.

The weather had turned colder; the forecast predicted a white Christmas. I hoped we could make it back to the island before a storm hit and driving became hazardous. Rainy settled the twins, wearing their keys to paradise, in the coffin in the back. Toop and the Bomb had to be forced in the hearse after them, and lay between the rollers looking at me as if I alone were responsible for life's reasonless mess.

Rainy held the ice cream bucket containing my mother's urn on her lap next to Given, who lay on top of my stash in his Moses basket. She insisted we swing by the mall on our way out of town. I parked in the place reserved for Santa's reindeer but kept the motor running. There were still a few "stay beautiful the year round" Christmas trees left, and these had been marked down. Rainy got out, opened the back doors, reached for the closest tree, and tossed it in. A man who looked like he was used to getting paid walked towards us as Rainy vaulted into the front seat and drove her foot down on top of mine on the gas. She didn't remove it until Astoria had disappeared in the rear view mirror.

PART SEVEN

Given the world he created, it would be an impiety
against God to believe in him.
— John Banville, *The Sea*

By THE TIME THE FERRY DOCKED, TWO hours behind schedule, the island lay buried under four feet of snow. Even the protestors had stayed home. The road hadn't been ploughed and we careened from one side to the other. Cedar trees, their branches burdened with snow, bent towards the ground. We passed cars in ditches, and others, featureless white mounds, abandoned at odd angles, in the deep drifts that had accumulated at the side of the road.

Rainy had never seen snow before and wanted to know if it came in any colours other than white. She couldn't wait to see if she could walk on it. *Way Jesus walk on water but don't sink in.*

We drove back to the farm in a whiteout. I set Given on my lap, my seatbelt fastened tightly around both of us, a bottle propped in his mouth. Every so often he tried to stretch, but I had him well wrapped in a blanket so all he could do was exercise the muscles in his face.

The sign at the Christian vegetable stand said, "Lordy, Lordy, Look Who's Dead", the only thing that stood out in a landscape obliterated by snow. *Where his muhfo Chrimas spit-it?* Rainy said. *We stupposed to have peace and earth and goodwill to ward off men.*

We made it up our driveway but a hillock of snow blocked the barn's entrance so I had to park next to the mounting block. If the cold weather kept up we could be stuck here for days. I thought of the pioneers who had built this house, when there was no plow to make roads or driveways passable, and the Yaka Wind people who had lived here before them, who'd had to dig their way out, break paths through the drifts.

Aged Orange was not waiting in his usual place to play chicken with the hearse, and I worried that we had been gone too long, left him to his own resources until he got indignant enough, as cats will do, and taken off to find a more hospitable home. I didn't see any paw prints in the snow as I carried the quaking Bomb up the front steps, thinking of our neighbours in the suburb who kept their lawns heated in winter so they could still let their small dogs outside. I wouldn't be letting the Bomb out until the snow melted. He was too small, too white, and might easily disappear.

I lit a fire in the cookstove, and another one in the living room, where the twins sat on the chesterfield staring at the space where the television used to be. Rainy sat next to them reciting nursery rhymes, and decorating the ice cream bucket containing my mother's ashes with green and red ribbon. I removed the two remaining baggies from underneath Given's blankets, kept a flap for myself and put the rest in a jar to keep it dry, sealed the jar in a Ziploc bag, and hid it outside under the verandah.

I spent the rest of the morning unloading the hearse and sneaking into the bathroom to do lines. I fed the dogs, filled the cat's litter box and put it under the stairs so the Bomb wouldn't make a mistake in the house.

Don't wonder he be queer, Rainy said, *muhfo stupposed do his business in kitty litter.*

I took a break around noon, realizing I'd have to keep the U-Haul for at least another day, and lay down in my room upstairs with Given. I kissed each of his tiny perfect toes, watched as he responded with pleasure. *Nació de pie.* Like Angel, Given had been born on his feet, wary and wise to the ways of the streets before he was old enough to walk them. I used to look into Angel's eyes and think 'he could have picked a pocket or hot-wired a car with those newborn eyes.' Angel's eyes had moved independently of one another, as if he could see, right from the start, he had been born into a world where it was every eye for itself. I think he had learned, while he was still in the womb, to see movement, to sense danger. Given's eyes were more of a team, working in tandem. Where one went, the other quickly followed.

I kissed his eyes and tiny eyebrows, the smell of his skin like the incense of rain. I could feel him growing stronger every day; he lay quietly in his Moses basket, his hands clasped over his heart, as if he were teaching himself to pray. There was a time, before I lost Angel, when I thought prayer would protect you from things that hurt. But the day I left Angel behind, my prayers lost weight, like ashes in a fire, and floated away.

Having Given to care for I had started dwelling on Angel again, in the place inside myself where I kept him alive, in the dark, unloved part of my heart. I lifted Given into a hug, heard the soft moaning of the world inside me mourning itself. Rocking Given back and forth, I knew that Angel was somewhere out there waiting for me to let him go, that the roots of the guaiac tree had worked their way into his sorrowing body, and set his spirit free.

When Rainy came upstairs with the twins she wiped my eyes with a corner of Say Muh's veil and brought me a roll of "cry paper" so I could blow my nose. *Don't matter how many tears you let go, you end up blowing your nose.* It wasn't only tears that were causing my nose to run. I needed to stash my flap of cocaine somewhere other than in the Moses basket where it wouldn't be so easy to reach. As long as I had to walk from one room into another to cut myself a line, I could convince myself I didn't have a problem.

Before it got dark we dressed in the warmest clothing we could find and went back outside so I could show Rainy how to make a snow angel. Rainy decided, after testing the snow with one bare toe, it wasn't safe to walk on anything that white, and stayed in the house, watching me from the doorway. I found a clean patch of snow, and lay down with my hands at my sides, drew them up over my head, then got to my feet, carefully, so as not to disturb the impression.

Rainy had asked me, once, if I'd ever seen a real angel. I said not in the flesh, though there'd been one in the room with me the day my baby was born.

Rainy wanted proof; what proof did I have that an angel actually existed?

How much proof did she need? I asked.

A pair of wings, she said. *Even a feather would do.*

৶ ৶ ৶

After we had eaten, and Given had been bathed, Rainy wanted to trim the tree. While she struggled to get it to stand up straight in a bucket full of rocks, I searched through my mother's boxes for the treasured ornaments she had wrapped in red or green tissue paper, on which she had attached a history of where each one had been purchased, along with the year, and how much it cost. Some of them dated back to my childhood; I remembered being allowed to choose the wooden snake though my father said he couldn't see what a snake had to do with Christ's birthday. When he chose a dill pickle, the following year, I made the same argument, but now, holding the fragile pickle in my hand, I appreciated my father's oddball choice. I hung the pickle at the very top of the tree, where the angel was supposed to be. The papier mâché angel had been eaten by rats the year my mother made the mistake of storing the Christmas decorations in the attic.

I dug out the gifts I had brought with me from the mainland, and arranged them under the tree. Later, when we sat down to listen to the news, Rainy said she would rather watch the snow.

I followed her gaze out the window. A full moon had risen over the trees and hung motionless in the sky like a frozen bloom. In so much brightness I could see the shadow of the smoke from our chimney on the snow. I picked up Given from his basket and carried him to the window where we both stood, bathed in moonlight, until he kneaded his head into my chest his lazy eyelids closing out the light, then carried him upstairs to bed.

I couldn't sleep, and when he had drifted off I got up and set to work cleaning the house. I scrubbed the floors, the walls, the insides of cupboards, scoured both the upstairs and downstairs bathrooms. I dusted, and when Rainy tried to help by sweeping the shadows in each room, it raised even more dust. I watched her trying to sweep the dust into the dustpan; no matter how carefully she swept there was always a thin line of residue that eluded her. The line got smaller and smaller until you couldn't see it anymore, but she knew, and I knew, it was still there. Letting us know there was always more, that the sweeping, the dusting of our lives, would never be finished until our day was done.

And, later still, when her twins lay in their coffin, dreaming, and I lay awake, still unable to sleep, I heard the sound of weeping below my window. I got out of bed and looked out to see Rainy, lying in the snow next to where I had made my snow angel, lifting her arms over her head, bringing them back to her sides, then getting to her feet to see what kind of impression she was made. There was nothing, no sign of her having laid her body down in the snow. She tried again; she tried over and over. Finally she stopped, and looked up at me out of all that white emptiness, and I thought in this moment Rainy had finally come to believe that her life, as she had known it, was over. Rainy understood now that she was dead, and that when death came, it would not go away.

§ § §

The snow fell all through Christmas day. It fell in clumps, hiding the hearse under a downy shroud. It covered the angel I had made and it covered the emptiness where Rainy had lain.

I opened the kitchen door and watched Toop kicking up joyfully in the snow. I wouldn't let the Bomb follow him and he whined at the door for an hour before curling up like an albino cashew nut by the fire in the living room.

I'd stuffed an eggplant, in lieu of a turkey, for our Christmas meal, but when I took it from the oven it looked like a collapsed heart and I didn't have the stomach to enjoy it. Instead I watched Given, dressed in a red velvet one-piece outfit lying in his Moses basket, in the middle of the table like a Christmas centrepiece. His cheeks were fire-engine red to match and he looked uncomfortably hot. I undid the little zipper and let him kick loose, his legs working overtime as if he were trying to run away from this life. Rainy figured I should find someone who'd be like a father figure to Given, someone to teach him Nintendo games and how to program a VCR.

At 9:00 I turned on the news. Police were still investigating Vancouver's suicide bombing, and continued their search for the mother of the baby abducted from Our Lady of Mercy Hospital. A human ear had been found in a paint can outside a Colour Your World paint store in Astoria but police did not believe there was any connection to the kidnapping. Farther afield, in the Persian Gulf, sailors prayed for peace while sweeping the sea for mines. The twins complained that it was better to watch the news on TV instead of trying to listen to it happen on the radio in someplace you couldn't see.

When the news was over I set Given's basket under the tree so he could enjoy the decorations while we opened our gifts: Rainy insisted my mother's urn be allowed to watch as the twins unwrapped the look-alike dolls I had been forbidden to touch. The twins undressed the dolls and drew circles around their eyes with a permanent black marker pen, then chewed off their hair. Say Muh pinned her doll between her knees, and every now and then turned it over and beat its backside with the flat of her hand. Her twin was a little gentler. She stroked her doll's butchered head muttering what sounded like death threats, then laid her, face down, in the woven willow coffin.

They never get the motherin they need, Rainy said, remorsefully. I didn't know if she meant her twins, or the dolls.

Rainy opened the paint scraper Frenchy had stolen for her from the Colour Your World Paint Store so Rainy could scrape the Evolve sign off heathen's cars. Before I let her open her present from me I made her guess what it was. "I'll give you a hint. It's long and it's straight."

Rainy stuck out her lower lip and narrowed her eyes, as if contorting her features helped her think. *A dead leg?* she said.

I had a flash of Al's naked legs as Hooker and I hefted him into the hearse. "Guess again. "It's long, straight, and blue."

A dead leg — wid jeans on?

"Go ahead," I said, "open it."

Rainy ripped apart the shiny red paper. *An underbrella!* she exclaimed, raising my mother's blue umbrella — something my mother would never have done inside the house — and twirling it above her head. *Now it be rainin inside me, but on the outside I be dry.*

Frenchy had even shoplifted presents for the dogs, and we opened these last. Toop got a Santa bandana and a rawhide bone with a green and red ribbon around it; the Bomb a box of animal crackers shaped like humans, and a pair of holiday "rein-dog" antlers.

When Rainy opened the gift I had set aside for Frenchy — my mother's endangered-species vanity set — her face began undoing itself, her mouth moving from side to side. Rainy looked in the wrong side of the mirror, but this time I didn't take it away from her and turn it around. I understood, finally, what she had always known. Rainy had no reflection, the same way she had no shadow or couldn't leave an impression in the snow.

Rainy set the mirror on the floor, picked up the tub containing my mother's ashes, and began shaking it, angrily, as if she had had enough of the hurt she suffered, holding in her secret. That's when she told me she'd seen a vision: Frenchy, with her whole nine fingers and her ugly spot, in my mother's cremated remains.

She'd opened the ice cream container, she confessed, the same day I'd rescued it from the freezer. She'd heard Frenchy's voice, listing off sniper rifles, and prayed the Lord's Prayer that Frenchy would show her face again. Not only did Frenchy reveal herself to Rainy, she insisted she had living proof that the God Rainy believed in was dead. The vision of Frenchy, and her voice, she said, as she began to pry the lid off the urn, were growing stronger and more argumentative each day.

God be God, when he dead he don't have to stay dead, Rainy said, speaking directly down into my mother's ashes. *He come back any time he choose. God be actual. He be a Glad bag layin there in some alley, got a hole in the bottom where shit fall through.*

Rainy tipped the urn towards me so I could see Frenchy, too. Her face crumpled when she saw the barely contained bewilderment in my eyes.

At first I thought there'd been a mistake, as I sat peering into the ashes for longer than it would take most people to realize what they were looking at. My mother's ashes didn't look like ashes at all, though I'd never seen cremated remains before. These were like coarse sand, pasty white, mixed in angry fragments of bone. There was a final indignity in the fact that my mother had been reduced to something resembling cat litter.

Given had just fallen asleep in my arms when the phone rang. I froze, letting it ring until the answering machine clicked on.

"Merry Ho Ho Ho," a familiar voice said. "I know you're there. Pick up the phone."

I held Given in one arm, cradled the phone between my shoulder and my ear. I had been afraid it was Grace (scared she wanted to reclaim her baby) and had hoped it might be Hooker. "I thought I'd been barred from talking to you," I said.

Vernal laughed, something I hadn't heard him do in a long time. "I am allowed to make one call. A compassionate call, because it's Christmas." He paused, and when I didn't say anything, he said, "I've been worrying about you."

"How's rehab," I said. "I didn't think you'd last."

"I'm not allowed to drink, but other than that, okay," he said, ignoring my last statement. I began picking at a wayward piece of skin at the side of my thumbnail. "It's been *really* good, actually, since Gracie arrived."

I stopped picking. Vernal had checked into a place for rich fuck-ups; Grace couldn't have afforded to pay for half an hour at the Outer Planet Hotel.

"The band council agreed to pick up her tab if she turned herself in," Vernal said quickly. "She got here this morning — she's doing well. We both are. I just called to say that, well, thank you for taking care of everything for us. We won't forget how much you've done for us. We . . . "

Us? We? He kept talking, but I didn't listen. I held the phone away from my ear with the vague thought forming that Vernal should not be speaking so openly about what "we" had done. I worked it out: Hooker had taken the baby from the nursery and helped Grace make her escape. He called I-5, then left Given for me in the dumpster because he knew, everyone knew, I'd be the best one to look after him.

"I just don't want there to be any more lies," Vernal said, as if I were the one who'd been duplicitous. I could smell the scent of baby powder over the long distance.

☙ ☙ ☙

The night had swelled to blacken everything. I found a flashlight and went outside, descended the steps, stooped and entered the cobwebby darkness. I shone the torch around, and saw a clutter of pop cans that had blown out of the recycling box, faded newspaper flyers, a section of black plastic hose, and, next to the jar I had sealed my stash in, a syringe.

Most of my second baggy was gone. I pocketed the remaining ounce and went back into the house. Rainy was asleep in the living room, slumped bonelessly in a chair. I glanced at her arms to see if there any track marks but she had changed into my long-sleeved prison-issue pyjamas.

I woke her up, told her what I had found under the verandah, and accused her of stealing from me.

Rainy appeared discountenanced but recovered herself quickly. *What a verandah?* she asked.

৯ ৯ ৯

Sometime during the night the twins manifested themselves into a north wind that banged around the farm making the house shudder and Toop whine to be let outside. The Bomb cried at the door until I brought him upstairs with me and let him lie fretting at the foot of my bed.

Rainy couldn't sleep. I think she knew her twins were leaving her that night. I couldn't help her; she wanted to know where the wind came from and where it went after it died.

It was still dark when she left our room and went out into the blizzard, and stood, both hands outstretched, trying to catch the snow. I watched from the window until she was barely visible. And then, because I was afraid she would freeze, or let the snow bury her, I drew a blanket around my shoulders, put on my cold, wet gumboots, and went to bring her inside. I apologized for being angry, said I would share the last baggy of coke with her and when it was gone we would both have to quit, face life with the skin torn away. Rainy said she was sorry, too. She swore she would quit the stealing habit she'd picked up from Frenchy, also. *I never make the same mistake once.*

We stayed up the rest of the night, hitching up the reindeer. I kept opening the door, so the twins, or Toop, could blow in, but there was nothing out there except the wind and it didn't seem interested in the tainted warmth we had to offer.

The blizzard let up at first light. I expected Toop to be at the door, and so did the Bomb. He raced from window to window, leaping at the glass until I had to threaten to tie him up. I wanted to drive out to look for Toop, but when I checked the driveway I knew we were snowed in, I wouldn't be going anywhere until the snow began to melt.

I told Rainy about Vernal's phone call, and that he and Gracie had hooked up. *She be wantin her kid back, she get done rehabilitatin. Then what you gon do? She leave him in a dumpster — next time he might not get so lucky.*

I heated water, prepared a bottle. Wherever I moved, Given's large eyes followed me, and I worried for him. Mine was not a world to bring a child into.

I sat holding him against my breast, sniffing the top of his head, inhaling the new life that was both his and my own. He was so new. He made small contented sounds as his eyes fixed on me. Small moments of grace: shouldn't these be enough? I smiled down at Given, thinking, for the first time since I had escaped, what good fortune to be alive, what beauty mercy sometimes brings.

§ § §

I know you're not supposed to tell your New Year's resolution beforehand, but I did, I told Given I was going to be the best possible mother to him. Given's eyebrows went shooting up, as if he was happy for me, as if he'd been afraid some part of me had been slipping away and leaving him, the way he'd been left before.

"When you're dancing with the devil, make sure you get the steps right." I remembered the Tranquilandian saying. I never thought for a moment that I needed help. In less than a week I had undone all the good staying straight for twelve years had done me.

What, if anything, had I learned? That pain is what we do, what we must have, in order to feel alive?

How could I begin to list the number of things that had happened to escalate me from a simple state of painful being into the excruciatingly nauseated state I found myself in the morning of New Year's Eve? I only knew what day it was because Rainy came to tell me Vernal was back at St. Jude's after almost choking to death on a balloon he was blowing up for an AA dance at the rehab centre for rich fuckups.

Grace had left a message on the answering machine. Just as Rainy had predicted, she wanted her baby back. *She have a changin mind.*

It had stopped snowing and the sun had come out, which made me feel more disgusted with myself for having returned so quickly to my old ways. The sun seemed to illuminate the black holes I wanted to stuff myself into. I found myself praying for rain; there was nothing holier than rain when it came to an excuse for getting obliterated. Rainy said I was praying up the wrong tree. *God no bell-hoppin nigga; you don't just go pushin on buttons get things sent up.*

I knew what had to be done. I got out of bed, dressed, filled a thermos, packed a diaper bag — formula, wet wipes, diaper rash cream, two changes of clothing including mittens, a scarf and a tuque — then swaddled Given in blankets and laid him in the Moses basket. Rainy said Given seemed so glad to be with me she couldn't believe anyone would ever think I wasn't doing the best thing for Gracie's boy. I wasn't demanding ransom payments, and threatening to cut off his ears and send them to the welfare office if they didn't pay up. I told myself, too, it wasn't as if the couple waiting to adopt him had had time to get to know him, or fall in love with him, and were praying for the safe return of the child they had already started a college fund for: it wasn't as if Given was loved more by anyone than me.

Which was why I would do what I needed to do. I planned on getting my life back before it got all the way lost again.

Rainy didn't want me to leave. The roads would be bad, she said. She hid my boots and when I said I'd wear shoes she ripped the shoelaces out. How did I know that when I got to Hooker's cabin there would be anyone home to look after Son Jesus, she said?

If Toop had gone, I said, reassuring her, it could only mean one thing: he'd seen Hooker in the wind that had blown from the north, and he had gone home. I remembered Hooker saying wherever I am, Toop will find his way back to me. I told Rainy I had to take Given back to where he rightfully belonged. Given was a miracle crack-baby who'd survived on Coffee-Mate and been left in a dumpster. I figured if he'd made it this far, he'd survive whatever came next.

By the time we were ready to leave, in the early afternoon, the hearse doors were still frozen shut. I used a hair dryer on the end of an extension cord to thaw the locks, then set Given on the front seat in his basket. I let the Bomb sit between us, where he would keep us both warm. I found an old collar, and a leash; Rainy insisted he wear the rein-dog antlers Frenchy had stolen for him at the mall. Given seemed unusually fussy, and drank both bottles I'd filled for him before I even got the key in the ignition.

The engine coughed into life on the third try, and I coaxed it to a whine as Rainy brushed the snow from the roof; I watched it falling around her body as if she were the centre of her own storm. Afterwards she brushed the snow off the rear windows and used the scraper Frenchy had stolen for her to chip away at the ice that had formed on the windshield.

I went into reverse, and the tires started spinning. I put my head down on the wheel, fearing I could be stuck here until the sun had enough strength to melt the ice, but Rainy disappeared into the house, after telling me not to budge, and when she came back I could hear her, behind the rear wheels, muttering to herself. After a while she told me to go ahead, try backing up again, and when I went into reverse, this time I had traction: Rainy had scattered the Bomb's cat litter on the icy driveway under my tires.

You be da bomb now, road sister, she cried, waving her arms over her head as if she were making a snow angel in the air. *You be catchin up wid me later, yo own self.*

I waved goodbye as Rainy skated barefoot over the icy driveway, falling and laughing, then picking herself up and straightening her neck so her head sat in the right place. A couple of times I felt the rear wheels slip under me, as the hearse skated sideways. I reached out with one arm, instinctively, to stop the Moses basket from being thrown off the seat onto the floor, while I tried to straighten out the tires, and crept forward in first gear through a ghostly silent landscape.

There was no message today at the vegetable stand, no Christian vegetables for sale, but a few poinsettias in green plastic pots, marked down after Christmas.

The road was clear all the way to the village. When we passed the turn-off to the dump I saw it had been closed off by yellow crime-scene tape. Gracie's house had been cordoned off, also. The tape looked recent and was the most blatant reminder yet of the trouble I might be in.

I drove past the Uncle's place, Matt's Yaka-Way, past Lawlor Moon's memorial pole. When a raven flew across the road in front of me by the church, a piece of red and green ribbon in his beak, I thought of my mother's ashes in the ice cream bucket back at the farm and that's when it came to me what Rainy had done: when she let go of her twins, somewhere inside that broken brain of hers she had decided it was time to let Frenchy go, also.

It wasn't cat litter she'd spread under the rear wheels of the hearse, it had been Frenchy. Frenchy, who, in Rainy's tragic mind, had manifested herself in my mother's ashes.

§ § §

I supposed my mother wouldn't have minded being backed over by a hearse; the idea might have amused her in a morbid way. Hadn't she always said that in death she still hoped she would go on being useful?

I parked at the end of Dead End Road and got out, making sure every part of Given's body was covered, except his nose. I sang to him as I broke a new trail, the sun shearing off the snow, and heard wind high in the trees and knew it was the dead out there, singing back to me, their bottomless love. He didn't look anywhere near ready to sleep, but I think my lullabies were to soothe *me* as much as they were to keep him from fussing as we walked.

We stopped, briefly, so I could introduce him to all his relations, especially Baby Born and Died. I had begun to feel an attachment to those whose graves I passed by each time I had come this way, as if it took death to awaken my feelings. Somehow it was easier to love those who had left us, the way I'd begun to love Rainy and Frenchy after they were executed (and before I knew they'd be coming back). How much easier to admire not only those we will outlive, but those who could teach us, who have ceased to speak to us, their closed mouths full of dirt.

Today, with the way the snow had tiptoed up to some of the graves and dusted them, and come down heavily, obscuring others and weighing the cedar branches, I felt in awe of the world again, as if it were no longer death, but Given's presence that had awakened me, halfway through my life, to the unbearable loveliness of existence.

The dry, bitter air slapped my face. My boots squeaked in the snow. I held tight to the Bomb's leash, and he kept getting underfoot, the snow going *crunch crunch crunch,* as I approached Hooker's cabin; I suspected the Bomb had never been in a forest before. Charlie and Ralph, so shiny they looked like they'd been polished with bootblack, took flight from the raven-feeder, but didn't sound off the way they normally did. I liked to think they recognized me.

There was no smoke coming from the chimney — I figured no smoke, no Hooker. I didn't knock, but used Given's weight to push the door open. Toop lifted an ear and then sat up and began licking himself, as if he were embarrassed to have been caught sleeping on the job.

The Bomb and I made a great fuss over him, lots of where have you beens, you had us worried half to deaths. Toop began panting enthusiastically when I told him I was going to the beach — I wanted to take my shoes off and walk in the foam, let Given taste the salt on his tongue. "If you're coming with me, you look out for the Bomb," I said, bending to unclip his leash. "He's a city-slicker, not like you." Toop stopped panting and gave me his "do I have to?" look.

I felt the tickling moisture of Given's breath falling softly on my neck, his chest heat-fused to mine in the sling I carried him in as I set out over the mossy point, still covered with deep snow in places — the rays from the late afternoon sun turning the white surface to a faint salmon — and then down onto the sand.

The sea glittered with jumpy light, as if someone up above had scattered a box of shiny new pins across the surface. Foam covered the whole beach, right up to the tideline, as far as the ocean could go before being pulled back out. A crust of snow still clung to the driftwood making it too slippery to walk on. Given dozed on my chest, his body wrapped around my heart. My heart felt safe with him. I felt holy.

I remembered one of my last days on Tranquilandia when I climbed Nevada Chocolata, with Angel in my arms, to have him baptised. It was a day clearer than any other, from that time in my life — the ten-foot sorrowing Virgin in white and blue plaster presiding over the Church of Our Virgin of Mercy as a small white coffin was unloaded from a garishly painted truck.

Angel had Holy Water sprinkled on his head, and the Salt of Life on his tongue. When the baptisms were over, the priest prayed to God Almighty for the babies' souls. Afterwards he held a funeral, as if birth and death, like tears and laughter, were born joined at the hip. And I guess it's true, they are joined. Only when you're holding a baby, you don't remember death.

When the coffin was carried from the church to the Cementarios de Ninos with its endless rows of forsaken graves, sulking up the slopes of Nevada Chocolata where the crucifix orchids bloomed, a black mass of clouds appeared suddenly over the peak of the mountain and I swear I felt Angel's small body shrink beneath his white robe, as if to say can there be any place lonelier on earth than this? I remember the earth cracked, as if those down below had moved over to make room for more, and the priest asking us to help him pray, as if that cracked earth had taken his courage away. That time I even prayed with him.

I was lost in my own remembering, wasn't watching the dogs, so that when the eagle swooped and plucked the Bomb out of the foam, I didn't see it happening until the Bomb was no more than a white blur, with bobbing antlers, in the eagle's talons. Toop raced back and forth at the water's edge, whipping the foam into suds, hurling himself as far out into the surf as he could before the waves dragged him back. The eagle flew with the Bomb in a straight line towards the thin pink rind on the western horizon. And then, when the giant bird disappeared from sight, everything was the same as before.

I watched the sun go down, almost audibly, into a gulf of gold, but I don't remember racing back through the foam, or the sky darkening around me as if the eagle's wings had blocked out the last of the sun's glow. I don't remember stumbling into Hooker's cabin, or the door being ajar; I don't remember registering any of this at the time. It still surprises me how much memory is framed by things we might not notice, or pay much attention to, when it is happening. I stood in the doorway, holding Given, squeezing him so hard that if he'd wanted to cry, right then for any reason, he wouldn't have been able to.

Hooker and I-5 lay entwined on the mattress in the middle of the floor. I could barely make out their faces beneath the white clouds of their breath, the steam rising off their naked bodies like little wispy ghosts into the cold cabin air. I didn't feel shocked, or jealous, when I think back on it, or even betrayed. Just in awe: how hot would a body have to be before sweat turned to steam!

Given made a sound like the newborn killer whale I'd heard on the radio, crying for his mother. Toop lifted his head and howled. Clutching Given to my breast, I stumbled back outside into what remained of the day.

☙ ☙ ☙

By the time I reached the hearse the sky had turned black in the north. I drove home, with Given next to me, erecting a chain-link fence around my heart. I didn't remember that it was New Year's Eve: what did it even matter? I tried not to think about the Bomb's last moments as he was carried out to sea, or of Hooker and I-5 either, how their bodies became one flesh, the colour of white and dark chocolate melted together.

When I reached the house an icy rain had begun falling. I got out with Given's basket under my arm, and took the front steps two at a time, nearly tripping over Aged Orange's crucified body, stiff and cold on the doorstep, his head in an Afro of blood. I dropped the Moses basket and fell to my knees, kissing the cat's liquid eyes where the dark blood had pooled.

Rainy heard me wailing on the verandah and flew to the door. Her face turned bare light bulb white when she saw me, kneeling before the bloody crucifix. *Best we bail ourselves on out of here*, she said, *'fore Son Jesus end up bein killed on down.*

"Who would do this to a cat?" I cried, until my voice grew hoarse. There was only one person I could think of. The man at the Christian vegetable stand.

I left Rainy holding Given, ran upstairs and stuffed all my belongings in my prison-issue duffel bag. The radio was on: police were close to making an arrest in the case of the abducted baby, and the mysterious slaying of an island man. A RCMP spokesperson said it was too early to say for sure, but they had reason to believe the kidnapping and the murder were connected.

The ice rain pecked at my window. I grabbed my bag and ran back downstairs, shouting to Rainy to get in the car. Everything — the trees, the birds, the wind — had been silenced by the hard, cold rain.

Rain be like needle stickin, Rainy said, as I sped down the treacherous driveway. *Take me where I don't want to go.*

I turned right at the driveway's end and headed towards the Bend. As I braked for the stop sign I saw the billboard with its big question looming up in front of me where, hours ago, there had been a sale of poinsettias at the Christian vegetable stand. I drove straight at it as the world began whirling away from me into that familiar weightless dream. Rainy screamed *pump yo brakes* as the hearse went into a spin on the icy road, hit the billboard and back-flipped in mid-air through

ETERNITY
WHERE DO YOU THINK YOU'RE GOING?

I flew headfirst through the windshield, with nothing to hang on to, as if I were freefalling towards the earth that was moving away from me even faster than I could fly.

Afterwards there was the usual, the morbidly curious crowd — neighbours, motorists who swore they'd seen it happen. When the police arrived I felt the world darken as if their gunmetal uniforms had just sucked up any light there was left to me. I had known all along they would find me, but it had taken them so long I could no longer remember what they wanted me for.

At first I assumed they'd come for the baby, or possibly because the hearse had been reported in an incident involving the theft of a Christmas tree. But then the heavy one with the greying moustache looked into my face and said, "It's me, Earl." In the shattered mirrors of Earl's sunglasses I saw the blood on my face reflected. "Do you know who I am? he said. Tell me who you are."

I like to look back on a situation and think about what I should have said, but whoever gets life right the first time? Officer Jodie Lootine, wearing Eternal aviators, said "how the fuck's she supposed to know who she fucking is?" as she bent over and kept asking me in loud, over-enunciated words, if I could hear anything she said. If they didn't know who I was, they couldn't have come to arrest me.

I let her words rain around me until they began to echo in repetition, *fucking doesn't know, who the fuck, doesn't know, who she is.* The Latrine had a fistful of Kleenex and kept trying to wipe my face. I could hear sirens. Another officer said "there's been an accident, an ambulance is on its way, don't try to move, we only want to help you." Why, then, did they have to put me in handcuffs? This meant I couldn't hold Given, and that's when I started fighting back and they put me in restraints. The Latrine kept saying they weren't going to hurt me, and every time I shouted for Rainy's help I saw the two officers exchange glances. *Cops got a way of turning everybody into nuttin,* Rainy said.

I heard people shouting in the streets, the sirens coming closer and closer. And I heard Given crying — he needed me, and I couldn't reach him. I thought of the mothers leaving the *curandero's* clinic on Tranquilandia, wrapping their babies in cheesecloth so they looked like little mummies in their coffins, how the women wailed at the gravesite: I would never forget that sound. Or the tears that made rivers in the dust on their faces as they stretched their arms toward their dead children they couldn't reach. How they crawled on their hands and knees, filling their mouths with dirt, stuffing the fresh grave-dirt into their ears and nostrils.

I turned to look for Rainy, who stood beside the wreck, her eyes heavy-lidded, her head rolling to one side, crying, but happily this time. She held Given in her arms and blew me a kiss. I mouthed the words, "look after him for me, I catch up wid you later," as an icy raindrop landed on Rainy's chin, melted, then travelled up her cheek, like a tear that had changed its mind.

AFTERWORD

When I finished *Cargo of Orchids* in 1999, I immediately began writing a sequel. I felt I wasn't done with my characters, nor were they finished with me. *Given* is the second book in what might well become a trilogy (at the time of this writing I still feel I am not done with my characters, nor are they finished with me.)

I believe this book stands alone and that readers do not have to have read *Cargo of Orchids* in order to enter Frenchy and Rainy's world, and the world of my first-person (unnamed) narrator. References to a hostage taking, the island of Tranquilandia, the birth and death of baby Angel, and the narrator's subsequent incarceration on Death Row allude to the world within *Cargo of Orchids,* and anyone curious to know more about the events leading up to this novel, *Given,* should hunt down a copy of *Cargo of Orchids.* (*Cargo of Orchids* was published by Knopf, Canada, in 2000, and is still in print. It was also published in Italy by Meridiano Zero, and in Australia by HarperCollins.)

In order to avoid divulging the actual location of the island of Kliminiawhit, and identifying the genesis of the Yaka Wind First Nation, I have used many phrases from the Chinook

Jargon, which are translated within the body of the narrative. Chinook Jargon became the official language of trade along the Pacific coast from Alaska to southern California in the 1800s (not to be confused with the more complex "Old Chinook" language spoken by the people living along the Columbia River, Chinook Jargon was an agglutinous, or "Pidgin" language, its words composed of morpheme, or word-element sequences.) Missionaries, in their zeal to convert the indigenous peoples, translated hymns and bible texts (as well as "The Night Before Christmas") into Chinook. The dialect is now seldom heard, except in ceremonial usage.

It has become fashionable to acknowledge great lists of people whose life and times have influenced the writing of any novel. I will refrain. There is one person, though, without whom this book, etc. etc. and that of course is my tireless editor and oldest, dearest friend, Seán Virgo. He has the skill, and the nerve, to resurrect the dead. As Rainy and Frenchy would put it, "he be da bomb diggity, best believe."

Susan Musgrave
Haida Gwaii, February, 2012